The Trouble with Secrets

ALSO BY NAOMI MILLINER

On All Other Nights: A Passover Celebration in 14 Stories

Super Jake and the King of Chaos

The Trouble with Secrets

NAOMI MILLINER

Quill Tree Books
An Imprint of HarperCollinsPublishers

Quill Tree Books is an imprint of HarperCollins Publishers.
The Trouble with Secrets
Copyright © 2025 by Naomi Milliner
All rights reserved. Manufactured in Harrisonburg, VA, United States of America. No part of this book may be used or reproduced in any manner whatsoever without written permission except in the case of brief quotations embodied in critical articles and reviews. For information, address HarperCollins Children's Books, a division of HarperCollins Publishers, 195 Broadway, New York, NY 10007.
www.harpercollinschildrens.com
Library of Congress Control Number: 2023944798
ISBN 978-0-06-331164-0
Typography by Andrea Vandergrift
25 26 27 28 29 LBC 5 4 3 2 1
First Edition

For Jesse
Your insightful feedback, creative ideas, and loving support made this book so much better.
Then again, you make everything so much better.

NOW

I DON'T HAVE a black dress.

I never needed one until two years ago, when Grandma Rachel died.

I didn't have a black dress then either, but my sister, Sara, lent me one she'd outgrown.

Now I've outgrown it, too.

Grandma Rachel's funeral was the first time I saw my dad cry. And the first time I saw a rabbi other than him lead the service.

Today will be the second.

"Becky?" a voice asks quietly at my bedroom door. "Can I come in?"

We meet halfway and she wraps her arms around me. "I am so sorry—" Her voice breaks and we hold on to each other. "Is there anything I can do?"

I pull out of her embrace. "I don't know what to wear."

I lead her to the closet filled with clothes in the bright colors I love: cheerful pinks, pretty purples, electric blues, and sunny yellows. She gently sorts through the happy colors that feel so wrong today.

"How about this?" She pulls out a black-and-white sweater and a black skirt.

I shake my head. "That's my concert outfit." But even as I say it—even as important as music is to me—suddenly it doesn't matter.

Nothing does.

"Whatever." I toss the skirt and sweater onto my bed, then close my eyes and try to shut everything out. Try to pretend everything is fine and nothing bad has happened and everyone I love is okay.

But we're not okay.

And I don't see how we ever will be again.

PART ONE

Before

1

MY HAND WAS on the doorknob, ready to go, but the rest of me wasn't so sure.

It seemed simple enough: leave my room, head up the hall and down the stairs—avoiding the third one from the bottom, since it creaked—then straight to the living room.

It was the next part I had trouble with. Specifically, the how-much-trouble-I'd-be-in-if-I-got-caught part. So I stood at my door, torn between convincing myself to stay put . . . or just doing it already before I lost my nerve.

After all, what was the worst that could happen? I got grounded?

For life . . . ?

I went to prison? Then again, could parents arrest their own twelve-year-old daughter? Was that a thing? Even if it was—and even if they did—Sara would bail me out. She always did.

Knowing she would be there for me, no matter what, I opened my door.

I crept down the stairs, silent and stealthy, then tiptoed into the living room like a spy on a top secret mission in the middle of the night.

And there it was, right where I expected, sitting innocently on the table by the lamp. I took a deep breath, reached for it, and—

"Becky!"

I was so startled I knocked it onto the floor and everything spilled out. But there was no time to worry about that because now I had much bigger problems.

I turned around and saw my seventeen-year-old sister standing there. Even in the darkness I could make out her face, and it did not look happy.

"What in the world are you doing up?" Sara asked, hands on her hips. "It's after midnight!"

When in trouble—which I now most definitely was—sometimes it helped to answer a question with a question. "What are *you* doing up?"

"I heard someone on the stairs," she said. "I came down to see if we were being robbed."

"Of course not!" Not exactly.

She aimed her cell phone flashlight at Mom's spilled purse, revealing Chapstick, a mini calendar, three pens, lip gloss, a little pack of tissues . . . and the reason I came down here in the first place.

Sara frowned in my direction. "So, what are you doing?"

"Um . . ." When in trouble, it also helped to change the subject. As I gathered the spilled contents, I tried to do just that. "Wow. Look at all this stuff. . . . No wonder her purse weighs a ton!"

Sara kneeled next to me and helped put it all back. "Don't change the subject."

"Whaddaya mean?" I asked as innocently as I could.

The only thing left was the wallet. We reached for it at the same time. I got there first and held on tight.

She waited for me to return it to the purse.

I didn't.

I couldn't.

"Becky . . . ?"

"Um . . . I kind of need to borrow this—just for a few minutes. . . ."

"Why?"

I sighed. "Promise you won't tell Mom and Dad?" Especially Dad. He definitely wouldn't approve of me taking Mom's wallet, since he was a—

She held out her hand and waited. I gave her the wallet. She dropped it into the purse, zipped it up, and turned to me. "Up. Stairs." Uh-oh. Sara only talked in one-word sentences if she was mad.

When in trouble, another strategy was to delay the inevitable as long as possible. "Could I get a drink first?"

"My. Room. Now."

Yep. Definitely mad.

She waited for me to climb the stairs, following so closely she would've bumped into me if I stopped. We padded down the hall and into her room.

She closed her door behind us, then stared at me like I was a criminal or something. Which I kind of was. Or would have been if she hadn't stopped me. "Start. Talking."

"Jon's leaving for college in two days."

"What? No one told me!"

I rolled my eyes.

Sara continued. "Is that why Mom went to the kosher market twice this week, then spent all day cooking for tomorrow night's dinner? Or why Benji took all afternoon trying to decide which stuffed animal to put in Jon's suitcase so he won't be lonely?"

Benji. Our little brother. The sweetest six-year-old in Maryland. Possibly the entire East Coast. Stuffed animals, special dinners . . . All of us just trying to do something nice for our big brother—including me.

"Sara, he'll be away for months! All alone in L.A.!" Except for all the people in his dorm. And his classmates at USC film school.

The point was he wouldn't be *here*. With us.

Sara crossed her arms. "That still doesn't explain why you need Mom's wallet."

"To get him a going-away present! I found the perfect thing—things—online. And they'll get here in one day, so he'll have them in time." I paused, hoping she would understand and maybe not be mad. Especially not mad enough to tell . . .

Sara sighed. "What did you find?"

"Forty-eight packs of those mint cookies he loves! And a hundred and twenty of those chai tea bags he has every day."

"That was nice of you, but—"

"The thing is, it costs over seventy dollars between them, and—"

"Seventy dollars?!"

"And forty-three cents."

"Becky! You can't just take Mom's credit card and—"

"I was going to pay her back! Honest! As soon as I get my Hanukkah gelt. And a little birthday money. Also, maybe if I get some for my bat mitzvah . . ."

My bat mitzvah.

It was more than five months away: January 28, to be exact. Whether I was ready or not.

And I most definitely was not.

Luckily, I already knew the prayers from a lifetime of attending services. The trouble was, I also knew how beautifully Sara had chanted them at her bat mitzvah, and how funny and well received Jon's speech had been at his bar mitzvah. And I knew I could never measure up.

So even though five months sounded like a long time, it really wasn't.

"Do you know how much trouble you'd be in once her

credit card bill shows up?" Sara asked, her thick, dark curls—the ones we all got from Mom—bounced around as she shook her head.

"Her what?"

"This is worse than taking those 'open house' balloons from next door for Benji's birthday party last year."

"I was only borrowing them! I was going to give them back. . . ."

"It's even worse than that time you—"

"Okay," I said. "I get it. I shouldn't have done it. Although, technically, I *didn't*."

"Only because I stopped you," Sara said. "Look. I know you mean well. You always do. But sometimes . . ." She shook her head again, only she was smiling this time, which meant she wasn't mad at me anymore.

I let out a long breath and felt my shoulders relax. Everything would be okay.

"What am I gonna do with you?" Sara asked, though I was pretty sure she didn't expect an answer. "You're turning into a juvenile delinquent—and you're not even a teenager yet!"

"Five more months." Plus one week. And three days.

She rolled her eyes, then handed me her phone. "Show me the links. Maybe we can figure something out."

She sat down on her bed and I joined her, feeling like partners in crime. But one thing was still worrying me. "You won't tell Mom and Dad, will you?"

Her hazel eyes stared into my blue ones. "Do you promise not to do anything like this ever again?"

"I promise."

"Okay then." She smiled again. "Your secret's safe with me."

The night before Jon left, everything was the same . . . and different. The six of us sat down to dinner, as usual. But instead of something quick and easy like pasta or meat loaf, Mom went all out with turkey and stuffing and—

"Is it Thanksgiving?" Benji asked as he scooped gooey marshmallow into his mouth and left the sweet potato on his plate.

"We're not even halfway through August yet!" I said.

"Think of it as an early Thanksgiving," Mom said, "in case Jon doesn't make it back for the real one this year."

As delicious as the food was, I kind of lost my appetite after that. How could Jon not be home for Thanksgiving?

Once dinner was over, Dad left for one of his weekly meetings; Mom went off to do a last load of laundry for Jon's suitcase; and I went upstairs to be alone for a while—or, rather, alone with my flute.

My flute always cheered me up and calmed me down. It was always there for me, like a best friend. And since my human best friend, Nipa, was still in India visiting her extended family, the flute would have to do.

Sara called it my secret weapon. Jon called it my superpower. Sometimes it really did feel that way. Anytime I felt inferior around my genius big brother or super-talented sister (which was basically every day), my flute made me feel special, too.

I warmed up with a few scales—all in minor keys, to match my melancholy mood. Then I played "Somewhere Over the Rainbow," "Let It Be," and Pachelbel's Canon in D, just to mix it up. Besides, school was starting soon, and I wanted every flute solo my band teacher, Ms. T, had to offer.

Pachelbel done, it was time for my favorite sad song of all, Leonard Cohen's "Hallelujah." I was a few measures in when my bedroom door opened and a very familiar voice said, "Uh-oh. Someone's feeling sorry for herself."

"Nipa!" I put down my flute and raced to the door, where my best friend stood with a grin as wide as mine felt. We hugged like we'd been apart six years, not six weeks. "I thought you weren't coming back for three more days!"

"I wanted to surprise you."

"It worked!" I laughed. "How was India? How are your grandparents? How was your cousin's wedding? What did you eat?" I love Indian food.

I plopped down on my bed. "Tell me everything!"

Nipa sighed and sat down next to me. "I feel terrible that you didn't miss me at all," she joked.

"Nope. Not one teeny bit." I grinned again. "Now tell me everything!"

"Jaipur is *a-mazing*! They call it the Pink City, because a lot of the buildings are pink—it's really pretty. If you like pink."

"Which we do."

She nodded. "We did some really fun things, and I kept wishing you were there with me."

"Like what?"

"There are all these old palaces, and this place that has kulfi—it's like frozen custard, with pistachios or mango or saffron...."

"Yum! Why didn't you bring me some?" I joked.

"What I really wanted was to go on this safari and ride a hot air balloon—but it was the rainy season, so they were both closed."

"Why didn't your cousin get married some other time of year?"

"Because Kabir got accepted to graduate school in the fall, in Texas, remember? He and his wife wanted to get married first. She has a really big family, and there's no way they all could've come to the United States."

"Gotcha. So...? How was the wedding? I need details—and pictures!"

Nipa pulled out her phone and started at the airport. She'd just gotten on the plane when Benji raced into my room. "It's Monopoly time!"

"Thanks. I'll be down in a minute."

He raced out again, probably summoning Sara next.

Nipa looked at me. "Since when do you like Monopoly?"

"Since Jon's leaving tomorrow."

We both stopped smiling. "Oh. I thought that was next

week!" Nipa said. "I would've waited. . . ."

"No. It's okay. I'm glad you're here."

Nipa smiled the way she always did when she had a surprise. "You'll be even gladder when you see what I brought you." She handed me a small box I hadn't even noticed.

I opened it and found a dozen purple metallic bangles studded with gold glitter. "I love them so much!" I took them out and put them on right away, six on each arm, tilting them in the light and admiring how much they sparkled. Then I gave her a tight side hug. "Thank you!"

"I got myself some turquoise and crimson ones, so we can mix and match if you like."

"Yes! For the first day of seventh grade!"

"Brilliant!" Nipa grinned. "Two weeks from today!"

Two weeks felt like years from now; Jon was leaving in a few hours.

As usual, Nipa read my mind. "Hey—it'll be okay. Want me to come over tomorrow night to cheer you up?"

"Duh."

A few minutes later, her mom came to pick her up. I gave Nipa a hug and waved as she rode away, then I headed to the living room.

It was time for Monopoly.

Spoiler alert: I am not a big Monopoly fan. It goes on forever, but then again, that meant more time with Jon.

Part of me wanted to spend all night with him; part of me

wanted to go to my room, close the door, and just be sad. It felt like half of him was still at home and half of him was already in California. And all of me was going to miss him.

I decided to focus on what I *did* like about Monopoly, which was knowing exactly how things would play out.

We gathered around "Mom's mah-jongg table" in our usual seats (me across from Sara; Benji across from Jon). Like always, Sara distributed the colorful paper money, I organized the deeds, Jon shuffled the Community Chest and Chance cards, and Benji handed out the tokens. (Except for the dog, which he always kept for himself. So far that metal dog, and the gazillion stuffed animals in his room, were the closest he got to a real pet. But he never gave up hope.)

As usual, he gave Sara the race car and smiled. "Don't get caught on the speed cam this time!"

Sara rolled her eyes good-naturedly; she really had gotten a ticket for speeding, so we all teased her about it. "It was one time."

Jon raised one eyebrow. "One time that we heard about..."

Sara waved a gold five-hundred-dollar bill in his face. "Careful—I might forget to give you this...."

Jon grabbed it from her and they laughed.

"Here, Becky..." Benji handed me the thimble.

"Thanks."

We waited for him to give Jon the top hat, like always. But he hesitated, then gave him the dog token instead.

Jon looked at Benji a few seconds, looking as surprised as

I felt. Then he said, "Thanks, buddy. That's really nice of you."

And that's when I realized things were *not* going to play out the way they usually did.

"You know what would be great right about now?" Jon asked. "A cup of chai."

I smiled at Sara and she smiled back. What was more fun than keeping a secret? Jon was going to love his gift.

"Savor it while you can," she told him.

"I doubt they serve it in the dining hall," I chimed in.

Jon put his hand to his heart. "Benji, can you believe how cruel our sisters are?"

Benji shook his head in a complete show of solidarity with his big brother.

"Fine," Sara said. "I guess you can have one last cup."

"I'll help." I followed her into the kitchen, where we'd stashed his going-away gift. Sara had bought it with her own credit card, and I'd promised to pay half (once I had the money).

We quickly made chai for Jon and cocoa for the rest of us. Sara carried the tray with steaming mugs and I carried the wrapped gift.

"What's this?" Jon asked as I handed it to him.

"It's a going-away gift. From Sara and me."

"Open it!" Benji looked as excited as if it were his own present.

Jon peeled off the paper and showed Benji the box. "A hundred and twenty bags? That's enough to last the whole semester! Thanks, you guys."

"It was Becky's idea," Sara said.

Jon smiled and so did I, and for a second it felt like we were back on track. But as soon as we started moving around the board, things got weird again. Jon kept passing up the chance to buy properties, and Sara went crazy buying everything.

"Sara!" I shouted after she bought the most expensive property in the game. "What are you doing? You already have, like, a zillion properties. Plus, Boardwalk is four hundred dollars and"—I looked over at her very small pile of money—"you barely have any money left."

"Bec's right," Jon said. "What are you doing?"

"Taking a chance," she answered. "Isn't that the point of the game? No risk, no reward."

Normally, this was one of the things I loved most about Sara. The fearless way she jumped right in without hesitation, never worrying about consequences.

Unfortunately, our parents didn't feel the same. "I don't know." I shook my head. "Mom always says, 'Look before you leap.'"

"Moderation in all things," Jon said in a deep voice. Our father was all about moderation. And rules. I guess that came with being a rabbi. He *always* had to follow the rules.

Everywhere we went, people knew him. Nipa said he was like a movie star; unfortunately, he was nowhere near as glamorous. Or rich. And he constantly had to be careful what he did, what he said, even what he ate: the congregants were always watching.

Trouble was, they were always watching the rest of us, too....

Benji took his turn, then handed me the dice. I rolled.

"Uh-oh!" Benji cried. "Becky has to go to jail again."

It was the third time this game. I was starting to feel like I really had stolen Mom's credit card....

I moved the thimble to jail, then watched Jon *not* buy another property, and Sara mortgage two so she could buy something else.

"I feel sorry for your future boyfriend," Jon said, rolling the dice. "After one month with you, he'll be broke."

"But he'll still be super cute," she joked.

"As long as he's Jewish." Dad had walked into the room without our even noticing. He smiled, but we all knew he was *not* joking.

"Abba!" Sara was the only one who called Dad the Hebrew word for "father." "That's so old-fashioned! This isn't *Fiddler on the Roof*! Times have changed."

"Not in our family," he said. There was no trace of a smile on his face now.

"So, just to clarify," Jon said, "Sara could date a ninety-year-old serial killer as long as he was Jewish?"

"Only if he came from a good family." Dad winked at him.

Sara shook her head. "I am done with all of you."

And suddenly I was, too. It was too sad sitting there, knowing it was our last night with Jon until Thanksgiving—or longer. He'd never been away so long, or so far, before. My fingers itched to get back to "Hallelujah."

I faked a yawn. "I'm kind of sleepy." I turned to my siblings. "You guys can split my properties or whatever." I got up, said a quick goodnight, and headed upstairs.

A few minutes later I was in bed, staring at the twinkly stars above me. Jon had put them there a few years ago because I was afraid of the dark. The thought of him caring enough to come up with that idea, then climb a ladder to stick dozens of glow-in-the-dark pieces of plastic on my ceiling made my heart ache.

I hadn't even told him how much I'd miss him, or wished him luck, or anything. I was thinking about going back downstairs when my door opened. "You don't look 'kind of sleepy' to me." Sara closed the door behind her and came in. "Move over, Becster."

She snuggled in and wrapped an arm around me. "I'm gonna miss him, too."

"So why are you up here with me when you can be down there with him?"

"Mom's putting Benji to bed, and I figured Dad might want some time alone with his firstborn—you know, share some of that rabbinic wisdom. Remind Jon not to eat ham sandwiches or shrimp cocktails . . ."

She could always make me smile. "I'm glad you're here," I told her.

"I'll always be here for you." She squeezed my shoulder. "I promise."

I smiled in the darkness. When Sara made a promise, she kept it.

2

THE WEEK BEFORE Jon left, I kept thinking things like, this will be the last time we go out for pizza together. Or, this is the last time we'll hang out and watch funny videos on YouTube. Or even, this is the last time we'll play Monopoly 'til he comes back home.

But once he actually left, Nipa and Sara kept me so busy, I barely had time to miss him at all, and the last two weeks of summer flew by. Sara convinced Mom that I needed some new outfits for school, so we spent more than a few hours at different malls and boutiques.

And Nipa and I lounged around the neighborhood swimming pool, made tons of homemade ice pops, and binged our favorite TV shows. And like every year, the night before school we got together to figure out our first-day-of-school outfits. It's a good thing we're about the same size; as usual, we liked each other's clothes more than our own. I borrowed her stretchy teal leggings and purple waffle-knit T-shirt, and Nipa took my skinny jeans and red smock top. Plus, we each took four turquoise bangles, four crimson, and four purple.

We were as ready as anyone could be for the first day of seventh grade.

After a quick breakfast, I took a last gulp of orange juice, brought my plate to the sink, and got a goodbye kiss from Mom. I leaned over and gave Benji a hug, careful not to choke him while he ate his sugary cereal. "Have fun in first grade."

"You have fun, too!" He grinned, revealing a mouthful of colorful mush.

I didn't exactly love school, but it would be "fun" to see who was in my classes, get first impressions of my teachers, and of course hang out with Nipa at lunch.

I grabbed my backpack and flute case, headed out, and walked three blocks to school. It was strange seeing so many kids swarming around in front of the two-story brown brick building after seeing an empty parking lot all summer. Some sat on the blue benches near the entrance; some went straight inside.

"Becky!"

I turned just as Nipa stepped off the bus with a backpack, a violin case, and a big smile. We met halfway and shared a hug even though we'd seen each other twelve hours earlier.

"Seventh grade!" Her smile got even bigger. "Can you believe it? This time next year, we'll practically be in high school!"

We let the other students move around us. It was easy to tell the upper grades from the sixth graders. The older ones met up with friends and hung out in front of the building, like we were doing; the new kids rushed through the massive double doors, class schedules clenched in their hands, looking terrified. I guess Nipa and I looked that way last year.

"Guess we'd better head in, too," I said.

Nipa nodded. "See you at lunch!"

"Not if I see you first!"

If we did see each other before lunch, it would be pure chance. We already knew we didn't have any classes together: Nipa had French while I had Spanish; Nipa had orchestra and I had band; I'd signed up for honors English; she'd signed up for honors everything else.

We waved goodbye for now and headed to homeroom in opposite directions. I smiled at some familiar faces as I made my way down the crowded hall to my classroom and took a seat just as the bell rang. I was about to turn off my brand-new cell phone (Sara convinced Mom and Dad I needed one), when I saw a new text message from my sister:

Do you hear the people sing?

I smiled and knew exactly what it meant: Sara's high school musical this year was going to be *Les Misérables*.

Les Miz was one of our favorites. Sara must be thrilled. She'd be singing the songs a gazillion times between now and mid-November, when the show went on. There was no doubt in my mind she would get a starring role. She always did.

My sister was pretty much amazing at everything, but musical theater was her One True Love. Everyone who had ever heard her sing or seen her perform knew it was only a question of time before she starred on Broadway. And I knew I would be in the front row, clapping and cheering my heart out for her.

I quickly texted a smiley face, then turned off my phone. I tried to focus on what the teacher was saying, but in my head, I was hearing the opening notes from *Les Miz*, and wondering which role Sara wanted and which one she would get. They were probably the same thing.

My next two periods were nothing bad but nothing special, either. And then it was time for my favorite class and my favorite teacher: band with Ms. Tennyson, aka Ms. T. Nipa thought she looked like Beyoncé; I thought she was even prettier.

Ms. T had thick black hair she wore in long box braids; light hazel eyes; and, according to my sister, "impeccable fashion sense." Sara always said if there were a contest for best-dressed teacher, Ms. T would win hands down. She'd already been voted best teacher—twice. And she deserved it. Most teachers spent the first day of school talking (and talking); Ms. T spent it listening.

I walked in and saw the piano off to the side, the drums way at the back, the music stands all set up and waiting for us. I did my best to walk, not run, straight to my place—at least, the place I sat last year: end of the first row, stage left.

First chair, which meant any flute solos would be mine. And I wanted every one of them.

Since basically all of us had been in band with Ms. T last year, we knew what to expect from her—and what she expected from us. So, unlike my other classes, we all settled in and settled down pretty quickly.

Ms. T watched with an approving smile as we got our instruments out without her even asking and waited for her instruction.

"Welcome, musicians! In fact, I can say welcome *back*, because I had the pleasure of working with almost every one of you last year." She paused and looked over at Ben, who was a decent trumpet player but also the class clown.

"Well," Ms. T said with a smile, "*mostly* a pleasure."

Ben laughed along with the rest of us. We all knew each other well by now: class clowns, show-offs, team players, soloists. . . . I was most definitely a soloist. At least, I hoped so.

"Okay," Ms. T said, "let's warm up with some scales, starting with B-flat."

We went through three scales with only a few mistakes (mostly Ben and his fellow class clown, Daniel, who also played trumpet). I looked around the room, happiness flowing through me. And even though I knew not everyone loved band the way I did, it still felt like family.

"Very nice," Ms. T said, interrupting my thoughts. "Now let's see if we've lost any ground over those long, lazy months of summer, or if anyone actually practiced once or twice."

I locked eyes with her and smiled; I had practiced, all right. Every. Single. Day. And I hoped it showed.

"All right. Let's turn to page seven in your exercise books."

Charlotte, the cute, chatty blond girl who played next to me, let out a sigh. "I am so sick of this one! It doesn't even have a name."

"Sure it does." I grinned. "Exercise number nine."

She groaned.

I admit, it wasn't the catchiest number, but it wasn't trying to be. It was all about dynamics—soft and loud and in-between. We played it through twice, some of us better than others.

"Ugh!" Charlotte sighed again. "I always mess up the fingering on that last measure."

"It's tricky," I said, even though it wasn't for me.

"You make it look easy," she said.

I shook my head. "Measure three should've been louder. It's supposed to be forte."

"I think you're the only one who noticed, or cared. Except for Ms. T."

Just then, Ms. T looked straight at me. "Nice job, Becky."

I tried to smile modestly, but I felt like taking a bow or doing a little happy dance. "Thanks, Ms. T."

"That reminds me." Ms. T smiled. "As of January twenty-first, I will be *Mrs*. Davis." She lifted her hand and showed us all a sparkly diamond ring.

The boys in the class played it cool, but the girls were

really excited—especially since Mr. Davis taught chorus and drama, and was almost as popular as Ms. T.

The bell rang, but luckily lunch was next, so I let the other kids talk to her first. "Congratulations," I told her when we were finally alone. "I'm so happy for you!"

Ms. T beamed. "Thank you, Becky. I've actually been thinking about you...."

"You have?"

She nodded. "You were one of my strongest musicians last year, and I can already tell you *definitely* haven't lost any ground. I want you to consider trying out for Junior All-County Honors Band this year. It's for outstanding musicians in seventh through ninth grade, and I think you have an excellent chance."

"You do?"

"I do. Auditions aren't until November, so you have more than enough time to get ready if you're interested."

"I am! Definitely!"

She grinned. "I was hoping you would be. There are six rehearsals starting early January, and the concert is mid-February—"

Before she could tell me more, Mr. Davis walked in. It was just as well, because I was too excited to hear any more details, let alone remember them. I congratulated him, too.

"Thank you, Becky." He beamed at me. "How's that sister of yours?"

"Fine, thanks. She still says you're the best teacher she's ever had."

"What about me?" Ms. T asked, pretending to look hurt.

"Second best. For sure," I said. And it was true. Sara loved anything and everything musical, but she was much better at singing than clarinet.

"Well, you tell her we said hello." Mr. Davis put his arm around Ms. T.

I promised I would, then floated to the cafeteria in a big puffy cloud of happiness to find my best friend.

Nipa and I had a tradition of trading food, although I definitely had the better deal. Since her family was vegetarian and mine was kosher, it was easy to share. Plus, Mrs. Sachdeva was an amazing cook. In exchange for her foil-wrapped samosas or spicy vegetable curry, I gave Nipa a bag of chips or a store-bought pack of snack cakes (neither of which Nipa's mom ever bought, so we were both happy with the arrangement).

By the time we'd caught each other up on our day so far, Nipa had demolished the bag of pretzels, but I'd barely touched the rice pudding she brought for me. It was studded with raisins and pistachios and was one of my favorite desserts ever, but I was too excited about All-County Band to eat.

"That's amazing!" she said. "You're totally going to get in."

"You think so?" I smiled.

"Of course!" She took a sip of lemonade. "When is the concert?"

"I don't know exactly. Sometime in February? Ms. T said the audition's in November and rehearsals start in January."

I started wondering what the audition pieces were. Then I started wondering what we'd play at the concert. . . .

And then I noticed Nipa's face was no longer smiling. In fact, it was doing the opposite.

"What?" I asked. "What's wrong?"

"Nothing. It's just . . . How will you have time for All-County *and* your bat mitzvah?"

"Oh." I hadn't thought about that. "I'm sure it'll be fine. . . ."

"Look," she continued, "I know you think Jon's speech was the best ever—"

"It was."

"And," Nipa continued, "I know Sara sang perfectly—"

"She did."

Nipa sighed and put on her serious face.

I sat up a little straighter and did my best to tune out the lunchroom noise all around us and focus on her words; I knew they would be important.

"Becky"—she leaned closer across the table—"the only way you can manage your bat mitzvah *and* All-County is if you stop comparing yourself to Jon and Sara. Otherwise, you're going to put so much pressure on yourself that you'll never do anything! Plus, your head might explode."

"I know." And I did. I also knew how little progress I'd made on my bat mitzvah—the part I had to sing and the part I had to write. Plus I still had to figure out my mitzvah project.

I knew how far I still had to go before I was ready . . . if I ever would be. "You're right. I need to stop comparing myself to them and just focus on the work."

And also All-County.

I didn't say that part aloud, but I sure thought it.

It was all I could think about.

3

WHEN I GOT home, I went straight upstairs to see Sara. We had so much to talk about: *Les Miz*, Ms. T and Mr. Davis, and, most of all, All-County!

As I approached her door, I heard her singing Eponine's showstopper "On My Own," and it was clear which role she wanted. It was also clear she would get it. I stood in the hall and listened to her hit every note and waited until she finished, then knocked.

"Enter if you dare," she called out.

"That," I told her as I walked in, "was amazing."

She wrinkled her nose. "You think? Some parts were a little rough."

"No way. It was perfect."

"Thanks, Becster. Maybe once it's polished, I can use it for my college audition tapes. Either that or something from *Wicked*."

"Oh—like 'For Good'? I love that one."

"Me, too. But I was thinking maybe something more upbeat and fun, like 'Popular.'"

"Ooh—that *would* be fun."

"Thanks. We'll see. . . ." She plopped down on her bed. "Enough about me—for now." She laughed. "So . . . how was your first day of seventh grade?"

I flopped down next to her. "Band was amazing! Ms. T asked me to stay after class, and—"

"How's she doing?"

"Fine. But guess what? She and Mr. Davis are engaged!"

"What? I can't believe it! My two favorite teachers are getting married! We've got to do something!"

Oh boy. I'd never get to All-County now; Sara was "off and running," as Dad liked to say.

"I know!" She grinned. "Let's throw a surprise bridal shower! We can do it in the band room!" Sara loved throwing parties.

I nodded. "That sounds like fun!" Before she started jotting down ideas and making an invitation list, I kept talking. "Speaking of fun—Ms. T wants me to audition for All-County Band!"

"Wait. What? That's fantastic! Why didn't you tell me that first?"

"Ummm . . ."

"Never mind. This is so exciting!" She pulled me in for a sideways hug.

"Thanks. But I haven't gotten in yet. It's only an audition," I said, trying not to sound as confident as I felt.

"Uh-huh," Sara said, knowing me too well. "It's a no-brainer. You'll practice, you'll nail the audition, and you'll get in," Sara said with her usual confidence.

"You make it sound so easy," I told her. "What about school?"

"Seriously? This is an incredible opportunity!"

"I know, but . . . what about my bat mitzvah? Rehearsals are the same month. . . ." Plus, I hated practicing. My bat mitzvah tutor's voice was so monotonous. Every time I listened to the MP3 file of Mr. Rubenstein chanting the Torah portion on my phone, it literally put me to sleep.

The section I was chanting was all about God asking for materials to make a portable sanctuary the Israelites could carry. It went into tons of detailed instructions, and it was my responsibility to talk about all of it as part of my speech. To be honest, I found it all pretty boring. I should've asked Dad for help a while ago; now I was embarrassed I'd waited so long.

Sara put her hands on my shoulders and looked me in the eyes. "Hey. You've got this."

"What about Mom and Dad? Even if I don't think it's too much, they will."

"Timing is everything with them," she said. "We'll just have to wait for the right moment. It'll all work out."

The way she said "we'll" made me smile. Plus, those last

four words were almost like a promise. And promises were important in our family. They weren't given, or taken, lightly; Dad made that clear to each of us early on. I still remember the first time he taught *me* about promises. . . .

I was even younger than Benji—maybe four or five. I thought Dad had promised to take me to a movie, and I was super excited because he hardly ever had any free time, let alone time to spend just with me. But, as usual, a congregant needed him for something, and he had to cancel.

"I'm sorry, Rebecca." Dad was the only one who called me by my full name. "Mrs. Sherman is in the hospital," he continued, "and I—"

"You promised!" I probably crossed my arms and stomped my foot to show I was upset.

"No." He covered my tiny hand with his big one. "I *wanted* to take you to the movie, but I didn't promise. A promise is sacred, like the truth."

I remember he took a piece of paper and my blue crayon and wrote two Hebrew letters. "This is aleph," he said, "the first letter in the Hebrew alphabet. This"—he pointed to the second letter—"is tav, the last letter. And this"—he wrote a third letter in between the others, "is mem, which is right in the middle of the alphabet.

"When you put them together, they spell *emet*, which means 'truth.' Truth is the center of everything." He smiled and kissed me, his thick beard tickling my cheek. "The *truth* is, I have to go now," he said gently, "but I *promise* to take you to that movie as soon as I can."

He did, too, the very next day.

Ever since then, I've taken promises very seriously, whether the promise is *for* me or *from* me.

Once Sara promised everything would work out, I believed it. I believed *her*.

The two of us talked a little more, then I split the rest of my night into three sections: homework, bat mitzvah study, and flute (only one of which was fun). I loved that my sister and I were on parallel paths, both of us passionate about music, both of us chasing our dreams, like Mom always said we should.

When she was in high school and college, Mom's dream was to be a singer. She had a four-octave range, like Ariana Grande and Miley Cyrus (Adele's is only three). And even though she didn't end up singing professionally, Mom did sing in the synagogue choir when she wasn't too busy. And she sang at home all the time: ballads, show tunes, folk songs, jazz . . . pretty much anything. And all of it was beautiful. Sometimes I would stop whatever I was doing and just listen to her.

I took my flute out of the case again and played the same songs: ballads, show tunes, folk songs, jazz . . . pretty much anything.

And the whole time I played, I wondered if anyone would ever stop what they were doing just to listen to me.

NOW

I WISH
   Mom could still sing.
   I wish
   Dad could still explain.
   I wish
   Sara could still dream.
   I wish
   Jon could still joke.
   I wish
   Benji could still laugh.
   Most of all, I wish
   I could still
   imagine a happy ending.

4

THE ALL-COUNTY AUDITION was the only thing I thought about for the next ten days. If I wasn't sitting at school or doing homework, all my free time was spent working on sight-reading, scales, and the sample etudes Ms. T gave me last week after class. Actually, "working" was the exact opposite of how it felt. I loved every second of playing these short exercises for practice.

But I couldn't wait to see the real etudes for the audition, and I wouldn't get those until one of my parents signed the permission slip for me to participate.

Which was why I was perched on the end of my sister's bed, talking on the phone with Nipa, instead of downstairs helping Sara and Mom and her sister, Ruth, in the kitchen. As usual, Aunt Ruth and Uncle Jacob were visiting for Rosh Hashanah. They used to bring Cousin Miri, too, but the past few years she'd been too busy getting straight As at Princeton.

Then she started NYU medical school and since then, she's been even busier.

Miri was the best. Sara and I loved when Miri visited. Even though there was an eight-year age difference between her and my sister (and thirteen years between her and me), Miri never minded hanging out with us. She was fun and smart, and we both thought of her as an older sister.

"I still don't see what you're freaking out about," Nipa said. "You're totally going to nail that audition!"

I looked at Sara's clock radio for the third time. Since Aunt Ruth was staying in my room, I was staying with Sara, which suited me just fine. Sara sleepovers were one of my favorite things. I got up from her bed and started to pace. "I don't even know if I *can* audition! Ms. T kept me after class today and said the permission slip is due this Friday or I can't even try out," I told Nipa.

"Oh," she said, immediately understanding my problem. "Sounds like you can't put off asking them any longer. . . ."

"Exactly. Luckily, Sara says this is the perfect night to ask them because they'll want everyone to be happy and in the right frame of mind to pray."

Before Nipa could respond, there was a knock on the door and Benji ran in.

"You're supposed to wait before you come in," I told him for the millionth time.

"Wait for what?"

"For me to—never mind. . . ."

"Mommy says dinner's ready!" And then he ran back out again.

It was barely five o'clock and I wasn't even close to hungry. I sighed. "Nipa, I've gotta go. Dinner's early because—"

"It's the Jewish New Year and your dad has to get to synagogue," she said with a smile in her voice. "Becky, we've been best friends since kindergarten. I know the drill."

"Sorry. I'm just nervous about All-County. What if they say no?"

"They know how important music is to you."

"I hope you're right."

When I got to the dining room, everyone and everything was in place. Two white candles in crystal candlesticks waited to be lit and blessed. The deep blue goblets we used only for holidays were filled with grape juice or wine. And a golden-brown challah, braided and fragrant, sat on the wooden cutting board Dad had gotten in Israel.

Since we were leaving for synagogue right after dinner, everyone was already dressed in their High Holiday clothes. Dad and Uncle Jacob were in suits, even though Dad's would be mostly hidden under his white prayer robe. Mom and Aunt Ruth were in what they called "tasteful and understated" skirts and blouses, and Sara and I were in modest dresses with the silver Star of David necklaces we always wore. Even Benji wore a navy blazer and khaki dress pants.

As I sat down at the table, Mom stood up. She lit the candles, waved her hands in front of her face three times, then closed her eyes and recited the blessing. Next, Dad chanted a longer blessing over the wine, and finally Benji got the honor of blessing the challah.

"*Baruch ata Adonai Eloheinu melech ha'olam hamotzi lechem min ha'aretz.*"

He said it with such pride, I had to smile. We all answered "amen," and each of us tore off a piece and tasted the yummy, eggy bread.

"And now for the real food," Uncle Jacob joked.

"Hush, you." Aunt Ruth kissed him on the head and stood up.

Mom got up, too, and smiled at her sister. "I don't know what I would do without your help."

"I don't know what I would do without your brisket." Dad grinned at Aunt Ruth.

No question; he was definitely in a good mood.

Sara must have been thinking the exact same thing because she gave me a pointed look and tilted her head. I smiled and nodded back.

Mom and Aunt Ruth went to the kitchen and came back with platters overflowing with noodle kugel and honeyed carrots and Dad's beloved brisket.

The food was delicious, but my stomach was in knots because Sara was right: it was absolutely the best time to ask about All-County.

For one thing, both of my parents really were in a great mood. Dad always felt hopeful when the New Year was just beginning. And Mom always felt happy when her big sister was around, just like I did when Sara was around.

And, speaking of Sara, the cast list for *Les Miz* came out today, and that was sure to make Mom and Dad even happier. They were always so proud of her.

Sure enough, a few bites into Mom's tender brisket and the rich noodle kugel brimming with raisins and cinnamon, Sara leaned in and announced, "I have a little news."

"The audition!" Mom leaned in closer toward Sara, and Dad beamed an expectant smile her way. We'd all heard her singing the show tunes for days now. Everyone was excited to hear which part she got.

"So," Aunt Ruth prompted, "which role?"

"Eponine," Sara said with an enormous grin.

"The lead," I said, in case someone wasn't familiar with *Les Miz*. "And the part she wanted," I added. I was so happy for her!

"*One of* the leads," Sara corrected. She was always modest, but her excitement was clear.

"I knew it!" Mom said.

Uncle Jacob smiled. "Mazel tov!"

"There won't be a dry eye in the house when you sing that duet with Marius when you're dying," I said.

"Spoiler alert." Sara laughed.

"Are those friends of yours in the show, too?" Aunt Ruth asked. We all knew exactly who she meant. Sara had been doing shows with Cassidy and Jenna ever since they met at theater camp when they were around my age. I called them her "theater BFFs"; Mom called them "the Three Musketeers."

"Jenna got Fantine, and Cassidy is Madame Thénardier."

"Wait," I said. "Isn't she Eponine's horrible mother?"

Sara laughed. "We're already joking that she should be really awful to me just to get in character."

"Well," Dad said, "I can't wait to see it. Mid-November, as usual?"

"Yup!" Sara grinned. "Opening night is November sixteenth."

Three days before the All-County audition.

"When do rehearsals begin?" Mom asked, no doubt mentally adding them to the overbooked calendar she depended on to keep sane.

The last thing I wanted was to steal Sara's glory. Or ruin a really nice meal. Or upset Dad before one of the most important and well-attended services of the entire year. Still . . . it really did feel like now or never.

"Speaking of rehearsals . . ." Everyone turned to me. I looked over at Sara.

"Becky has exciting news, too." She nodded at me, which was all the encouragement I needed.

"Oh?" Dad raised his eyebrows.

"Ms. T wants me to audition for All-County Honors Band." Mom's hands flew to her heart. "Becky, that's wonderful!"

"Very exciting!" Aunt Ruth chimed in.

"Thanks." I smiled at Sara, who was grinning from ear to

ear. This was going way better than I'd expected!

"I'm sure it's an honor to be asked," Dad said. "However, between schoolwork and your bat mitzvah, I'm not sure this is the best time—"

"Dad, no! No 'however.' Please . . . I really, *really* want to do this. At least let me try. I might not even make it!"

Mom smiled. "You'll make it."

"They'll be lucky to have you," Aunt Ruth said.

"So I can audition?" I looked at Mom and held my breath. Unfortunately, she looked at Dad.

"Rebecca," he said, "we appreciate how much you love music. But last I checked, you hadn't made any progress on your speech, let alone come up with a mitzvah project yet. Am I right?"

He knew he was right, on both counts. And so did I.

"Abba," Sara said. "Her bat mitzvah isn't 'til the end of January. She's got plenty of time!"

"She has already had 'plenty of time.'" He turned back to me. "When is this concert?"

"February," I said softly.

He sighed. "Which means rehearsals will also be in January . . ."

"Ari . . ." Mom didn't say another word, but that was enough. I knew she was on my side. She was all about us following our dreams.

"Tell you what," Dad said. "After we're back from synagogue tonight, I'll listen to you chant your Torah portion. If you've made progress, you may audition."

Jon and Sara always teased me about my poker face—or lack of one. So I knew one look at my face told Dad how little progress I had actually made. It was hard enough *reading* the Hebrew words—without vowels—let alone *chanting* them. I stared at my still-full plate of food, knowing I wouldn't eat another bite.

He sighed and shook his head. We both knew the Torah portion should be at least partly ready by now.

Unlike me, though, Sara wasn't giving up. She looked at Mom. "Eema. Abba . . . if Becky needs any help with her bat mitzvah, I'll work with her."

"That's very generous of you," Dad said, "but Mr. Rubenstein is a fine tutor, and *your* plate is already very full."

"No, it isn't," Benji piped up. "She only has a little brisket left."

Sara smiled at him. "He means I'm very busy." She smiled at me. "But I always have time for Becky. And Mr. Rubenstein isn't very . . ."

Dad tilted his head and waited.

"Mr. Rubenstein puts me to sleep," I blurted out. "Every time I listen to his voice."

Mom covered her smile.

Dad took a sip of wine and considered. "Rebecca. You are a talented musician, and I am very proud of you."

"Thanks." I crossed my fingers.

"And I have no doubt you will have many opportunities to

audition for All-County—even All-State. But you will have only *one* bat mitzvah, and you need to be ready for it. I'm sorry, but the answer is no."

I wanted to argue. I wanted to beg.

I wanted to cry and scream and run to my room and slam the door.

But there was no time for any of that. I had to go to synagogue and pray . . . for a happy New Year.

I walked into the building as familiar as my own house. Where Dad's office was, full of books in English and Hebrew. And the sanctuary, with its beautiful stained glass windows and the large wooden ark that housed three Torahs. Where there were rows of seats and rows of plaques with the names of loved ones who had died, including all my grandparents. Where Dad had been the rabbi since before I was born. Where I always felt welcomed and accepted and loved.

I walked into that building and said hello to dozens of congregants, who'd known me all my life and greeted me with the warmest of smiles. And I smiled back, but I felt like crying.

I sat and stood and listened as my father led the congregation. Heard his booming voice talk about endings and new beginnings. About forgiveness and second chances and new opportunities.

About hope.

I heard him wish everyone a good and sweet New Year. It

was the traditional thing to say, but for the first time, it felt like he was wishing it for everyone except me.

I tried to pray, but all I kept thinking about was how little I usually asked for. How I was always fine with hand-me-downs like Mom's paperbacks, or several days in a row of leftover sandwiches from a turkey or brisket dinner. How I never asked for trendy clothes, like Sara, or a fancy new gaming device, like Jon—or even a puppy or kitten, like Benji.

All-County was the *one* thing I wanted that was shiny and new and just for me. And each time I tried to listen as my father led his congregants in prayer on one of the most important and holiest nights in our religion, all I could hear was "I'm sorry, but the answer is no."

5

WHEN WE GOT home, Sara went to take a shower and I went straight to her room, since Aunt Ruth was in mine. I was desperate for some quiet time, but I kept replaying the voices from a few hours earlier.

"They know how important music is to you."

"Becky has exciting news, too."

"They'll be lucky to have you."

"You are a talented musician."

But none of it mattered. The answer was still no.

I thought about calling Nipa again—we wouldn't see each other for the next two days because I'd be spending them at the synagogue—but it was late, and there was nothing she could do to cheer me up anyway.

I thought about calling Jon. He could always find something funny to say about pretty much anything. It was three hours earlier in Los Angeles, but I remembered one of his roommates had invited him for Rosh Hashanah dinner with his family, so he was probably in the middle of that. Besides, I doubted even my big brother could come up with something funny about this.

I got in Sara's bed and reached over to turn off the lamp when there was a knock at the door.

The door opened and Mom came in. At first, she just sat down next to me and didn't say a thing, just stroked my hair like she did when I was Benji's age. It was soothing and comforting and it felt like she knew how *I* felt.

"I've been thinking," she said softly. "Would you like me to talk to your father? About All-County? It might not make a difference, but—"

"Yes!" I sat up. "Please! He'll listen to you...."

"Well, we'll see about that." She smiled. "But I'm happy to try."

"Thank you!" I hugged her tight and she hugged me back.

"As soon as the High Holy Days are over, I'll—"

I pulled back. "But that's ten days from now. There's not enough time!"

"You know how busy he is this time of year. There won't be a good time to discuss *anything* with him until after Yom Kippur."

"I can't wait that long! I need written permission by this Friday."

"I'm sorry, Becky. If I ask him now, when he has so much on his mind, he'll just say no again."

"But what about dreams?" I asked her.

"What?"

"You know. Dreams! For Jon it's directing. For Sara it's Broadway. For me, it's All-County!"

"Becky—"

"Mom! Just because you gave up on *your* dream doesn't mean I should give up on mine!" As soon as the words came out, I felt bad. She was only trying to help, and—

"Oh, honey. I didn't give up on my dream. I met your father . . . and my dream changed." She touched my cheek, her fingers feather soft. "I wish I could do more, but talking to Dad *after* Yom Kippur really is the best I can do."

It wasn't the best *I* could do.

It felt like the day had already gone on way more than twenty-four hours—but, according to Sara's clock, it was only a little after ten. Benji was asleep, Mom was in the living room, spending time with Aunt Ruth and Uncle Jacob, and Sara was in Jon's room talking with one of her theater BFFs.

Which meant that Dad was alone in his study. This was nothing new—he always spent time there—but especially during the High Holy Days, when he had even more work and even more sermons to write than usual. He said he always did his best thinking at night, when it was quiet. I needed to do my best thinking, too.

I needed to think of something he couldn't possibly disagree with—something to convince him to let me audition.

I got out of bed and opened the door; sure enough, there was light coming out of his study. As I padded down the hall, I thought maybe Mom was wrong. Maybe this was the perfect time to talk to him, just the two of us, when everything felt full of possibility.

"Dad?" I called outside the closed door.

"Rebecca?" I heard his chair move away from the computer, heard his footsteps approach.

"Are you busy?"

"Just working on the sermon for tomorrow morning." He opened the door and motioned for me to come in and take the seat across from his, which was an excellent sign.

"How's it coming?" I asked, figuring that was a good place to start.

He shrugged. "It's coming." He narrowed his eyes at me, the same way Nipa did when she could tell something was up with me. "But I'm guessing you aren't here to discuss my sermon," Dad said.

"Actually, I am. Kind of," I admitted. "I've been thinking about Rosh Hashanah."

"Is that so?" He looked surprised but pleased.

I nodded. "I've been thinking about how you said that the New Year is a time for new beginnings and opportunities...."

He took off his glasses, rubbed his eyes, then put them back on. "Is this about that All-County audition?"

I felt my cheeks turn red. "I'm sorry to bother you when you're so busy, but—"

He raised his hand to stop me. "You know I always have time for you, sweetheart. And I appreciate what you're saying."

"You do?" My heart beat faster, and I leaned forward in the chair. "Does that mean I can audition after all?"

He looked at me for a second or two, then reached out and took my hands in his. "I'm sorry. But I can't approve of a new commitment when you're nowhere near completing your first. You need to put more time and effort into your Torah portion, your speech, your mitzvah project...."

"I can! I promise!"

"I know you *can*. But you haven't." He shook his head. "Your bat mitzvah is a once in a lifetime event. It will be your day, Rebecca. Your ceremony. Your celebration. Your achievement."

There was nothing more to say and we both knew it.

When he took his hands away, mine felt cold and empty.

I went back to my sister's room. Took off my dress clothes. Let them fall to the floor. I threw on my soft pajamas and added my fuzzy slippers just as Sara walked in. She was headed my way, then stopped when she saw my abandoned clothes on her rug.

"Sorry about that." I went over to pick them up, but she beat me to it.

"No worries." She brushed them off and hung them up. "We all skip the closet once in awhile."

"I was making a statement."

"I see." She reached for my skirt and blouse. "Want me to throw them back on the floor?"

I tried not to smile.

She touched my shoulder. "Hey . . . I'm really sorry about what Dad said."

"You already heard?"

"Did you not notice me at the dinner table?"

"Oh—I thought you meant just now."

"Just now?" Sara echoed.

"I talked to him again. Or, tried to. I was hoping I could change his mind."

Sara squeezed my hand. "Maybe if you work extra hard on your bat mitzvah, he'll reconsider. I'll help you."

"That's okay. Besides, we both know once he makes a decision . . ."

We sighed in perfect unison.

She sat on her bed and I followed. Neither of us spoke. Hopelessness set in. I felt completely exhausted.

"I think I'm gonna go to sleep," I told her.

"Okay," Sara said. "Enough with the moping."

"I wasn't moping . . . much."

"Well, I'm very sorry to interrupt your *not* moping," Sara said, "but maybe instead of feeling sorry for yourself, we could do something fun."

I sat up a little straighter. "Fun?"

"Did you forget we're having a sleepover?"

"No, but . . ."

"Do you honestly think we're going to call it a night already?"

I no longer felt exhausted. "What did you have in mind?"

"Oh, I don't know. Maybe a little something you've been pestering me to do for half a year?"

"Spa day?" Ever since she had a spa day last spring break with Cassidy and Jenna, I'd wanted one, too.

"Spa *night*, anyway . . ."

"Is this because you're feeling sorry for me?" I asked.

Sara smiled. "Maybe."

"I accept your pity." I jumped off the bed.

"Okay." She grabbed her phone and started typing rapid fire. "Do we have . . . cucumbers and avocado?"

"I thought we were having spa day, not making salad!"

Sara laughed. "You're gonna have to trust me on this, okay?"

I nodded easily. There was no one I trusted more.

"Go to your room and get your robe," she instructed.

Three minutes later I was putting on my favorite fuzzy blue bathrobe when she peeked into my room. "A *nice* robe. Not that ratty blue one."

I sighed, put it back on the hanger, and took out the plush purple one I always thought was too nice to wear.

By the time I got to the kitchen, Sara was already at work adding slices of avocado to a bowl with coconut oil and honey. Then she looked at her phone and frowned.

"We're missing lavender oil."

"I've got this...." Before she could ask where I was going, I ran upstairs, certain I'd seen it somewhere. I looked around for a minute or two, then grabbed the fancy little bottle and ran back to the kitchen. "Did someone say lavender oil?" I handed it to her proudly.

My sister looked pleased—then suspicious. "Wait a second." She looked toward the living room, then whispered, "Isn't this Mom's?"

"It's only four drops," I whispered back. "She'll never miss it!"

She shook her head, then carefully squeezed four drops into the bowl. She held the bottle under my nose. "What do you think?"

I breathed in the flowery fragrance. "Nice."

"It's supposed to help you relax."

"Maybe I should use it before math tests," I joked.

Sara capped the bottle and I stirred everything together into a gloppy paste while she cut four slices of cucumber.

"So, what's all that goop for?"

She smiled. "You're about to find out...."

I followed her back upstairs, returned Mom's lavender oil, and went to Sara's room. She put the bowl and the plate of cucumber on her dresser, then grabbed her phone and turned on the Bluetooth speaker. "Classical, rock, or show tunes?"

"Surprise me." Although I knew what she would choose already.

"*Fiddler* or *Wicked*?"

"Tevye," I named the hero—such as he is—in *Fiddler on the Roof.*

She hit play and we both smiled as Isaac Stern's gorgeous violin filled the room. I was finally starting to relax—maybe lavender oil really did work!—when Sara stuck a brush into the bowl and headed in my direction.

"Uh . . . no way," I told her.

"But this is the face mask," she said, like that made a difference.

"Nope."

"Oh, come on—it's half the fun. Besides, you're the one who wanted a spa day."

"N. O."

"Fine. I'll put it on myself first." I watched as she slathered goop all over her face, leaving only her lips and eyes untouched. "It feels really nice. And it'll make your skin glow. . . ."

I was still nowhere near convinced, but then my favorite song, "Matchmaker," came on and she started humming and before I knew it, I was, too. Sara seized the moment and covered my face in avocado goop.

It actually did feel really nice.

"Okay," she said. "Now lie on your back and close your eyes."

I lay down and a second later she put two cold slices of cucumber on my eyelids. And then I heard a click. "You did not just take a picture of me!"

She laughed. "Don't worry. I'll let you take one of me before I wash it all off. Okay?"

"Fine. But no one ever sees it unless I say so."

"I promise."

She lay down beside me and we listened to the music. "Ever wonder what the story would be like if Tevye had five sons instead of five daughters?"

"Not really." I took one of the cucumber slices off so I could look at her. "Why?"

"I feel like he would've gone easier on them if they were boys. Especially Chava."

She took off her cucumber slices and turned to me, her face serious—or, as serious as a face covered in goop could be. "Tevye let his first two daughters be with the guys they loved. Why not her?"

"Because he wasn't Jewish!"

"So?"

"So . . . she broke the rules!"

Sara sat up. "She fell in love. There are no rules for that."

"There are according to Dad." I sat up, too. "And God. Remember the Ten Commandments? Thou shalt not kill? Thou shalt not steal? Thou shalt not . . ." I let out a breath. "I can never remember all of them."

Sara rolled her eyes at me. "Seriously? You're talking to *me* about breaking rules? About stealing? What about stealing Mom's credit card?"

"I didn't steal it! But if I had, it would've been for a good reason."

She lay back down. "Exactly! You would have broken the rules *for a good reason.*"

"Why are you getting so worked up about this, Sara? Are we still talking about Chava?"

She looked at me, *really* looked at me. Like she was about to tell me something. Then she stood up. "We should wash the goop off our faces before we fall asleep."

A few minutes later, teeth brushed and faces goop-free, we were back in her bed. She leaned over and turned out the lamp. "Listen," she said in the darkness, "you know I love Abba, right?

"Of course!"

"But that doesn't mean I always agree with him." She leaned in so close, I could smell her minty toothpaste. "I think maybe, sometimes, rules need to be broken."

"What rules? When?"

"I think we all have to figure that out for ourselves."

I heard her yawn. Felt her roll away from me. Before I knew it, her breaths were soft and even, and I could tell she'd fallen asleep.

But I didn't. I couldn't.

I was too busy trying "to figure things out" for myself. . . .

6

I DON'T KNOW how or when I finally fell asleep. But it was definitely before I figured out which rules should be broken, how to break them, or when.

There was one thing I *had* figured out, though: I did not want to go back to synagogue for the morning service.

I did not want to listen to my father give a sermon from the pulpit.

I did not want to smile and say hello to the other congregants all over again.

I did not want to act like I was happy. Like nothing had changed.

I did not want to pray, or even try to.

I didn't even want to get out of bed.

I was about to roll over when the door opened.

"Hey, sleepyhead," Sara said. "If you get up this second, there might still be some of Uncle Jacob's world-famous chocolate chip pancakes left. If Benji hasn't finished them all."

I doubted they were world-famous (though they should have been). Back in the old days, when Miri still visited and Jon was my age and I was Benji's age, we'd all race down the stairs for those pancakes. Miri would tell us stories about college, Jon and Sara would see who could eat the most pancakes the fastest, and I sat there, soaking it all up. But the old days were gone, and so were Miri and Jon.

And my chance of trying out for All-County Band.

"He can have 'em."

Sara came over to the bed and put her hand on my forehead. "Are you okay?"

I shrugged. Spa day—or night—had been a fun escape, but reality had set in again, and all I felt was tired. And sad.

Before she could investigate further, Benji walked in, his mouth smeared with chocolate. "I saved you some of Uncle Jacob's pancakes," he announced. "They're leaving tomorrow, so we won't have them again 'til next year!"

"Thanks, but I'm not hungry."

Benji approached the bed, eyes huge. "Are you sick?"

"She might be," Sara said before I could answer.

"Oh no!" Benji gasped. "I'll go get Mommy!" He ran out.

"I'm okay," I told Sara. "Just didn't get much sleep last night."

"Maybe you should stay home."

"From synagogue?" I felt my eyes grow as wide as Benji's. "It's Rosh Hashanah morning! We never miss that service."

I paused. "Wait . . . is this one of those rules we're supposed to break?"

Sara shrugged and smiled at me. "You need to figure that out for yourself."

"What's this about you not feeling well?" Mom hurried into the room, her face full of worry. She felt my forehead.

"She hardly got any sleep," my sister said. "I felt her tossing and turning all night."

"Even though *you* were asleep?" Mom pointed out, eyebrows raised.

"Well," Sara said, "I mean—"

Mom cupped my cheek with her soft hand. "You do look tired, Becky. Maybe you should skip this morning. If you get a good rest, you can join us tonight."

I guess Sara was right; some rules were okay to break.

A little while later, everyone left for services. Everyone except me.

It was the first day of the Jewish New Year. I was supposed to be at synagogue. My family was there, and I was here. It felt like I was doing something wrong.

If this was breaking the rules, I didn't like it. It didn't feel good. It didn't feel right.

It just felt lonely.

So I did what I always did when I felt lonely—reached for my flute. Without thinking, I automatically played the opening notes of the practice etudes Ms. T gave me for All-County.

Then I stopped.

What was the point if Dad wouldn't even let me try out for it?

What was the point of Ms. T inviting me to audition?

What was the point of all those hours I'd practiced?

It felt like the one thing that always made me feel better—made me feel special—was taken from me.

And that felt awful, and totally unfair.

And there was absolutely nothing I could do about it.

I returned the flute to its case, then put the sheet music back in my band folder ... and saw the All-County permission slip, still waiting for one of my parents to sign at the bottom.

Suddenly Sara's voice popped into my head: "I think maybe, sometimes, rules need to be broken."

Was it possible this was one of those times?

I thought about what would make me feel worse: forging a signature or missing the audition.

I thought about it while I showered. As I got dressed. When I ate a bowl of cold cereal by myself.

I thought about it while my family was at synagogue, praying on the very first day of the Jewish New Year.

And then I went into my parents' bedroom, found an old receipt in one of the drawers ... and copied Mom's signature the best I could.

7

"YOU DID WHAT?" Nipa's eyes were bulging.

"Shh." I looked around the lunchroom. Luckily, as usual, no one was paying attention to us. "I had no choice."

"You did have a choice—and you chose to be a *criminal*!"

"I think you're overreacting." I ignored my brisket sandwich and took a bite of her mom's yummy spiced lentils instead.

"Yeah? Well. Enjoy that curry while you can. They don't serve it in jail, you know."

"Hey. You're supposed to be on my side."

"Not when you forge your mom's signature!" Nipa crossed her skinny arms across her chest and looked as angry as I'd ever seen her—which still wasn't all that scary.

"I shouldn't have told you." I took another bite; this one was really spicy.

"No! You shouldn't have *done* it!"

I started coughing. "Whoa! This is super spicy!" I coughed some more and took a gulp of milk. "Did your mom use an entire jar of cayenne pepper?" I grabbed my milk and drank some more, only it wasn't helping.

Nipa just shook her head, ignoring me. "I can't believe Sara didn't talk you out of this."

"I didn't exactly tell her," I said, gasping for air.

"You didn't 'exactly' tell her? What does that mean?"

"I didn't tell her, okay?"

Her eyes managed to get even bigger, and I worried she might pass out. "No! Not okay! Since when do you keep secrets from Sara?"

She was right; that had been the worst part of all.

My nose was running and my eyes were tearing and I didn't know if it was from the spicy food . . . or something else. "I wanted to tell her! Honest! But I knew she would try to talk me out of it. Sara never breaks the rules."

Nipa looked around the cafeteria. Then she leaned across our table and whispered, "Okay. Forget Sara. What're you gonna do when your parents find out?"

"You need to stop worrying so much! I've got it all under control, okay?" She looked at me and I looked at her and we both knew I had nothing under control. At all.

When in trouble . . . lie to your best friend. "It'll be fine. Besides, I might not even get into All-County. Then all this worrying will be for nothing."

My stomach was killing me and my hands were sweaty

and my head was spinning with what-ifs. So I did what I always did when someone was upset with me: changed the subject. Besides, one of my favorite nights of the year was less than three hours away, and I wanted to enjoy every minute of it.

I had to miss all the high school sporting events that fell on Friday night or Saturday afternoon, which was Shabbat. But when they were other times, I got to sit in the bleachers instead of the sanctuary. (Spoiler alert: the bleachers are way more fun.)

"What should we wear to the football game tonight?"

"Don't try to change the subject," Nipa said.

"I'm thinking my white skirt and—"

"White skirt? To a football game? Have you seen those bleachers? And what if you get nachos? You know you'll spill them all over yourself."

I sighed. "You're right. . . . Hey! We should wear the turquoise bangles!"

She smiled. "That's a great idea! Like the school colors!"

I nodded. "When we get to high school, we can wear turquoise all the time!"

"It is a very flattering color," Nipa said. "For both of us."

And, just like that, Operation Change the Subject was a success.

Sara and I made it to the high school forty-five minutes before the first football game of the season, and the parking lot was already almost full. We made our way to our usual meetup spot at the snack shack, where Nipa, Cassidy, and Jenna were already waiting.

I loved football. Actually, I loved the pep rallies. Specifically, the pep *band*. I couldn't wait to be part of it in two years! I always begged to go to as many high school games—and concerts—as I could.

Nipa and I exchanged a quick hug, then admired our matching turquoise bangles.

Sara shook her head and smiled. "You guys are too much." She turned to her friends. "Can you save me a seat? I'll take the 'twins' here to their favorite spot."

Her friends went one way while Sara guided Nipa and me to the best seats in the house: directly behind the pep band.

"You are such a band groupie."

I grinned. "Guilty as charged."

"I'll check up on you at halftime," she reminded me. "Try to stay out of trouble." She went off to find her friends as Nipa and I settled in and watched the musicians gather in front of us.

"Hey," I said to her. "I know I have some stuff to figure out, but can we please not talk—or even think—about it tonight?"

She looked at me for a second, then smiled. "Okay."

I closed my eyes so I could soak up everything all around us: the banter, the camaraderie, the jokes, the music.

"Becky!" Nipa nudged me. "They're about to start!"

I opened my eyes. We looked at each other and grinned.

The band director was Mr. Silverstein, a tall, skinny guy in his early thirties, and he always led his band with a perfect mix of authority and fun. After a few songs, he stepped aside and a short white girl with a long blond braid stood up in front of me. She put her trumpet down, took Mr. Silverstein's place, and started to conduct.

I leaned in to get a better view and accidentally hit her trumpet. The mouthpiece fell out and disappeared!

I couldn't believe it! A million thoughts raced through my head: I'd be kicked out of pep band before I even got to high school; the lead trumpet player wouldn't be able to play; and, most of all, Sara would kill me.

Plus she'd never take me to another game.

"Becky!" Nipa looked at me wide-eyed. I could tell that half of her was horrified and half of her was trying really hard not to laugh. I, on the other hand, was one hundred percent horrified.

"Did you see where it went?" I shouted so she could hear me over the band.

She shook her head, still trying not to laugh.

"It's gotta be somewhere! I have to find it!" I bent over and scanned the bleachers, but there were so many feet and backpacks and soda cans and popcorn bags and a thousand other things. . . . It was hopeless.

I looked at Nipa. "What am I going to do?" My voice sounded as shaky as I felt.

Before she could answer, I heard a voice ask, "Looking for this?"

I looked up. A slender boy with reddish-blond hair and bright blue-green eyes was smiling down at me. He opened his hand and showed me the most beautiful sight I'd ever seen—the trumpet mouthpiece.

He held his finger to his lips, looked around to be sure no one was watching, and quickly put the mouthpiece back on the trumpet, where it belonged.

I wanted to thank him. I wanted to hug him. I wanted to tell him he just saved the day—and probably my life.

But before I could even form the words, he smiled, said, "Enjoy the rest of the game," and disappeared down the bleachers.

Nipa grabbed my hand. "OMG!" She squealed. "It was like something out of a movie! He's, like, a real-life superhero! Like Captain America!"

I nodded, still searching for him in the crowd. But he was gone. I turned to Nipa, who was still grinning like this had been the best thing ever. "I don't even know his name...."

"Maybe your paths will cross again," she said.

"Sure," I told her. "I cross paths with cute high school guys all the time."

She shrugged. "You never know."

The crowd went wild—someone must have scored a goal or something. We stood up along with everyone else and cheered.

NOW

HEY, NIPA TEXTS me. **Pep band's playing tonight. Wanna come with?**

I think for about two seconds, then text one word back: **No.**

She immediately texts back: **Why not?**

You know why.

Might make you feel better . . .

Could it? Could anything?

I think for a few seconds more, then text again.

No.

"SEE YOU ALL next week," Jon said over the computer screen. The six of us were wrapping up our Saturday evening video chat. It was hard to believe it was the last week of October already, and we'd been doing these calls every week since he left. Seeing him smile when he talked about the second short film he was working on, hearing funny stories about his three roommates that made us all laugh, feeling his excitement about being a production assistant on someone else's big project . . .

I loved seeing him so happy. But it was hard, too.

During the week, I had so much going on: schoolwork, practicing for the All-County audition, and every once in a while even working on my bat mitzvah. And because I was so busy, I missed my big brother a little less. Then Saturday night rolled around, and I'd seen him and listened to him, and it was nice and everything, but it made me miss him all over again.

After we said our goodbyes, Mom switched the screen back to her email and Sara stretched her arms over her head, probably anxious to get to another *Les Miz* rehearsal. Dad stood, ready to write next week's sermon, and I had to work on my bat mitzvah speech, or at least try to.

But before any of us left the room, Benji spoke up. "I was wondering, since my birthday's tomorrow, and since Jon's gone . . . can I get a puppy?"

I knew his chances were somewhere between zero and none, but I had to give him credit for asking every single day the week before. He did not give up easily.

"We are not replacing your brother with a dog!" Mom said.

"How 'bout a cat?" Sara suggested with a smile.

"Or a bunny?" I threw in for good measure.

"None of us have time for a pet right now, sweetie." Mom ruffled Benji's light brown curls. "I'm sorry." She looked over at Dad—also known as her ally in all things, especially animal related.

"I don't know," he said, giving me the shock of my life. I held my breath to see what happened next.

"Ari!" Mom was clearly as surprised as we were. "You can't be serious."

Dad tilted his head to the right, the way he always did when giving a matter his full consideration. "The kids are all old enough now to take care of a pet. . . ."

Mom shook her head. "Yes, but—"

"I'll help!" Benji cried out.

"Me, too," I said.

"Count me in," Sara said. "Especially once my auditions are over." When she wasn't doing homework or performing *Les Miz*, she was working on college applications. Since she was applying to musical theater programs, every application included an audition tape. It was a lot of extra work, but she didn't seem to mind. Just like I didn't mind practicing extra flute.

Dad put an arm around Mom's shoulder. "Let's think about it, Jill." Which was as close to a yes as Benji might ever get, but still closer than I'd expected.

Mom and Dad walked out together, and Sara was close behind. But my little brother didn't move a muscle. "Becky? Can we look at the Barks website again?"

It was the third time we'd looked this week. His best friend, Tommy, had an older sister who volunteered at the Barks Animal Shelter and had shown him the page. It had postings of dogs and cats and all sorts of animals that needed homes.

If I spent as much time on my bat mitzvah as he spent poring over those photos . . . "I don't know, Benji. I really should work on—"

"Please?"

I sighed. Those big brown eyes, the freckles, the missing front tooth . . . who could say no to that face? "Fine. But just for a few minutes, okay?"

He grinned like I was the best person ever. And I knew I wasn't—but it made me want to be.

So, we looked at the same cats and dogs and bunnies and birds we saw the last two times. "Let's see if there's anything new," I suggested.

"Like what?"

"I don't know." I clicked around and came to a page titled "Wish List," with tons of items they needed people to donate: toys, food, supplies. . . . It looked like they needed everything!

I gave Benji a hug, printed the page, and jotted down the main phone number.

I finally had my mitzvah project.

I went to my room and was reading over the wish list again when Sara texted me a photo.

What do you think? We already have the ingredients!
You and I can make it tomorrow morning.

It was a picture of a cake: the perfect one for Benji's birthday party.

I sent her a smiling emoji and texted **YES!**

"I promise you'll go next, okay?" Sara gave our birthday boy a hug, then helped one of his friends take another blindfolded whack at the SpongeBob piñata.

The SpongeBob theme was Sara's idea. Benji had been torn between Marvel and *Star Wars* when Sara came up with a third option. After she explained that it would be funny to serve Krabby patties, since we kept kosher and didn't eat crab (or Krab), Benji thought it was hilarious.

As usual, Rabbi Dad and Overextended Mom were happy to go along with whatever Sara came up with. And, as usual, I was happy to play second fiddle . . . and even happier to play the flute.

Still, it was nice to take a little break, and Benji's party was as good an excuse as any. As luck (plus a little help from Sara) would have it, he was the one who finally broke the piñata, and a dozen six- and seven-year-olds cheered and dived for the miniature candies like they were the last sweet things on earth.

Then, in case that wasn't enough sugar, we brought out the cake Sara and I made. We used chocolate cake for the patty and yellow for the bun; colored icings for ketchup, mustard, and lettuce; and white jimmies for sesame seeds. It had taken us all morning, but the huge smile on Benji's face when we brought it out was worth it.

He took a deep breath, made a wish, and blew out all the candles.

While Mom sliced up the cake, Dad scooped ice cream, Benji grinned with a face covered in red and yellow icing, and Sara recorded it all for Jon, I made a wish of my own.

As my way-too-busy family hit the pause button for a change and just enjoyed the moment, I wished we could *stay* paused: Mom and Dad didn't know about the forgery, and I still had a shot at All-County. In a strange way, it was the best of both worlds. Then again, part of me wished to skip the pause button and hit fast-forward: the audition was still three weeks away!

Every day I grew more anxious, and every night when I

finished practicing and it was time to go to sleep, all I could do was stare at my star-covered ceiling and think about wishes.

When Grandma Rachel used to visit us from Florida every spring for Passover, she and I would snuggle in my bed, stare up at those same stars, and laugh and talk long into the night. When I started getting sleepy, she'd tell me to picture whatever it was I wanted most and to make a wish on one of the stars over our heads.

"Of course, it might not come true . . ." she would always say. "Then again, you never know with wishes. When you want something with all your heart, my darling, sometimes it really can happen." And she'd hold me close and I'd pick a star and make a wish.

She was right; sometimes they did come true. Once I wished for this really cute purple coat, and I got it. And another time, I wanted to go away with Nipa and her parents for a weekend at the beach, and I got that, too. But other times I didn't get my wish. Like when I wished Grandma Rachel would move to Maryland and live with us.

Whether they came true or not, wishes were simpler back then. If I made a wish to get into All-County and it came true, my parents would find out about the forgery for sure. And their anger—or disappointment—could feel worse than my wish not coming true at all.

So I stared up at my stars-covered ceiling awhile longer, trying to figure out what to wish for.

9

THE DAY AFTER Benji's party, I was sitting at my desk, highlighting the items I thought would be easiest to collect for Barks Animal Shelter, but my thoughts were elsewhere. Some were with the mysterious boy who rescued the trumpet mouthpiece and me; some were about how amazing it would be if I really did make All-County; and the rest were wondering how—or even when—to tell Sara about the permission slip forgery. Ever since her rehearsals started taking up more time, it felt like I never saw her anymore. Or, if I did, either our parents were there, too (so I definitely couldn't talk about the forgery!), or she was working on her college applications.

I was very busy trying *not* to think about that when my door opened without a knock, which meant it could be only one person. "What's up, Benji?" I asked, not even bothering to see if I was right.

"I did something bad," he said in a wobbly voice.

I turned around, saw tears streaming down his freckled cheeks, and hurried over to him. "Benji, what happened?"

"Mommy's gonna be mad at me."

"I promise it'll be . . . Is that blood?!" I grabbed his hand. "Are you hurt? What did you do?"

"I tried to clean it up but—"

"Never mind. We need to clean *you* up first. C'mon."

Whenever one of us got hurt, we always went straight to Mom. But she was out running errands, Dad was off doing rabbi things, and Sara was at rehearsal.

Which meant it was up to me.

"Do you know what to do?" Benji stared at me, equal parts helpless and hopeful.

"Of course!" I said, trying to convince us both. For the record, I was not a fan of blood. At least, not when it was on the outside. But there was no choice. I took a shaky breath. "We'll get you cleaned up good as new." I washed the cut—luckily it wasn't deep—then covered it with an Ironman Band-Aid. "Okay. Now you can tell me what happened."

He sniffled. "I was playing with my Frisbee. . . ."

"Inside?"

He nodded. "That's why I'm in trouble! Plus, I broke Mommy's vase."

"You know the rules—" I cut myself off. Who was I to lecture him about breaking rules? "Show me."

I followed him down to the living room. Between the sofa and the side table, there were shards of jade green scattered all over the floor.

"I tried to pick them all up. . . ."

"Oh, Benji. No wonder you cut yourself! I'll be right back. Do not touch anything, okay?"

Two minutes later, I was back with a broom, dustpan, and vacuum. I used the broom and dustpan for the bigger pieces, and let Benji vacuum the really small bits.

"Good job," I told him when he was done. "You can't even tell anything broke!"

"But what about Mommy's vase? I'm still gonna get in big trouble. . . ."

I put my hands on his scrawny shoulders. "Listen. Everyone gets in trouble once in a while. The trick is knowing how to get out of it."

I searched the area for another vase, but no luck. I grabbed a decorative plate from a nearby shelf and put it where the vase had been. "There you go. She'll never notice!"

He blinked. "You mean, we're not gonna tell her?"

"Sure we will—if she asks. If she doesn't, it'll be our secret, okay?"

His face lit up. "Our secret!"

I nodded, even though the last thing I wanted was another secret. We put the vacuum, broom, and dustpan back where they belonged. Then I poured us each a glass of chocolate milk.

"Thanks, Becky." He took a sip.

"Hey, it's okay. I've got your back." I handed him a napkin

to wipe his chocolate mustache.

"Becky? Does everyone really get in trouble?"

"Sure." I took a drink.

"Even Mommy?"

"Oh. Well. Maybe not . . ."

"And Daddy?"

I smiled. "Definitely not."

"How about Jon? And Sara?"

I put my glass down. "Not that I can remember."

"So, only you?" He slurped his milk and leaned back in his chair.

I sat up straighter. "Whaddaya mean?"

"Like that time you stole those balloons for my birthday party last year?"

"I did not steal them! I *borrowed* them."

Just like I "borrowed" Mom's signature.

Was he right? Was I the only one who ever got in trouble? The only one who broke the rules? I ruffled his curls and tried not to feel like the criminal that maybe I was. "Never mind. Just . . . finish your milk."

He reached over and put his bandaged hand on my shoulder. "It's okay, Becky. I've got your back, too."

Another person who had my back was Ms. T.

Even though she'd offered to help with my audition back in September, I'd felt funny taking her up on it, especially after I turned in the forged permission slip. If she knew about that, I doubt she'd be helping me at all. Still, it was hard doing it on my own, and I needed to do my best.

"I really appreciate this," I told her. It was the third time she'd stayed after school to help me and, as usual, I felt a weird mix of gratitude and guilt.

"It's my pleasure," Ms. T said. "I see tremendous improvement in both etudes already. But the question is, what do *you* see?"

I put my flute down. "What do you mean?"

"Becky. You could play the scales perfectly. You could perform the etudes flawlessly. Even sight-read without one mistake. But you need to *believe* in yourself. You need to look confident, even if you're not. Sometimes, if you look confident often enough, one day you'll realize that you truly are."

"I thought you saw 'tremendous improvement.'"

"I did. I have. But I can't help feeling that something is holding you back. That you're holding *yourself* back."

I wanted to tell her everything, but she would never look at me the same way if I did. And she certainly wouldn't spend any more time after school working with me. Plus, she would have to tell my parents, and then everything would be over before I even found out if I was good enough. All her work, and mine, would have been for nothing.

I settled on a half-truth. "You're right. I am holding myself back. I'm feeling guilty about . . . spending time on this audition instead of my preparing for bat mitzvah. I want to do both, and I want to do them well."

Ms. T smiled at me. "I completely understand."

"You do?"

"Sometimes I feel the same way, especially these days. I don't want to shortchange my students, but I don't want to shortchange my wedding planning either! Both are very important to me."

"So, what do you do?"

She shrugged. "The best I can. That's all any of us can do, right? If your bat mitzvah and this audition are both important to you, I think you'll find a way to do them both justice. You just need to have a little faith in yourself, Becky." She smiled again. "I do."

10

THE NEXT FEW days were a busy blur of activities: school, more Jewish holidays (Sukkot and Shemini Atzeret), practicing for the audition (only ten days away!), and working on my bat mitzvah. The speech and the chanting hadn't improved much, but I was definitely making progress on the mitzvah project.

I'd highlighted the wish list items for Barks, then separated them into things I could find at home and things I might be able to get from friends and neighbors. The first list had things like cardboard box top lids (the shelter uses them as litter boxes), smooth peanut butter, and gently used blankets and towels; the second had things like dry and wet food for cats and dogs, kitten nursing bottles, and baby wipes.

I had already taken an unopened jar of peanut butter from our kitchen cabinet, and an old blanket from my closet, and was checking them both off my list, when Sara was at my door.

"Hey, do you have any—" She walked over to me. "You do know there's an open jar of peanut butter downstairs, right?"

I turned to her. "This is for my bat mitzvah project," I said proudly.

"Huh?"

"I'm collecting donations for Barks!"

She looked confused. "That shelter Benji is obsessed with?"

"That's the one." I handed her the lists. "We already have a ton of this stuff right at home!"

She scanned the papers. "Sure, but . . ."

"But what?"

"This is more Benji's thing than yours."

I shrugged. "It's still a mitzvah, right?"

"Sure, but . . . it's not something you *really* care about."

I took the papers back. "What I *care* about is getting it done. What I *care* about is having one less thing to worry about right now."

She was about to say something else when Dad stuck his head in. "Rebecca? We're leaving in fifteen minutes," he announced.

I paused, confused for a moment, then mumbled "okay" and sighed. I'd totally forgotten I had another lesson with my bat mitzvah tutor!

"I'm leaving soon, too: rehearsal!" Sara ran out of my room to get ready.

I looked at my Barks list a little longer, then grabbed my bat mitzvah folder, put on my shoes, and headed down the hall.

I made it downstairs just as Sara was at the front door. I could see her theater BFFs already waiting in our driveway.

I'd always liked Cassidy because she reminded me of Tinker Bell, with her cute blond pixie cut. And I'd always liked Jenna because she'd played clarinet back in middle school with Ms. T, and she had already offered to help us with the surprise shower in January. Jenna also had gorgeous, wavy auburn hair, which both Nipa and I envied, but we agreed that she wore way too much makeup. Cassidy and Jenna were always friendly when we crossed paths, but it made me sad that these days, they saw Sara more than I did.

"Have fun at rehearsal," I said, wishing we could've finished our conversation.

She turned to me with a wicked smile. "Have fun with Mr. Rubenstein."

I restrained myself from sticking my tongue out at her (only because Dad was nearby), then noticed something about her was different. "Wait—did you put on makeup?" It wasn't a big deal or anything, it was just that Sara always preferred the natural look—and with her looks, that was more than enough.

A strange expression crossed her face. "A little."

"You're not turning into Jenna, are you?"

"We're just having some fun."

Then I noticed her hair was different, too; she'd straightened her curls. "Did she tell you to change your hair, too?"

She reached up and touched it.

"I mean, it looks nice. Just different."

She laughed. "Meaning it usually looks hideous?"

"Only sometimes," I teased.

"Thanks so much for that. See ya later!" She ran out of the house.

"Yep," I told the closed door. "See ya."

A few minutes later, Dad and I walked into the synagogue. "After you're done with your lesson, and my meeting is over," he said, "maybe the two of us could go to Millie's. What do you say?"

Normally, that was a rhetorical question. We both knew I never turned down a trip to Millie's Milkshakes—or the chance to hang out with him, just the two of us. It hardly ever happened; he spent countless hours at synagogue every week, attending meetings, leading services, and officiating at baby namings, weddings, and funerals.

But I was pretty sure this invitation was because he felt bad—maybe even a little bit guilty—about not letting me audition. As much as I love ice cream, though, it would take a million cones to make up for that.

On the other hand, I was feeling guilty myself about the forgery, so I said, "Sure. That sounds good."

The way he smiled when I said yes made me feel ever guiltier. "I'm thinking rocky road," he said, "or maybe—" Before he could finish his sentence, a voice asked, "Rabbi Myerson?"

We both turned to see a tall man with a warm smile. His hair and beard were red, streaked with gray, and he wore a clerical collar. I knew right away he was a minister.

One of the things I loved most about Dad was that even though he was a rabbi, he was very involved with the churches and mosques in our community. I was used to seeing him with priests and imams and other clergy all the time at interfaith events, but I hadn't seen this man before.

Dad gave him a warm smile and they shook hands. "Thank you for taking time to meet with me."

"Thank you for inviting me," the man said.

Dad turned to me. "Reverend McCormick, this is my younger daughter, Rebecca."

The reverend shook my hand, too.

"Actually," I told him, "everyone else calls me Becky."

Reverend McCormick smiled. "Well, Becky, it's a pleasure to meet you." He turned to include Dad in the conversation. "Both of you. In fact, everyone I've met here has been extremely kind. My son and I are very grateful for the warm welcome."

"The reverend and his son recently relocated to Maryland," Dad explained.

Before I could find out more, Mr. Rubenstein walked in, said hi to my dad, and led me down the hall to his empty eighth grade classroom.

We sat on opposite sides of his desk, and I immediately wished I had spent less time on the mitzvah project and more on my chanting.

"So, shall we start at the beginning?" He put his hands under his bearded chin.

"Uh..."

"Or," he added, "is there a particular section you'd rather focus on tonight?"

"Oh... uh..."

Poor Mr. Rubenstein. He took a deep breath and put a smile on his face.

I knew that smile. He put it on every time we met. It was the same smile my math teacher used when she explained how to do an equation in class... again and again. "Let's start at the beginning, then," Mr. Rubenstein said, "shall we?"

I tried my best, mostly because I felt sorry for him. He couldn't help it if his monotone chanting put me to sleep.

Still, I felt sorrier for me. I was the one who had to learn this. I was the one who would be standing on the bimah in front of the entire congregation. Standing there, looking at my brother with his funny speech, and my sister with her flawless voice. If only Sara could do the chanting, and I could accompany her on my flute! Mr. Rubenstein cleared his throat, interrupting my wishful thinking. "Let's try the next three lines," he said.

I was pretty sure he was suffering as much as I was.

But at least he was getting paid.

Thirty painful minutes later, we were finally done. Dad's meeting was over, too. He met me in the lobby, and we exited the synagogue and walked to the car.

Ten minutes later, I was at Millie's Milkshakes, stirring hot fudge into my sundae. "Reverend McCormick seems nice."

"He is. I hope he and his son will be happy here." Dad sipped his cherry shake and got a little pink ice cream on his mustache.

I pointed to my upper lip, like I'd seen Mom do a zillion times. He smiled and reached for a napkin.

"Where did they live before?" I asked.

"Los Angeles."

"Wow. I hope they've got winter coats. And boots. And snow shovels."

Dad laughed. "It's a good thing you didn't tell him that. You might have scared him off."

"Can reverends get divorced?" I took a sweet, melty spoonful of sundae.

"Why do you ask?" He pointed to his upper lip.

Guess it was my turn for a napkin. "He mentioned his son but not his wife."

"Ah. You're a very good listener. I'm afraid his wife passed away a year and a half ago."

"That's so sad!"

"It is. She sounded like a lovely woman—very musical, in fact. You probably would have liked each other."

Before I could ask more questions, the bell above the entrance jingled and Cassidy and Jenna walked in . . . without Sara.

"I'm gonna get a cup of water," I told Dad. "Want some?"

He shook his head as his phone chimed.

I walked over to the counter and asked for a cup of water,

then said hi to Cassidy and Jenna.

"Hey, Becky," Cassidy said.

"How's it going?" Jenna asked, friendly as always.

"Fine, thanks." The guy behind the counter handed me a small plastic cup with water, then I turned back to my sister's friends. "Where's Sara?"

Cassidy looked at Jenna, like she didn't know the answer to a hard math problem or something.

"Oh, um . . . She had to . . . stay late—" Jenna looked at Cassidy.

"Right . . ." Cassidy looked at Jenna. "To work on her solo."

"So, how is she getting home?" I asked.

"Oh, I'm sure one of the other actors will bring her back," Jenna said.

"Yeah." Cassidy nodded again.

"Okay . . ." I said. "But—"

Their milkshakes arrived just then, and they grabbed them and said goodbye before I could ask another thing.

It was all very strange.

I took the water I hadn't needed and headed back to the table as Dad ended his call. "Mrs. Parizer just lost her father. I'll drop you off at home before I head over to her house."

We were halfway to the car when he turned to me. "Did I see Sara's friends just now?"

"Yeah. They said Sara had to stay late to work on her solo and would get a ride from someone else."

Dad nodded, but I could tell his thoughts were already

with Mrs. Parizer and her family.

He dropped me off and I walked into a quiet house, which meant Benji was asleep, Mom was in her bedroom reading, and Sara wasn't back yet. I went to my room to tackle the math homework I'd avoided earlier.

I was struggling with the last two problems left when I finally heard the front door open. I finished the problem I was on and was halfway down the hall when I saw Sara heading toward me.

"How was rehearsal?"

"Great! I would've been home sooner"—she touched her Star of David necklace—"but Cassidy and Jenna wanted to hang out awhile, so we went to Millie's after rehearsal."

"What?" I asked, certain I had misheard.

"Millie's," she repeated. "Maybe you've heard of it? They serve the best shakes and sundaes in town." She smiled. "So, how was your meeting with Mr. Rubenstein? Did you manage to stay awake this time?"

She waited for me to laugh, but I couldn't. Laughing was the last thing I felt like doing.

For the first time in my life, Sara had lied to me.

Part of me wanted to ask why she would do that, *how* she could do that. But I couldn't get those words out. Instead, I said, "I . . . need to finish my math homework."

Sara stared at me, confused. I hurried back to my room and shut the door. I wanted to slam it. I wanted to run back into the hall and ask what was going on. But there were so many emotions swirling inside me, all I could do was stand there and try to process them all.

I was angry that she would lie.

And shocked.

And hurt.

I felt betrayed.

I felt dizzy.

The person I trusted most in the whole world, even more than my mother and my father and best friend, had just lied to my face.

I felt sick.

I turned off the light, got into bed, and pulled the blanket up to my chin.

If I couldn't believe in Sara, how could I believe in anyone?

And then I thought of an even scarier question: What if this *wasn't* the first time Sara had lied to me?

11

"MAYBE IT WAS just a misunderstanding," Nipa suggested at lunch the next day.

I'd barely slept last night and had purposely stayed in my room that morning until Sara left for school. For the first time ever, I didn't want to see her.

I had no clue what happened in my first two classes, and even band wasn't as fun as usual. I just kept seeing Sara look me in the eyes as she lied.

"Nope." I shook my head. "No misunderstanding."

Nipa took a chocolate-covered doughnut out of the bag I gave her and chewed thoughtfully. She was already on dessert, and I hadn't eaten a single bite of her mom's chana masala curry, even though it was one of my favorite things on the planet. "Okay." My BFF looked me in the eye. "If there's no misunderstanding, we need to figure out why she would lie."

I couldn't help but smile at the "we," especially after the

way she'd reacted to the Great Forgery. "There has to be a reason she didn't leave with her friends."

"Jenna and Cassidy were acting kind of strange, too. They kept looking at each other, like they weren't sure what to say when I asked where Sara was."

"You think they know what's going on with her?"

"Good friends tell each other everything," I said. And then, because I couldn't resist, I added, "even when they commit a criminal act."

"Hilarious." Nipa sipped her milk. "The point is, Sara might tell them, but they wouldn't tell anyone else if it really was a secret. You know, out of loyalty."

"Which means it really *is* a secret. And Sara really *is* keeping secrets—from *me*." It felt like someone knocked the breath out of me as I put my head in my hands.

"Hey..." Nipa gave me a pity smile. "I'm sure it's nothing," she said unconvincingly.

"It's *not* nothing. My sister lied to me!"

She handed me the last doughnut. "Well, for what it's worth, I think it has something to do with the show. Or maybe someone *in* the show..."

"Wait—you think it's a boy?" That would explain the makeup and straightened hair. . . .

"Don't you?"

"I don't know. But we're going to find out. We're going to the play rehearsal. Tonight." I took a big bite of the doughnut and dug into the curry.

"What? We can't just go in there! And even if we could, which we can't, what would we say? Or do? Just sit in the audience and . . . spy on your sister?"

"Of course not!" I took another spoonful of curry: delicious as always. "Not exactly. We'll look around. See who Sara hangs out with when she's not onstage. Maybe talk to some of the cast members when she's busy."

"Are you serious right now? This is a terrible plan! We can't even *get* to the high school on our own! And we definitely can't sit in on a rehearsal uninvited! Plus, there is no way I'm talking with a bunch of high schoolers I don't know!"

I looked at her. "You're right."

She exhaled. "Thank you."

I shrugged. "I'll do the talking."

Nipa's mom dropped us off at the entrance closest to the theater. Before Nipa could even open her mouth, I said, "I know what you're thinking. But we didn't lie. We *do* need student service hours. We can't graduate high school without them!"

"Yes, but no one said we could earn them *at* the high school!"

"No one said we couldn't. . . ."

Nipa stared at me. "Who are you, and what happened to Becky?"

I was wondering the exact same thing myself. Of course, I couldn't let her know that, because the second I admitted it, Nipa would try to talk me out of my plan. So I marched straight for the double doors, trying my best to look confident, even though I totally wasn't.

"Becky, it's going to be locked."

I paused for a moment. I hadn't even thought that far ahead. She was probably right. Still . . . I pushed on the door and it opened right up. "Or not." I walked straight in while she stayed behind.

"Are you coming?" I asked, seeing the panic spreading across her face.

As we made our way to the theater, she whispered, "I still don't see how this will work. We don't have permission to—"

"Nipa, stop worrying! Leave it to me." I put on a smile and strode into the theater, channeling my sister's confidence. "Hi," I said to some tall, skinny kid standing near the entrance. "We're here for student service hours. Do you know how we can help?"

"Uh . . . Not really. You should probably talk to Mrs. Keller." He motioned to a well-dressed but frazzled-looking woman on the stage.

"Hmm," Nipa said. "She looks kind of busy. Maybe we should come back another—"

"That's okay." I talked over her. "We don't mind waiting."

The guy shrugged and left, and Nipa stared at me. I smiled, then headed to the back row so we'd be less conspicuous.

She followed and took a seat next to me. "Now what?"

"Now we wait."

We waited, but after five minutes, Nipa whispered, "I don't see Sara, do you?"

I shrugged. "Maybe she's backstage."

"Let's move down a few rows."

"What for? We can see the stage just fine from here."

Nipa grinned at me for the first time since we'd walked into the theater. "But we can see the cute actors better if we're closer."

I rolled my eyes and considered arguing, but she was doing this for me, after all. The least I could do was let her get a better look at some cute guys.

We found seats farther up. They weren't exactly hard to come by, considering practically every one was empty. A few cast members were scattered here and there, texting or trying to study. I still didn't see my sister anywhere.

"Look at the guy in the red shirt," Nipa whispered and pointed. "He looks like Michael B. Jordan."

"He does!" It only took a minute for me to figure out which part was his. "He's playing Jean Valjean. The lead."

Nipa pointed to another actor. "How about that one? The guy in stripes. He looks like a young Tom Holland!"

"Tom Holland *is* young."

"Can you tell which part he has?"

A second later he was joined by a short, curvy blond girl. "I think he's Marius. The one Sara's character is hopelessly in love with. And that must be Cosette." Sure enough, they started singing their duet. Marius had a great voice; Cosette's was okay but nothing special.

I was about to ask Nipa what she thought of their performances when her cell chimed. "It's my mom. I'll be right back." She got up and walked out to the lobby.

Marius and Cosette finished their number, and the girl playing Cosette exited the stage while a bunch of guys walked on: Marius's revolutionary friends. They were all pretty nice-looking, but one boy immediately stood out, and I instantly knew he was playing Enjolras, their leader. It wasn't only his movie star looks; he had the kind of energy and charisma that was impossible not to notice. The kind that reminded me of someone else...

Someone who had lied to me.

Before I could pay closer attention to the other actors, Nipa was back. "Well," she said, "I think it's safe to say Sara's not sneaking around with the Michael B. look-alike."

"How do you know?"

She smiled. "I saw him making out with Cosette."

I nodded toward the stage. "I'm betting it's Enjolras, the guy in the purple shirt with the dimples."

"Whoa. He's super cute."

I nodded again.

"Hey—you'll never guess who else I saw in the lobby."

"Sara?"

"Nope. The guy from the football game. The one who saved you!"

"Mouthpiece guy?"

She laughed. "Mouthpiece guy."

"I never got to thank him."

"Now's your chance."

"Okay, but keep an eye out for Sara." I went out to the lobby and spotted him at the vending machine. He punched some buttons, and a can of soda came out. He popped it open, took a sip, and noticed me.

"Trumpet Girl! Is that you?" He smiled. "Are you here to destroy the pit orchestra one instrument at a time?"

I felt myself blushing. "It's actually Flute Girl."

"Oh yeah? Is that right?" He shrugged. "Hey, flute's cool. Just do me a favor and stay away from the lighting equipment, okay?"

"Is that what you do?"

"I dabble."

"Cool," I said. Then I remembered why I'd left the theater. "I never got to thank you. For finding the mouthpiece."

"All in a day's work." He smiled again. "Well, I'd better get to it. Don't want to leave any actors in the dark." He waved and headed toward the theater.

"Wait!" I shouted after him. "I still don't know your name."

He turned around and smiled. "I'm Sean. And you are . . . ?"

"Becky. Myerson."

He raised an eyebrow. "As in, Sara Myerson?"

I nodded. "You know Sara?"

He smiled. "Doesn't everyone?"

I smiled back because it was true.

"Anyway, Becky Myerson, nice to meet you," he said. "Officially."

"You, too."

He walked toward the theater, and I went to the water fountain and took a long drink.

"Becster?"

The water went down the wrong way and I started coughing.

"Are you okay?" Sara asked.

I nodded.

"What are you doing here?"

I coughed some more, mostly to stall for time while I figured out what to say. "I thought we . . . Nipa and I . . . could help with the show for student service hours?" It sounded way more like a question than a statement. I could tell from Sara's expression that she saw right through it.

When in trouble, stick to the truth . . . as much as possible. "Actually, I just wanted to see you. You're so busy with the show and everything. You're hardly around anymore."

"I know. I'm sorry."

Before we could continue the conversation, Nipa appeared.

Sara raised her eyebrows. "Look, if you want to sit in on rehearsal, all you have to do is ask. Mrs. Keller would be cool with it. Either way, you don't need to make stuff up; you can always talk to me."

Nipa and I looked at each other and I knew we were

thinking the same thing: Sara was one to talk about making stuff up.

"Listen," my sister was saying, "we're gonna be rehearsing at least another ninety minutes. You're going to be bored way before that."

"Nipa's mom is picking us up in half an hour," I told her, which wasn't exactly true. We were supposed to call when we were done. The question was, were we?

Sara touched my shoulder. "That sounds good. When I get home, you can tell me what you think of it so far."

"I think Enjolras is really cute," Nipa said.

We both stared at Sara to see her reaction.

She laughed. "I'll be sure to let Jeff know—that's Enjolras's real name. He and Alex like to keep track of how many fans they have."

"Which one is Alex?" I asked.

"Marius."

"He's cute, too," Nipa commented.

We both stared at Sara again, but she didn't give anything away.

She turned to me. "I really am sorry I haven't made time for you lately. I will tonight, okay? I promise."

I nodded. I wanted to believe her. And in spite of everything, I *did*.

She headed backstage and Nipa texted her mom to pick us up in thirty minutes. Then we walked back into the theater, where Mrs. Keller was working with Jean Valjean.

"Look," Nipa whispered. "Sara's coming onstage."

"Maybe she's going to perform her song. Wait until you hear it!"

We watched Sara sit down on the front corner of the stage, waiting for the director to call her. Marius—or Alex—joined her. They sat close together, speaking softly, their heads almost touching.

"They look cozy," Nipa commented.

I shook my head. "I was so sure it was Enjolras."

"Speaking of . . ." Nipa said.

We watched as Enjolras/Jeff approached Sara and offered her a bottled water. Their hands touched. Did their fingers linger longer than necessary?

I didn't know what to think. I was about to get Nipa's opinion when Mrs. Keller finished talking with Jean Valjean and called Sara.

The whole time Nipa and I had been watching the rehearsal, the actors did their scenes, then left the stage. But when my sister started to sing, no one moved. I guess no one wanted to walk away from magic.

Sara drew me in from the first notes, singing softly and intimately, like she was letting me in on a secret. Her loneliness felt sad and real, and her longing to be with Marius broke my heart. She took me with her on a journey from happiness to hopelessness; from the dream of being with him to the reality of being *on her own*.

When she hit the highest, most powerful note and held

it, I found myself holding my breath along with her. Nipa reached over and took my hand, and there were tears in her eyes—and mine. And it was impossible to stay mad at Sara.

When it was over, no one in the room spoke for a few seconds. We had all witnessed something special, something... real. And I guess we all wanted to hold onto that feeling.

"That was... wow," Mrs. Keller said. "I have nothing."

"What does that mean?" Nipa asked.

"She has no notes—there's nothing to improve."

And how could there be? Even without a prop, a set, or a costume, Sara made you believe.

12

NIPA AND I spent the entire car ride back discussing Marius/Alex versus Enjolras/Jeff. But when her mom dropped me off, we were no closer to solving the mystery of who Sara liked than when we left the theater—or got there in the first place.

I walked into the house and immediately thought of all the things I needed to do before I went to sleep: study for my Spanish quiz, practice for All-County, and try to stay awake when I listened to Mr. Rubenstein's sleep-inducing bat mitzvah recording.

"Becky!" Benji jumped up from the kitchen table and greeted me with a big smile. "Wanna play KerPlunk with me and Mommy?"

"I'd love to," I told him, "but I've got so much work to do!"

"Oh." His smile disappeared, and all of a sudden, I heard myself telling Sara how she wasn't around anymore.

"But . . . I suppose I could make time for one game."

Benji's smile returned, and I knew I'd made the right call.

One game turned into two, and then I went upstairs to tackle homework and practice flute. By the time all that was done, three hours had gone by and all I wanted was to relax with TV or just go to sleep. But I wanted to see Sara even more. Plus, I felt guilty not working on my bat mitzvah chanting.

I put in my earbuds and managed to stay awake through the first few lines, but was starting to nod off when my door opened.

"Becster!" Sara walked in and plopped down on my bed as I pulled myself into a sitting position. "Were you falling asleep again?"

"No." I yawned.

"You know, it might help if you didn't listen to the recording in bed."

"I don't. Not always. Sometimes I'm at my desk. But it doesn't matter. You know Mr. Rubenstein's voice always puts me to sleep!"

"Maybe you should sell it on eBay as a cure for insomnia. After your bat mitzvah, of course."

I flopped back down on the bed. "There won't be a bat mitzvah at this rate. What if I really can't learn this? Can you imagine what people will say if the rabbi's own daughter doesn't have a bat mitzvah? Or if she does, and it's a total disaster?"

"What's the worst that could happen?" Sara asked. "They fire him?"

I sat back up. "Could they do that?"

"You should see your face right now." She laughed. "I'm kidding!"

"It isn't funny."

"You are being completely ridiculous." Sara shook her head. "If you're this worked up about your bat mitzvah, I can't wait to see you on your wedding day."

"Sorry to disappoint, but there will be no wedding day. I am never getting married."

"Speaking of marriage," she said.

This was it! She was finally going to tell me about Marius/Alex. Or Enjolras/Jeff . . .

"We need to start working on that surprise shower for Ms. T and Mr. Davis."

So much for that. Still, maybe there was a way to circle back and—

"For now, though, let's focus on your bat mitzvah."

"But—I thought we were going to talk about your rehearsal."

"We will. *After* this."

I groaned.

"I have an idea. Give me your phone." She put hers down and took it, then we listened to my bat mitzvah tutor chant the first couple of lines while we followed the words on my hard copy. Then she did her own recording of the same lines on my phone.

It was so much better than Mr. Rubenstein's.

She played her version. "What do you think?"

I smiled. "I think there's no way anyone could fall asleep listening to that."

"In that case, I'll do the first couple paragraphs and we'll see if it really helps. Deal?"

"Deal!" I gave her a hug. "Thank you."

"You're welcome. I'm going downstairs to get us some snacks. You keep at it, okay?"

"Okay." I hit play and sang along with Sara's voice. It was already working better. I was about to try it again when her cell phone chimed and a text message showed up.

You were amazing tonight. As usual. XO, Sam.

Sam?

What happened to Jeff? And Alex?

What was going on with Sara?

And who the heck was Sam?

NOW

I SAW SAM again for the first time since . . .

"Hey," he said.

"Hey," I said.

We stood there and looked at each other.

So much had happened, and it all still felt so unreal.

Neither of us knew what to say.

Or maybe we just didn't know how to say it.

13

MY AUDITION WAS less than a week away now. I was practicing sight-reading and scales every chance I got. And, thanks to a few after-school sessions with Ms. T, the etudes were getting better all the time: they were almost as perfect as they needed to be.

But I could only practice them at home when no one was around. Mom heard me playing a few days ago, after she got home from the kosher market and before she visited a sick congregant with homemade matzo ball soup.

I used to love that she cared enough to stop whatever she was doing and listen to me play, especially since she was always doing something: driving Benji here and me there, helping Sara navigate all the college craziness. And on top of all that, she spent tons of time at her other full-time (also nonpaying) job: being the rabbi's wife.

When both Dad and the cantor were unavailable, she would visit sick congregants at the hospital, even sit with them when they were so ill they were in hospice. Sometimes if a Hebrew school teacher had a last-minute emergency, Mom would substitute with no notice at all. And Saturday morning, whenever they were shorthanded, Mom helped in the synagogue kitchen, preparing the oneg for after the Saturday morning service. Basically, anytime anyone needed her, she was there.

But when she stopped to listen to me last week, it was different.

I was different.

"Becky?" Mom stood in my open door, a smile on her face. "That was lovely!"

"Oh, thanks." I quickly glanced at my desk to make sure my All-County folder was covered; luckily it was.

She came in and looked at the sheet music on my stand. "Is that a new piece?"

"Uh . . ."

"It sounded pretty advanced for seventh grade band."

"It is. I mean, it's not. For band." I bit my tongue so I would stop babbling.

Mom stood there with a question mark on her face.

"Ms. T gave it to me." At least that part was true.

"Oh?"

I shrugged modestly. "She said I needed 'more challenging material.'" I made air quotes with my fingers.

"Ms. T is right. Will you be playing this at the winter concert?"

"Oh. I don't know about that. . . ."

"Well, I hope you will. It really did sound lovely."

"Thanks, Mom." I tried not to sound, or look, as impatient as I felt. It wasn't that I didn't love her being there, or listening to me play. I just wanted her to stop asking questions so I could stop telling her lies.

Mom gave me a quick kiss on the top of the head and left. I packed up my flute and sheet music, then glanced past my music stand to my bat mitzvah speech notebook. My blank bat mitzvah speech notebook. Okay, not totally blank. I'd written down a few notes and some random thoughts. But I still had no idea what to write, or talk, about. And it was way past time to figure it out.

Switching gears, I sat down at my desk and pulled out the Torah portion, determined to come up with something. As I read the passages for the third or fourth time, one phrase jumped out at me: "I will arrange My meetings with you there...."

Of course I understood this was God explaining that he would meet with Moses ... but all I could think about was Sara meeting with Sam, and my mind filled with questions.

Did they meet during school? After school? Outside of school? And where had they met in the first place?

Was Sam involved with *Les Miz*, too? Was he there when I was at the high school with Nipa? Did he have a supporting role in the show? A small, background part, maybe?

Or maybe he wasn't in the show at all. Maybe he didn't even go to her high school!

And then there was the biggest question of all: Why was

Sara keeping Sam a secret—especially from *me*?

I don't know how much time went by before there was a knock on my door and Benji ran in. "Mommy says we're almost ready for dinner and she wants you to help." Then he ran out again. I closed my mostly empty bat mitzvah speech notebook and met my sister in the hall. "Hey," I said. "How's your audition recording going? Which one is it today?"

"Carnegie Mellon."

"Is that still your top choice?"

"I think? I'll be glad when all of them are over. After a while, I can't tell if I'm getting better or worse."

I felt exactly the same way about my flute audition. I wished I could tell her, but I couldn't.

"Maybe you just need to stop and take a breath," I said.

"You could be right. There is such a thing as overpreparing."

I considered that. Was I overpreparing? For the audition, maybe. For my bat mitzvah? Not even close. "I wish my speech was overprepared," I grumbled. "Better overprepared than not at all."

When we reached the bottom of the steps, Sara turned to me. "I really think you should talk to Dad about this."

"I can't. I should've asked for his help weeks ago. Now it would just look pathetic. Which it is."

She shook her head. "This is Abba we're talking about! He would be happy to help you."

"I don't know...."

"Girls?" Mom met us at the foot of the stairs.

We followed her to the kitchen, where Benji was already sitting, snacking on celery and hummus.

"We need something green," Mom said.

"Can it be a lollipop?" Sara joked.

"I was thinking more along the lines of a salad." Mom smiled.

"Bec and I are on it." Sara took some baby lettuce and shredded carrots from the fridge, and I grabbed some peppers and cucumbers as Mom's cell chimed.

Mom hated having her—or any—phone at the table, but it was a necessary evil with a rabbi in the family. Dad had his own, of course, but lots of times he couldn't answer, so Mom had to be available as backup.

"Is it Mrs. Lefkowitz again?" Sara made a face. Mrs. Lefkowitz called way too often and talked way too much; at least, Sara and I thought so. Mom probably did, too, but she was too polite to admit it.

"It's Ruth." Mom smiled and put the phone on speaker. "Hi, Sis."

But instead of my aunt's cheerful voice on the other end, all we heard was crying.

"Ruth? What is it? What's wrong?"

"It's . . . it's Miri."

I turned to my sister, who looked as scared as I felt.

"What happened? Is she hurt?" Mom started to pace.

"She ran off with that . . . that boy!" Aunt Ruth cried. "They eloped!"

"Start from the beginning." Mom turned the phone off speaker and left the room.

"Thank God." Sara breathed a sigh of relief. "I thought it was something terrible!"

I stared at her. "It *is* something terrible! Miri eloped!"

"It's not the end of the world." Sara tore up the lettuce. "Frankly, I don't blame her."

"What?" I couldn't believe what I was hearing. "What do you mean?"

"It's not like Aunt Ruth and Uncle Jacob were going to throw her a beautiful wedding."

I stopped slicing the red pepper. "Sara, what are you talking about?"

She took a deep breath and let it out slowly. "Miri's boyfriend—I guess husband, now—isn't Jewish. I heard Eema and Aunt Ruth talking about it on Rosh Hashanah."

"It's just like *Fiddler on the Roof*!" I gasped. "Wait, is *that* why you were so worked up about Chava on spa day?"

Sara sighed. "Look . . ."

"I can't believe you never told me!"

"It was no big deal." Then, in a softer voice, she said, "It's *still* no big deal."

"It's a big deal to Aunt Ruth! And to Mom and Dad!"

"Becky . . ."

"Dad says if we all marry non-Jews, there won't be any Jews left after a while!"

"That's absolutely ridiculous and totally not true. What

about all the Jews who marry non-Jews and raise their kids to be Jewish? What about the non-Jews who convert? What about—"

"What about the ones that don't? Mom says we'll lose all our customs and traditions!"

"And I say, if we care about our customs and traditions, we'll still pass them on to our children."

"But . . . how would you raise your children?"

"We'd raise them with love," Sara said.

"How can you be so calm? Aunt Ruth is sobbing! And Miri . . . What's gonna happen to her?"

Sara looked at me. "Becky, nothing is gonna *happen* to her. Once Aunt Ruth and Uncle Jacob get over their shock, they'll cool off and everything will be fine. Luke is a really great guy. They should be happy for Miri."

"But . . . Mom and Dad always say marriage is hard enough without—"

"Becky. Stop. This isn't your problem. In fact, it's not a problem at all—or it shouldn't be."

I shook my head in disbelief. "And you're honestly okay with this?"

"Yes. I am totally okay with this. You should be, too."

And I almost believed her, until she reached for her Star of David necklace.

It wasn't there.

"Where's your necklace?"

"What?"

"Your necklace," I said. "Where is it?"

"On my dresser."

"What's it doing there?"

"I take it off when I'm singing 'For Good' for an audition. It feels weird to be wearing a Star of David when I'm trying to channel Elphaba," she said, referring to her favorite character—the wicked witch—in *Wicked*.

"If you really want to feel like Elphaba, maybe you should paint your face green."

Sara stared at me for a few seconds, like that wasn't the only reason she took off the necklace. Like maybe she was going to tell me what was. But the moment passed. "You don't get it." She cut into the cucumber with such fury that all I could do was stare.

I looked over to see what Benji was thinking.

His mouth was open and his eyes were closed. He was probably dreaming of chocolate or *Star Wars* or superheroes. He looked so sweet and untroubled.

Sometimes I envied him.

NOW

I LOOK UP from the cold dinner I've barely touched and see Benji looking back at me.

His hair needs to be cut because none of us have the energy to deal with it.

His eyes have circles under them because—like the rest of us—he's not getting much sleep.

I wish I could give him a happy dream.

I wish I could give myself one, too.

14

AS UPSET AS I'd been with Sara ever since she'd lied to my face, and as curious—and baffled—as I was about Sam's identity, I was more than happy to put all that on hold, at least for now....

It was Sara's opening night!

Three years ago, her opening night freshman year, all six of us sat around the dining room table trying our best not to make her more nervous than she already was.

That first year—before we knew better—Mom had baked a huge veggie lasagna, since it was Sara's favorite. Jon had three helpings, but the only thing Sara could manage was a bowl of soup and a few crackers.

After the show, Sara's appetite was back, and she ate more than her share while we all discussed every detail of the show.

Ever since then, I've loved opening night as much as Sara. The last two years, Mom still made veggie lasagna, only none of us ate it until we got back from the show. Jon called it cruel and unusual punishment, but he still ate soup and crackers along with the rest of us.

Tonight, Sara's last opening night, there were only five of us around the dining room table. It was hard not to feel bittersweet as my family and I sipped soup, munched on crackers, and tried not to look at Jon's empty chair.

"I wish Jon was here," Benji said with a mouthful of cracker.

"Me, too," Sara said softly.

"Me, three," Benji said.

I laughed. "That doesn't make any sense."

Just then Sara's cell chimed, and her face lit up. "Jon's on FaceTime!" She turned her phone around and we all caught a glimpse of him slurping ramen.

"I figured it's the next best thing to being there." He raised a cracker in the air. "Here's to another opening night triumph, Sis."

We joined him in raising a cracker to Sara and touched them to each other's like glasses of champagne. Benji joined in a little too enthusiastically and his cracker broke.

"Uh-oh," Jon said, "looks like somebody's cracker cracked!"

We talked a few more minutes, then Sara left with Jenna and Cassidy to get to the high school early. Around ninety minutes later, the four of us headed out, too.

Dad, Mom, and Benji went into the theater, and I waited in the lobby for Nipa. She loved opening night as much as I did. While I stood there, I searched all the faces for Sam. Of course, I had no idea what he looked like, but if he and Sara were together, I was pretty sure he wouldn't miss opening night.

"Hey, you!" Nipa walked in and gave me a quick hug. "Any suspects?"

I shook my head, grateful for my partner in crime. "Not yet." I handed her a ticket and we squeezed our way through the crowd and into the theater, joining Mom, Benji, and Dad.

Nipa and I took our seats at the end of the aisle. "Let's check the program," she whispered. "Maybe there's a Sam in it."

"Ooh! Great idea!"

We looked through every name in the cast, from leads to chorus, but not one Sam.

I frowned, discouraged. "So much for that."

"Hey. What if we—"

Before Nipa finished her sentence, the lights dimmed, and a hush came over the theater. A moment later, the curtain rose. I instantly forgot about everything else and let myself get lost in the show.

Sara was right: everyone was awesome. The acting and singing were flawless, the pit orchestra was fantastic, the costumes were perfect, and the lighting was beautiful and dramatic. I remembered that Mouthpiece Guy—Sean—was up in the lighting booth somewhere, and wished I could tell him what a great job he was doing.

But as great as everyone and everything was, Sara shone

the brightest, like always. It was clear: any college musical theater program would be lucky to have her.

Before I knew it, it was intermission. Dad took Benji out to get a snack and Mom left for the lobby to buy flowers for Sara. Nipa and I spent the first few minutes agreeing that it was the best production we'd seen, then she said, "I was thinking. Maybe Sam's not in the cast. Maybe he's in the orchestra."

We searched the program again. "Look!" I pointed to a name under the orchestra. "Sammy Schwartz is percussion!"

"That must be him! Let's go over to the pit and see if we can find him. . . ."

But before we could follow through, Dad and Benji came back, my little brother's cheeks full of M&M's.

"Benji! You're not supposed to eat in the theater," I told him.

"Don't worry, Becky. I'm almost done." He poured a few candies into his sticky chocolaty hand. "Want some?" he offered Nipa.

She laughed. "Thanks, I think I'll pass."

Mom made it back just as the lights dimmed and the curtain rose again. Act two was even better than act one. And when the music started for "On My Own," a hush fell over the whole theater.

I'd heard Sara practice this song over and over the past few weeks, but nothing compared to seeing her perform in costume and makeup and beautifully lit. I was so proud of her. To me, she was clearly the star of the show.

The audience thought so, too. She got the first standing ovation of the night. In the other shows we'd seen, the only standing ovation came at the end, for the entire cast. But Sara earned it. I stood with everyone else, tears in my eyes.

That was my sister up there.

The rest of the show was great, too. Nipa and I teared up when Sara/Eponine died in Marius's arms. When the show ended, it was obvious from the thundering applause when she walked onto the stage to take her bow that my sister was the fan favorite.

I couldn't wait to see her, but I knew it'd be a while. My family and I took our time gathering our things and heading out into the lobby. Sara was backstage getting out of her costume and probably being congratulated and hugged by every single person in the room.

When we got to the lobby, Dad greeted some congregants who couldn't say enough about Sara's performance, and Mom exchanged compliments with the other stage moms. I was keeping one eye out for Sara and the other for Sean to tell him what a great job he did.

Nipa nudged me. "This is weird." She pointed to the program. "Since when did Sara start using her middle initial?"

"What?" I asked, looking at the program. Sure enough, it read "Sara A. Myerson." I shrugged. "Maybe she thinks it sounds more sophisticated or something." Honestly, I hadn't even noticed. Too busy searching for Sam, I guess. Or Sammy . . .

"Hey! Maybe Sara is Sam!" Nipa joked. "Sara A. Myerson—see? The first letters of each name spell out Sam."

I laughed. "That must be it. Sara is texting herself about how amazing she is."

Nipa giggled.

"What's so funny?"

We looked up to see Sara standing in front of us, cheeks flushed. I was the first to hug her. "You brought the house down!"

"What house?" Benji asked.

Sara swooped him up into a hug, then Dad took his turn. "You really outdid yourself tonight, sweetheart."

"You certainly did." Mom handed her the bouquet of flowers.

Sara beamed. "Thanks, you guys. I'm so glad you're here."

"Where else would we be?" I asked.

"Is it time for lasagna?" Benji always got straight to the point.

We dropped Nipa off, went home, and discussed the whole show while we ate our second dinner. Everyone raved about everything, and it was unanimous: Sara was the breakout role.

As Mom was cleaning up and Dad was starting Benji's bedtime routine, Sara and I made our way upstairs. I was about to open my door when I remembered something. "Hey!"

Sara turned back and smiled. "Hey what?"

"What's with Sara A. Myerson? I've never seen you use your middle initial for any of the play programs before."

"Oh. That." She shrugged. "A bunch of us did it for fun." She reached for the necklace that wasn't there.

Sara smiled. "No biggie. I'm surprised you even noticed."

"Actually, Nipa did."

She yawned and stretched. "I'm exhausted, and I've still got to get all this stage makeup off before I go to sleep." She gave me another hug then headed to her room. "We can talk more tomorrow."

I got in my pajamas, brushed my teeth, and turned off my lamp. Then I turned it back on and grabbed the program, wondering how many of the cast had included their middle initials.

She was the only one.

I checked the names under pit, too. No initials there, either. I thumbed through the names of stage crew, just for fun. Only one had a middle initial: Sean A. McCormick.

I stared at the page, at the name, so long my eyes watered: S-A-M.

I couldn't believe it; he was right there all along.

I didn't know what to do—especially because my go-to problem solver *was* the problem.

Sara lied to me. Twice. Why was she keeping him a secret?

He was nice. And funny. What was so terrible about Sean A. McCormick that . . . McCormick. Not exactly a Jewish name. In fact, the only other McCormick I knew was that reverend I met at synagogue. The widower with a son . . .

Was the rabbi's daughter dating the reverend's son?

15

THE NEXT DAY, we'd only been at school a few minutes when the fire alarm rang. All the students quickly emptied out of the building, but the only thing I cared about was finding my best friend, because our earlier conversation had been cut short.

I found Nipa by the playground and was out of breath by the time I reached her. "This is an emergency!"

"It's only a fire drill," Nipa said. Her voice was calm but her eyes were distracted.

"I'm talking about Sara and Sam!"

"That is not an emergency," she said. "And, like I told you last night *and* when I got off the bus half an hour ago, you don't even know it's him for sure."

"Who else could it be? And why else would Sara keep him a secret?"

"I don't know," she admitted.

I followed her gaze as she looked at the students around us. They were all chatting and laughing, happy to miss a few minutes of class.

I wondered if any of them were keeping secrets, too. . . .

"I hate this!" I told her. "I don't know what to say or do or even how to act around her anymore!"

"Maybe you're overreacting," Nipa said. "I mean, she's still Sara, right? No matter what."

"How could she keep a secret from me?"

Nipa raised an eyebrow. "Did you seriously just ask that? Seems like there's an awful lot of secrets in your family lately."

Before I could respond, another voice said, "Hey, Nipa?"

I'd been so caught up in our conversation, I hadn't noticed Ethan had joined us. He had curly brown hair and was the best trumpet player in band, but I didn't know him very well. I waited for Nipa to say hi or something, but she just stood there and stared at him.

"What's up?" I asked, partly because, apparently, she couldn't, but mostly because I wanted to finish our conversation.

Ethan looked at me, then Nipa. "I was wondering if you had a partner for that science project. . . ."

Again, we both waited for her to respond. And, again, she didn't. Finally, I looked at her and said, "No, right?"

Nipa nodded. Then she shook her head.

"So . . ." Ethan tilted his head in confusion. "You don't?"

She shook her head again. The bell rang and teachers

started corralling us toward the building.

Ethan smiled. "Cool. We'll talk." He turned to me. "See you later, Becky."

He disappeared into the masses and I turned to Nipa.

"What just happened?" she asked.

"So you *can* talk," I teased.

"Did Ethan just ask me to partner with him?"

"He did."

"And . . . did I say yes?"

"Yep. Well, sort of." I grinned at my best friend. "Speaking of secrets . . . is there anything you want to tell me?"

"No." It was the first time I had ever seen her blush.

"Let's get a move on, girls." One of the gym teachers tilted her head toward the building.

Nipa looked relieved.

"I will see you at lunch," I told her. "And you will tell me everything."

"Fine." She sighed. But she did it with a smile.

I spent the rest of school trying to picture Sara and Sean together, and trying to figure out what I should say, or do, about it.

I ran through different opening lines in my head, but in the end, I decided to go with the truth. Maybe if I was honest, she would be, too.

Maybe it was time we both stopped keeping secrets from each other.

When I got home, I went straight to her room before I lost my nerve. I was about to knock on her door when Sara opened it. "I was waiting for you," she said.

"Oh?" I was probably imagining it, but she didn't look all that happy to see me.

I looked past her to the dresser and saw her Star of David necklace lying there. And then I saw there was another gold chain around her neck and under her shirt.

"Did you get a new necklace?"

Sara reached up and touched the chain.

"Does this one go better with your auditions?" I asked.

"What?"

"You said that's why you stopped wearing the other one. Remember?"

"I remember," she said softly.

"Did he give you this one?"

"Who?"

"Sam."

She looked like Benji when he was caught doing something he shouldn't. "How did you . . . ?" Before I could answer, she pulled me into her room and closed her door. "How did you find out?" she asked, turning to me.

"How did you not *tell* me?"

"I . . ." She looked away from me and sighed. "It's complicated."

"I want to see it."

"What?"

"Your necklace."

We stared at each other a few seconds then she pulled it out. It was half of a heart with two words engraved in the center: "I know."

"I'm guessing his half says, 'I love you.'" Being a *Star Wars* fan, I caught the reference immediately. It was one of our favorite scenes in *The Empire Strikes Back*. Princess Leia—one of the best movie heroines of all time—finally confesses her feelings to Han Solo—one of the best movie heroes of all time. Sara and I always sighed at that part.

Jon always rolled his eyes.

Sara didn't bother answering; we both knew I was right. She tucked the heart back under her shirt like the secret it was. "I would ask if you have any questions, but it seems you already know everything." She sank down on her bed.

"How did you get together in the first place? Did you meet in homeroom or something?"

She shook her head. "Theater camp, actually."

"*Summer* theater camp?! So you've known Sam since . . ."

"Mid-June. And his name is Sean."

"Unless he's texting you."

"When did you see—" She broke off, suddenly putting it all together. "My phone."

"I wasn't snooping. We were working on the chanting, and you went down to the kitchen to get snacks."

She waited for me to explain the rest.

"Nipa and I—"

"Of course, Nipa was involved." Sara managed to smile, even though she still looked upset. "Wait—is *that* why you were at rehearsal that time?"

I nodded. "We thought maybe Sam was in the show. It was my idea—don't be mad at Nipa."

Sara sighed. "I'm not mad at Nipa—or you. I still don't see how you put it together that Sean was Sam. . . ."

"You two were the only ones with initials in the program: S-A-M. And once I figured out who his dad was, I knew why it was a secret." I waited for her to say something. But she didn't. "Sara, I get why you didn't tell Mom and Dad. But why didn't you tell *me*?"

"I was *going* to! I wanted to . . . then Miri eloped and you freaked out and . . . I thought you'd be mad, like Mom and Dad would."

Now I was the one who didn't know what to say.

"Besides," Sara continued, "there was nothing to tell at first." She touched her necklace. "We started out as friends. Then, when school started, I was the only person he knew, so . . ."

"What about Jenna? And Cassidy? Weren't they at theater camp, too?"

"Yes. But Jenna's obsessed with her boyfriend, and Cassidy's always got ten things going at once. . . . So the two of us started having lunch together, and then we both got involved with the show, and then . . . He's unbelievably sweet, and funny, and charming. . . ."

I was trying my hardest to stay mad, but it wasn't easy. I loved my sister and I wanted her to be happy. Plus, I'd seen Sam—or Sean—in action a couple of times, and he *was* sweet and funny and charming....

Still, she had looked me right in the eye and lied to me—at least twice. But really, who knew how many times? Part of me wanted to forgive her, but part of me was still angry.

"Whatever," I said. "I still can't believe you didn't tell me. I still can't believe you *lied* to me!"

"I'm sorry! I really am. But when Aunt Ruth called crying because Miri ran off with a non-Jew..."

I sat down on her bed. "You're not Miri. And I'm definitely not Aunt Ruth."

Sara gave me a small smile. "Promise you won't tell Eema and Abba?"

"I don't know.... I feel funny keeping a secret from them."

"Oh, really?" She put her hands on her hips, her hazel eyes staring me down. "How 'funny,' exactly? Funnier than you felt about signing Mom's name?"

I gasped. "How did you—?"

"I bumped into Ms. T at school. Mr. Silverstein was out sick so she came to work with the pit orchestra. During the break, she told me how happy she was about your All-County audition."

My heart stopped. "And what did you say?"

Sara looked at me. "Lucky for you, I'm an actress." She shook her head. "Relax. I didn't blow your cover."

My heart started to beat again. "When was this?"

She shrugged. "A few days ago."

"A few days ago? You've known all this time? Why didn't you tell me?"

Sara looked at me. "Why didn't *you* tell *me*?" Her face, and her voice, told me she wasn't angry; she was hurt.

"I thought you would disapprove."

"Don't you know by now that I'm always on your side? That I always have your back?"

I felt guilty, but also relieved. It felt so good *not* keeping a secret from her. I looked at her and she looked at me and maybe we were both trying to figure out what to do next.

"Listen," Sara said. "How 'bout we keep both these things between us, at least for now." She put her hand out. "Deal?"

I tried to think of all the reasons this was a bad idea. But all I could think was how good it felt that we were really talking again, that we could be there for each other like old times. And how badly I wanted it to stay that way.

There was only one thing to do: I took her hand and shook it.

And, just like that, I was keeping Sara's secret . . . and she was keeping mine.

16

THE TROUBLE WITH keeping secrets was that secrets led to lies, and one lie led to the next and the next . . . like a not-so-fun game of dominoes.

Still . . . it was finally the night of *my* big secret: the All-County audition.

This time the lie was telling my parents that Nipa and I were going to study together, which accomplished two things. First, I could follow Sara's lead and eat nothing but soup and crackers without my parents wondering why, or insisting I ate more. Second, Sara could pick me up from Nipa's house and drop me off at the audition, then pick me up and bring me home afterward without anyone being the wiser.

Sara had hatched the plan, and I was grateful. But between guilt and nerves, I was also feeling sick. Nipa hugged me at the door and waved to Sara, who waved back from the driver's seat of Mom's minivan.

I slid in next to her and, when she grinned at me, my nerves turned into excitement. After all these weeks, I was actually going after the dream I'd worked so hard for. Sara put on the soundtrack to my favorite show, *Little Shop of Horrors*, knowing it would help me relax. As we sang along to the first few tracks, I felt happier than I had in days.

If I didn't make All-County, at least I'd tried my best. Plus, I could stop keeping secrets from Mom and Dad—well, *my* secret, anyway. And if I *did* get in, all the forging and sneaking around would be worth it.

At least, that's what I kept telling myself.

"This is it." Sara pulled up in front of an unfamiliar high school. "I've got to run some errands for Mom. Text me when you're done, and I'll pick you up right here." She handed me my flute and my music folder, which she'd managed to sneak out of my room.

"If you weren't going to be a big Broadway star, you'd be a great spy."

She laughed. "Maybe I'll be both. Broadway can be my cover."

"Sounds good." I knew I should head inside, but now that it was time, my nerves reappeared with a vengeance. My palms were wet and my mouth was dry.

"Here." She handed me a water bottle and squeezed my shoulder. "Hey—you've got this."

"Thanks." I leaned across and gave her a hug, then ran up the stairs to the high school.

I checked in at a table in the lobby, then followed the signs to the gym. There were sixty or seventy other kids, every one of them warming up and, suddenly, it felt . . . real.

Tonight was only woodwinds, so I was surrounded by oboes, clarinets, and, of course, flutes. It was weird seeing so many in one place. And exciting. And nerve-racking.

I'd found a corner and was running through the scales when one of the volunteers called everyone with a last name between *G* and *N*. A bunch of us followed her down the hall to a row of hard plastic chairs outside the audition classroom. I sat there for almost half an hour, going through my fingerings and trying not to listen through the closed door as kids auditioned before me. Trying not to compare myself to them. Trying to stay focused and confident.

Just when I thought I couldn't wait another minute, a volunteer called my name. I entered the classroom and couldn't help feeling like Dorothy in *The Wizard of Oz*. The judges sat behind a curtain: I couldn't see them and they couldn't see me.

The volunteer showed me what music to play and in what order, then left.

I closed my eyes and saw Ms. T smile at me, felt Sara's arms around me, heard Grandma Rachel telling me to make a wish. I knew what I had to do, and I knew how to do it. I took a deep breath, opened my eyes, and let my fingers find the notes.

I started with two scales plus the chromatic, then did a

sight-reading and played the first etude. My focus was laser sharp. My fingers were flying. With each note, the knots in my stomach untangled a bit more.

Then, halfway through the last etude my mind went blank. My fingers froze. I couldn't believe it! This had never happened to me, all those times I practiced. Not even once! I wanted to melt into the floor . . . but that wasn't an option.

Instead, I kept breathing and tried not to panic. I remembered how Ms. T always told us to keep going, no matter what. So I regrouped and powered through and did the best I could.

The rest of the piece was perfect; I hoped I hadn't ruined my chance. I hoped my best was good enough. For now, at least it was over. I let out a huge breath as the volunteer returned, thanked me for coming, and said they'd contact me next month if I made it.

Next month! Hanukkah, Christmas, winter break . . . and the most important decision of my entire life.

Still, I thanked her, grabbed my flute, and made a quick exit back to the lobby and out the front entrance. I was about to text Sara, but she'd already texted me:

Mom needed the car. Don't worry! I'll figure something out. . . .

That meant Cassidy or Jenna to the rescue, so I stood at the designated spot and waited for a lime-green or cherry-red car to pull up. But when a car finally did, it was one I didn't recognize . . . with a face I didn't expect.

"Heard you needed a ride, Trumpet Girl."

"You're not Cassidy or Jenna."

"Very true. But I'm here and they're not. I suppose we could call them and see if they're available. . . ."

I let out a very dramatic sigh. "Never mind. I guess I'll just go with you."

He put his hand over his heart. "I am honored."

I refused to smile.

I climbed in. "I suppose this is the second time you rescued me," I told him.

He shrugged and smiled. "It's what I do. I'm kind of a superhero."

I flashed back to the day we met, when Nipa had said the exact same thing. It was hard not to smile after that.

He waited for me to put on my seatbelt, then pulled out of the parking lot.

"Where's Sara?"

"Let's see. . . . Your dad was visiting one congregant, and another called and needed help, so your mom filled in, and Sara had to stay and watch Benji."

"Oh."

"My mom used to do the same thing. If Dad was tending to one family and another had an emergency, she'd be there for them."

"So who was there for you?"

"When I was Benji's age, my grandpa lived with us. By the time he died, I was old enough to be on my own, or I'd go with Mom if she thought I could help."

"That was nice of you."

He shrugged. "It's what superheroes do."

We rode in silence, each of us lost in our own thoughts. Plus I didn't really know what to talk about. Did he know I was keeping him a secret?

When we were stuck at a really long red light, he turned to me. "So, how'd your audition go?"

"Good, I think—except for one part."

He nodded. "So . . . what happens if you make All-County?"

"Whaddaya mean?"

"I mean . . . will you tell your parents?"

I shrugged. "I'm not worried about it." Except when I was awake. Or asleep. Or trying to sleep.

He tapped his fingers on the steering wheel. "Maybe you should just tell them."

I looked over at him, this boy who'd been going behind everyone's backs with my sister. And I knew he had helped me out—twice now—but I couldn't keep my mouth shut. "Maybe Sara should just tell them about the two of you." *And maybe Sam should throw me out of his car.* "I'm sorry. I shouldn't have—"

"No." His face was sad and his voice was soft. "You're right."

"I am?"

He looked over at me. "I actually did tell my dad."

"What did he say?"

"He wanted to meet her. So I invited Sara over and they met."

"What happened?"

"They got along great. I said she should tell her parents, too. I'm not really on board with the whole sneaking-around thing. But she said she wasn't ready." He looked over at me. "Sometimes you have to give people a chance, Becky. They might surprise you."

A few minutes later he pulled up in front of my house. I was about to thank him for the lift when I realized something. "Hey—should I call you Sean, or Sam?"

He smiled. "Whichever you like."

"I think I like Sam."

"Then Sam I am."

"Thanks for the lift, Sam."

"Anytime." He smiled, waved, and drove away.

I was searching for my key when Sara opened the door.

"I'm so sorry!" She pulled me inside and gave me a hug.

"It's okay." I handed her my flute case and took off my coat and hat.

"How'd it go?"

"I messed up the second etude. I don't know what happened! I totally blanked for a few seconds. But it felt like forever."

"Don't worry," Sara said. "It probably wasn't as bad as you think. They might not even have noticed."

"Right. Like no one would notice if you missed a verse of

'On My Own' or got the lyrics wrong."

"Oh, they'd notice." Sara smiled. "But the audience would be so charmed by my grace and beauty they wouldn't care."

"Well, my audience didn't see my grace or beauty because they were behind a curtain."

"But they *heard* your beauty, Becky. Loud and clear."

Sara touched her necklace. "So . . . did you and Sean talk about anything on the drive here?"

"You mean Sam?"

"Sean, Sam . . . a rose by any other name, yada yada." She smiled. Then her face turned serious. "Becky. Honest, what do you think of him?"

I didn't answer right away. I could have; I already knew what I thought of him: he was sweet and kind and it was easy to see why Sara cared for him. But if I told her that, would it mean I was okay with her seeing him? With her doing something we both knew our parents would disapprove of?

It felt like I had to make a choice, then I realized I already had by agreeing to keep her secret. Just as she was keeping mine.

So I said the truth for once. "I like him."

"I'm glad." She hugged me and I hugged her back and it felt good.

It felt right.

"Hey." Sara pulled back and looked at me. "Don't worry about the audition. I have absolute faith in you."

NOW

I'VE BEEN THINKING about faith a lot lately.
   It's easy to have . . .
   until you really need it.
   And hard to find
   once it's
   gone.

17

I'D THOUGHT ONCE the audition was over, things would get easier. But they didn't.

Instead of practicing every chance I got, all I could do was wait for the result. What if, after all that work, I hadn't done enough?

Or, what if I had?

As usual, I decided to do what I did best: avoid thinking about it. Luckily, it was my favorite time of year, so I had plenty of distractions.

Every Thanksgiving, Mom and I gathered new recipes for side dishes and desserts, then had a lot of fun making them. And Dad made it a point to work less than usual, so we could all be together the whole four-day weekend, just the six of us. We ate too much and played endless board games and watched tons of old movies and had fires in the fireplace....

But this year was different.

To begin with, Jon was staying in L.A. It wasn't worth flying three thousand miles home for a holiday weekend when his semester ended just two weeks later.

And this year was different because Sara and I were keeping secrets.

One thing that wasn't different, though . . . Every year, since I was younger than Benji, my family helped out at a local soup kitchen the day before Thanksgiving. Over the years it became an interfaith event, with our synagogue and the local churches and mosques coming together to prepare the menu, get the ingredients, cook the food, and serve it to those who are in need of a hot meal. There were even greeters and waiters to make the guests feel extra special.

This year Dad signed us up for the afternoon shift. Sara, being the outgoing, charismatic one, would be part of the welcoming committee; Benji was in charge of refilling bread baskets, and Dad would take and bring orders. Mom and I would stay behind the scenes, cooking and plating the food.

I knew the community and the people we fed were grateful, but I was, too: grateful to do a mitzvah for those who needed help, and grateful that I always had enough to eat. This year, I was also grateful to *not* think about my secret, or Sara's, for a few hours.

Except, less than five minutes after we arrived—before we'd even gone to our separate stations—one of the secrets showed up in person.

"Reverend McCormick! Good to see you again." Dad shook his hand warmly, then turned to the person standing beside the reverend.

"Hi," he said. "I'm Sean."

Dad shook his hand.

Did Sara know they would be here? If she did, it might've been nice to give me a heads-up. I risked a look in her direction. Her eyes were huge and her mouth was open. It was clear she'd had no idea, either. I could only hope our parents didn't register her complete panic.

"You remember Rebecca," Dad said to Reverend McCormick.

Reverend McCormick smiled at me. I did my best so stay calm and smile back as I said hello.

"And this"—Dad put his arm around my sister—"is my other daughter, Sara."

"Hello," Sam's dad said.

My sister looked like she was about to run out of the building. Or faint. Or run out of the building and then faint.

"Wow," Sam said, taking in everyone in the room except my sister. "Looks like lots of hungry people. . . ."

Reverend McCormick nodded. "There certainly are." He turned to my dad. "Please. Show us how we can help."

"Let's start by greeting our guests." Dad smiled and led the way, Sam and his dad following closely.

Mom looked over at my sister, who may or may not have been breathing. "Are you all right? You look pale. . . ."

I had to do something, and fast! "Sara ... we'd better get to work!" I grabbed her by the arm—and not gently.

"But she's s'posed to be the greeter," Benji reminded us.

I ignored him, still clutching my sister's arm. Then, before Mom could say anything else, I whisked Sara into the huge kitchen, where half a dozen people were already hard at work. We walked quickly past them and through a door leading to a small parking lot behind the building.

In twelve years, I had never seen my sister look so terrified. Her breathing was way too fast, and I thought she might have a heart attack. It would've been funny if she weren't so upset.

"I don't think anyone suspects," I told her, hoping I was right.

"You need to find Mom and tell her I have to go home."

"That's a great idea. Not only will she ask why, but we'll be short two volunteers on the busiest day of the year."

"This is a nightmare! I can't think! I can't ..."

"Just breathe." I rubbed her back in circles, the way Mom did whenever one of us was scared. "It's okay."

But my sister was on a roll. "It's not okay! It's the opposite of okay! What if they find out? What if they *throw* me out?"

"What?! This is Mom and Dad you're talking about! They would never—"

"It'll be Miri and Luke all over again! Mom will have a meltdown and Dad will—"

"I thought you supported Miri and ..."

"I do, but her parents don't. Uncle Jacob acts like she doesn't exist! And every time Aunt Ruth talks to her, all she does is cry."

"What? How do you know all this?"

"Because I *do* support Miri. We call and text all the time. She says it's nice to talk to someone who's on her side."

I was still processing this new information, when I heard a familiar voice behind me.

"There you are." Sam came toward us, a sweet smile on his face despite everything.

I had never been so happy to see him as I was that moment. Ever since I discovered their secret, I'd been trying to wrap my brain around the two of them as a couple. But he looked at her with such tenderness that I could not only see it, I could feel it.

"What are you doing here?" she cried. "Why didn't you tell me you were coming?"

"I didn't know myself 'til half an hour ago. Dad asked if I wanted to help at a soup kitchen. I didn't know you were going to be here...."

Sara covered her face. "This is a disaster!"

"C'mere," he said softly.

Sara went to him and he wrapped his arms around her while I kept a lookout.

"Everything's gonna be all right," he murmured.

Sara stepped out of his embrace. "How can you say that? They almost found out about us!"

He shrugged, then looked over at me. "Becky found out about us and she hasn't gone screaming into the night." He smiled again. "Then again, it is daytime."

A very small smile appeared on Sara's face. "Becky and I always have each other's back."

Hearing her say that made me feel like I'd do anything to keep her secret. "We'd better go in before someone notices we're gone," I said.

"See you 'round," Sam said. He didn't kiss her or even touch her again, but the way he looked at her . . . I found myself hoping, maybe someday, someone would look at me that way.

She turned to me. "Hey. Thanks for helping. I owe you one."

I smiled. "No, you don't."

The rest of the time went by quickly and without a hitch—or one single clue that Sara and Sam were a couple. I knew, of course, that Sara was a great actor; I had no idea Sam was, too. My work was mostly in the kitchen, but every once in a while, someone needed me in the dining room, so I was able to see the two of them together—or, *not* together.

Sara stood at the entrance of the dining room, welcoming guests with her usual warmth and charm, while Sam scurried around, filling glasses and taking orders and making sure everyone had enough to eat. An innocent bystander (like Mom or Dad) would never have suspected there was anything between them. But I could see it. Every now and then, I caught Sara turning around and glancing his way, and sometimes I caught him looking at her, too.

Even without words I could see how much they cared about each other. It was hard to believe no one else saw it. But I guess that was a good thing.

After our three hours were up, the five of us got back in the van and headed home, another successful soup kitchen event behind us despite the unexpected drama.

When Dad turned onto our street, there was another unexpected turn of events: an airport shuttle sat in front of our house . . . and a very familiar passenger was emerging with suitcases and backpack.

"Jon!" Benji shouted.

He and Sara and I jumped out of the van and suffocated our big brother with hugs.

"I thought you weren't coming for Thanksgiving!" I said, tangled up in everyone's arms.

"We wanted to surprise you," he said.

"It was our little secret," Mom added as she pulled him into a hug of her own.

Sara and I looked at each other, and I knew we were both thinking about *our* secrets.

"All right, all right," Dad said. "My turn. Let me hug my firstborn."

"First and best," Jon teased.

"Says you," Sara said.

I raised an eyebrow. "Nice of you to show up *after* we

worked all day at the soup kitchen."

"I haven't even set foot in the house yet and you're already giving me grief." Jon wrapped an arm around my shoulder. "Good to see nothing's changed around here."

If he only knew.

Dad grabbed one of Jon's suitcases while Mom unlocked the door.

"Think you brought enough stuff for a four-day weekend?" Sara joked.

"Laundry," Jon said. "Plus I may have brought a few Hanukkah gifts. . . ."

"For me?" Benji asked.

"But Hanukkah's two weeks from now," I pointed out.

"He's staying through the first week of January," Mom announced with a big smile.

Sara looked at me. "Guess we'd better get him some Hanukkah gifts after all."

I couldn't stop smiling.

Jon smiled, too. "Finals are over. Let the fun begin!"

And it did. It was the best four-day weekend ever: the Thanksgiving feast, the games, the fireplace chats . . .

And the ending. The ending, most of all.

I'd brushed my teeth, gotten into my pj's and into bed, when I decided to check my email one more time.

There was a message. From Ms. T.

The subject was "All-County."

My hand hovered over the phone. Was it "Congratulations,"

or "Better luck next time"? I took a deep breath and opened the email.

I read it twice. Then once more.

And then I sprinted to Sara's room and ran in without even knocking. She glanced up from her phone, took one look at me, and knew. "You made it!"

I nodded and laughed and cried as she hugged me hard.

"I knew you would. Mazel tov!"

"It's an early Hanukkah present!" I said.

Suddenly, Sara's eyes sparkled the way they always did when she had an idea. "We should go out and celebrate!"

I laughed. "We're in our pajamas."

"We can get out of our pajamas!"

"It's after eleven."

"So?"

"So, everything in town is closed."

She sighed. "Fine. We'll wait 'til tomorrow. But we're going to celebrate, whether you like it or not."

"I like it very much. But right now, I'd better call Nipa before she falls asleep—if she hasn't already."

She gave me a smile and a gentle push toward the door.

I went back to my room and emailed Ms. T, then called Nipa.

"Hello?" She sounded as sleepy as I was awake.

"Nipa! I got in!"

"You did not!" she said in that happy way people do when they mean the exact opposite.

"Can you believe it?"

"Of course I can," my loyal BFF said.

"And guess what else? Jon's home!"

"What? I thought he wasn't back 'til winter break...."

"I know! He and Mom kept it a secret!"

"Lots of secrets going around these days," she said pointedly. I could almost see the disapproval on her face.

"Yeah, yeah ... Oh! And guess what else? You totally won't believe this! My whole family was at the soup kitchen, and *he* showed up."

"He who?" She gasped. "You mean, Sam?!"

"Yes!"

"OMG!"

We talked a few more minutes, then I heard Mrs. Sachdeva tell Nipa to turn out her light and go to sleep.

We said goodnight. I turned out my light, too, and stared up at my starry ceiling. I couldn't stop smiling: my wish had come true! I would never fall asleep now. I couldn't remember ever feeling this excited, this happy.

I loved sharing my news with Sara and Nipa, but I wanted to tell Jon and Benji, too.

I wanted to tell Grandma Rachel. I could see her face so clearly: the way her blue eyes had always crinkled when she smiled.

Then I saw my parents' faces, and my happiness took a nosedive. It was like on Passover, when—to remember the plagues and the Egyptians' suffering—we took ten drops out of our cups to lessen our joy. Knowing that I couldn't share my joy with Mom and Dad was kind of like that, only worse.

Much worse.

It was like emptying the entire cup.

18

EVER SINCE JON had come home two weeks earlier, life was busy and everyone was happy, maybe me most of all. Not only was our family all together again, but my winter break was just around the corner, I really *had* made All-County, and the past seven nights had been filled with candle lighting, dreidel spinning, latkes, and gifts.

Tonight was the last night of Hanukkah.

We not only lit all eight candles (nine, if you count the shammash), but we used four menorahs: the simple brass one Mom inherited from Grandma Rachel and would pass down to Sara or me someday; the one with the turquoise mosaics of birds; Benji's favorite, the animals in Noah's ark; and my favorite, the silver dove whose wings held four candles on each side.

Benji turned off all the lights in the living room and the six of us gazed at the flames of thirty-six colorful candles glowing in the darkness. Dad had one arm around Mom and the other around Jon, and I held hands with Sara and Benji. It felt like a perfect moment; it *was* a perfect moment. I felt safe and warm and loved and . . . lucky.

As the candlelight flickered and danced, we sang Hanukkah songs in Hebrew and English, my mom's and sister's flawless voices soaring in perfect harmony above the rest. It was all so beautiful, I suddenly felt a little teary. I looked over at Dad, who clearly felt the same.

Next came my family's traditional last Hanukkah meal, which always included crispy potato latkes made from scratch, and everyone's favorite, sufganiyot: jelly doughnuts! We all gathered around the kitchen table for the feast, then Benji brought out the bag of dreidels in all sizes and colors, which we'd collected over the years, and we each took one. Dad gave us each twenty pennies (though Benji and I liked it better when we used M&M's), and we all took turns spinning the dreidels to see which Hebrew letter they landed on: gimel was best—you got the whole pile of coins; hei meant "half"; nun was "nothing"; and shin was the worst, because you had to put another coin into the pile. As usual, Jon ended up with way more coins than the rest of us, and we all teased him about cheating at dreidel (which I'm pretty sure is impossible).

And then it was time for gifts.

This was my favorite part of Hanukkah, especially on the last night. We all gave, and received, a few small things the seven other nights, like jigsaw puzzles or paperback books or candy. But on the last night, everyone went all out.

We went back to the living room, where gifts in shiny, colorful wrapping paper covered the whole table.

"Me first!" Benji shouted.

Sara, Jon, and I pushed our presents in his direction, but he shook his head. "Mine for you," he explained, handing one to each of us.

"Thanks, buddy!" Jon smiled at Benji, then opened his present: a plastic Baby Yoda head. "Uh . . ."

"It's for toothpaste—I'll show you!" Benji jumped up and ran to the bathroom, then returned with a half-used tube of toothpaste. He unscrewed the top, replaced it with Baby Yoda's head, and handed it back to Jon. "Squeeze it!"

Jon did as told. Toothpaste oozed out of Baby Yoda's mouth.

Sara and I started giggling and couldn't stop. Jon managed to keep a straight face. "Wow." He looked at Benji. "I've never seen anything like this! Every time I brush my teeth, I'll think of you."

Our little brother had never looked prouder.

"Your turn," I told him.

Since his birthday party had been a hit, Sara suggested the three of us stick with the SpongeBob theme. Jon gave him a T-shirt, I gave him a DVD, and Sara gave him a mug, all with SpongeBob all over them. As she'd predicted, Benji loved them all.

Jon, Sara, and I had a Hanukkah tradition of gifting each

other last, so we all turned to our parents next. Jon handed three same-size gifts to Mom. "Turns out L.A. has some pretty awesome bookstores...."

Her eyes lit up. Mom's favorite thing on the planet, besides us, was books. She opened the first gift—a mystery by an author she'd followed for years.

"Look inside," Jon said.

"It's autographed!" She unwrapped the other two and they were signed, too. "Thank you so much! I don't know which one to read first!"

I gave her a gift certificate to a local spa, and Sara gave her one to her favorite bookstore. Both were very nice. And very expensive. As Mom thanked us, Sara and I looked at each other: guilt-ridden gifts, for sure.

And it went on and on. I felt especially pleased when Dad opened the gift card I got him for Millie's Milkshakes. He smiled at me and said, "I know just who I want to share this with."

"Is it me?" Benji asked, already salivating.

I laughed. "You can come along."

I saved Sara's gift for last because it was the one I was most excited about. Since *Wicked* was her favorite musical, I searched Amazon and Etsy and everywhere I could think of until I finally found a fleece blanket with images of the lead characters. It was soft and warm and—

"I love it!" Sara hugged the blanket to her chest, then hugged me and whispered, "Best gift of the night."

As for me? I got a music T-shirt from Jon with weird time signatures and a caption that read, "These are difficult times." Benji gave me a Baby Yoda pillow, which was the cutest thing ever. And Sara gave me an IOU to my favorite boutique, along with a promise to help me find my bat mitzvah dress there: it was the perfect gift.

We hadn't discussed how much I was dreading dress-shopping with Mom. She and I didn't exactly have the same taste when it came to clothes. But Sara had a knack for choosing styles that were just right for me. I hugged her and whispered, "Best gift of the night."

And it was, until Mom and Dad did two amazing things in a row. "Sara," Mom said. "Becky . . ."

"Your mother and I are very proud of you both for working so hard. . . ."

I looked at Sara and she looked at me and I wondered if she was feeling as guilty as I was. I pasted on a smile, but I knew whatever they were about to give me, I didn't deserve it. I tried not to think that, if Mom and Dad knew the secrets Sara and I were keeping, the last thing they would do is give either of us a special gift.

They handed us each a sealed envelope, which Sara opened faster than I did.

"It's a train ticket." She held it up for everyone to see.

"To New York City!" I stared at my identical gift.

"We're hoping it won't be too crowded after Christmas and before New Year's Eve," Dad explained.

"You'll stay with Aunt Ruth." Mom smiled. "She's looking forward to seeing you both again."

I looked at Sara again; she didn't seem very enthusiastic. "This wouldn't have anything to do with Miri, would it?"

"No!" Mom's smile got a bit shaky. "Of course not."

Dad looked at her.

"Well," Mom admitted, "not entirely."

Sara and I waited.

Mom sighed. "Ruth may have mentioned, in passing, that perhaps you"—she looked at Sara—"might have a word or two with your cousin."

"I'm always happy to see Miri," Sara answered, "but I am not getting in the middle of this."

She kind of already was, if you asked me. But no one did.

There was an awkward silence until Benji interrupted. "Can I have another doughnut?"

Dad smiled. "You may want to hold off on that. Your mother and I have one last present for the whole family. I just need to get it from next door."

"Why is it next door?" I asked, but no one answered as my brothers eyed the doughnuts, Mom waited at the front door... and Sara stood in silence. I knew she was upset about the whole Miri/Aunt Ruth thing, but I'd take any excuse to go to New York City. It was the best city in the universe!

Mom opened the front door and Dad walked in with a huge smile on his face... and two fluffy, fuzzy, furry things in his arms.

"Kittens!" Benji ran toward them.

"Be gentle," Mom said.

As cute as Baby Yoda was, he couldn't compare with these guys. The smaller one was gray and black and the bigger one was orange and white. Both had stripes and were incredibly soft. We all took turns petting one, then the other.

"They're brother and sister," Dad told us. "The orange one is the—"

Before he could finish his sentence, the kittens were already on the move, probably hoping to escape our well-meaning but terrifying little brother. Benji raced after them, and we raced after him.

"Take it easy, buddy," Jon said.

"Don't scare them," Sara said.

"Slow down!" I shouted, after nearly tripping over a bag of cat food that materialized out of nowhere.

After awhile, Benji and the kittens wore themselves out. Mom and Dad went upstairs for some much-needed quiet time, while the rest of us sat on the living room rug, enjoying the soft, fuzzy creatures that were now part of our family, whether they wanted to be or not.

"Think they need more water?" Sara asked as she looked at their still-full water bowl.

"Or more of those crunchy things?" I asked, even though there were still plenty of those, too.

Benji looked up from petting the orange one. "What they need is names!"

"How 'bout Luke and Leia," I suggested.

"Or Loki," Sara said, after her favorite Marvel character.

"And Black Widow," Jon said, after his.

"That's a better name for a spider than a cat," I said. "How about Pumpkin for the boy?"

"What'll we call the girl?" Benji asked. "Pie?" He laughed; no one else did.

The little tabby was purring contentedly in my lap, but it was Sara's turn. She cleared her throat and reached out and I handed her the kitty.

"Why don't you sing to her?" I suggested.

"Something from *Cats*," Jon joked.

Sara thought for a few seconds, then hummed "Castle on a Cloud" from *Les Miz*.

"Hey." I smiled. "What about Marius and Eponine?"

"Peanut butter and jelly!" Benji shouted.

A slow smile spread across Sara's face. "Belle and Beast."

"Perfect." I smiled, too.

"Not bad," Jon said.

"I guess Peanut Butter is kind of long." Benji yawned and suddenly we all realized it was way past his bedtime. "Okay. Belle and Beast."

"Go tell Eema and Abba the kittens' names," Sara told him, "then get ready for bed."

"Do I have to?" Benji whined.

"If you do it right now, I'll come tell you a story," Jon bribed.

As usual, it worked. Benji kissed the kittens on their noses, then ran upstairs, Jon close behind.

"Think I'll go make a phone call," Sara told me. We both knew who she was going to call.

She headed upstairs just as Dad came down.

"I was thinking of making some cocoa," he said. "Can I interest you in a cup?"

I smiled and nodded. We both knew I never said no to anything chocolate.

We gathered the ingredients, and while he heated milk, cocoa powder, and sugar, I checked on the kittens. They were curled up against each other on the sofa, sound asleep.

I wish I felt as peaceful as they looked. But as I returned to the kitchen and Dad poured the cocoa, all I felt was guilty. I flashed back to my conversation with Sam after the audition. "Sometimes you have to give people a chance," he'd said.

If I told my Dad about All-County—if I gave him a chance—would he support my decision? Be happy for me? Forgive me for going behind his back?

Or would he be so angry that he'd force me to quit before I even started?

As I sipped the sweet, chocolaty drink, I still wasn't sure what to do, or say, about All-County.

"I know we haven't talked about it," Dad said, interrupting my thoughts, "but I know what you've been up to."

I choked and practically spit the hot chocolate out.

"You do?"

He nodded. "Of course! And I'm very pleased."

"You are?"

"Collecting those items for the animal shelter is a nice thing to do. Very . . . practical."

My heart stopped pounding. My mitzvah project. Of course that's what he was talking about! Anything bat mitzvah—related was always on his mind.

"Thanks. But, Dad . . ."

He put his mug down and gave me his undivided attention, like always; it was one of the things I loved most about him. "Rebecca? What is it?"

"I could use your help . . . with my speech. I know I should have told you sooner, and I'm really sorry but—"

He reached across the table, took my hand, and smiled. "I thought you'd never ask."

NOW

AS I TEAR up my bat mitzvah speech, the only thing I feel bad about is that Dad helped me with it.

Then again, he always helps everyone with everything.

Doesn't matter what's needed, who needs it, or when. Dad is always there for all of us: family, friends, congregants, neighbors. . . .

For the first time, I wonder: Who's going to help him?

19

"HAVE I MENTIONED how much I love winter break?" I asked Nipa.

She laughed. "You may have mentioned it one or ten times since you got here."

"Have I mentioned that this is one of my favorite *parts* of winter break?" Because it was. As much as I loved spending the holiday season with my family, I had just as much fun with Nipa.

The first time I'd visited her house in late December, I was five or six and afraid to be anywhere near the Christmas tree. It's not that it wasn't pretty (it was) or didn't smell good (it did); but my family didn't have one, so I thought I was supposed to avoid it.

The next year, we played in the same room as the tree; the year after that, I threw a little tinsel on—after Nipa threw some on me. The year after that, I hung a couple of ornaments. It was fun, but deep down I still wondered if it was okay. And I was scared to ask Mom or Dad in case they said it wasn't.

So I asked Sara.

She said it was perfectly okay. She said she'd helped Cassidy decorate her entire tree—and had even gone caroling with her! "And it didn't make me any less Jewish," she reassured me.

After that, Nipa and I created our own holiday traditions. She came to my house for latkes and dreidels on the first night of Hanukkah; I went to hers on December 23 to help decorate the tree and make sugar cookies. She gave me a Hanukkah gift and I gave her a Christmas present and all of it was great.

Was it the same for Sara and Sam? Was it great for them, too? Would he give her a Hanukkah present? Would she help decorate his tree?

Would they kiss under the mistletoe?

"Becky!" Nipa waved her hand in front of my face. "Stop daydreaming! We've still got a lot of cookies to decorate and a ton of other stuff to do."

"Okay, okay." I grinned and took a snowman, then reached for the red gel. I put on a red scarf and a green hat, then Nipa added mini chocolate chip eyes and a gumdrop nose. When the cookies were all decorated, we'd eat a few with huge glasses of ice-cold milk, and she'd give me a bagful to bring home.

My brothers looked forward to those cookies all year long. And so did I.

But the cookies were only the beginning. Since Sara and I were leaving for New York in three days, Nipa and I figured we'd better start the decorations for Ms. T's surprise shower: it was less than three weeks away!

Nipa—who, unlike me, was very artistic—was going to teach me how to make hearts and flowers out of paper, and Sara and Jenna were going to help us make cute little sandwiches the night before the party.

Sara . . .

I reached for the green gel and knocked over the bag of mini chips. They spilled all over the table. "Sorry!" I started scooping them back into the bag. "Guess I'm a little distracted today."

"It's okay," Nipa said. "Hey. Would you rather do the shower decorations after New York? Maybe you'll feel better about everything once you spend some time alone with Sara, like on the train ride up and back."

"I hope. But we might as well start the decorations. I'll probably be super slow and not very good at it."

Nipa smiled. "I can't wait to see Ms. T's face—can you?"

I smiled back. I loved that we were doing something special for her; she always did so much for us. If it weren't for her, I would never would have auditioned for All-County.

"I love weddings," Nipa said. "They're so much fun, especially Indian ones! There were all sorts of parties and ceremonies and singing and dancing two days before my cousin even got married! It's called *sangeet*, and it means 'sung together.'"

"Three days to celebrate? Wow!"

She put the mini chips on the last snowman, and we separated the cookies into two piles: one for her family and one for mine. "And before the wedding, there was this big procession called *baraat*, with family and friends all around, and more dancing and singing, and Kabir rode in on a beautiful white horse!"

"A horse?"

Nipa nodded. "He told me that some grooms even ride an elephant!"

"Amazing!" I laughed. "I'd like to see someone ride a horse or an elephant into the synagogue for a wedding."

Nipa laughed, too. "You should've seen his bride! Krupa had these incredible henna designs on her arms and hands and feet, and wore this gorgeous red dress...."

"Red?"

Nipa nodded. "Red is a lucky color for Hindus. I think it's supposed to represent love and beauty and marital bliss."

"'Marital bliss.'" I giggled. Nipa did, too. Then I thought of Miri and stopped laughing. Maybe she should have worn red, too.

"I think red is way more interesting than boring old white," Nipa said. She carefully slid our snowmen masterpieces into a huge plastic bag, then handed it over just as the doorbell chimed. Nipa's dad opened the door and started talking to a very familiar voice.

"Is that . . . Sara? I thought your mom was picking you up?" Nipa said. She looked over at the kitchen clock. "Plus it's—"

I looked at the clock, too. "An hour early. That's so weird."

"Do we really have to share those cookies with Jon and Benji?" Sara asked as she entered the room.

"Hi, Sara!" Nipa smiled, always glad to see my sister.

"What are you doing here?" I asked. "You're early."

"Nice to see you, too." Sara grinned at me. "I was thinking we could check out that boutique you like."

"Now?"

"Why not? Like Abba says, 'If not now, when?'"

"Actually, I think Hillel said it first." At least, according to my Hebrew school teacher. Still, whether it was Hillel—this famous Jewish scholar who lived, like, over a thousand years ago—or Dad, "If not now, when?" was definitely Sara's motto. Why do something tomorrow when you could do it today? Why wait ten minutes if you could do it right this second?

Why say no to your sister when she offered to hang out with you?

Still, Nipa and I had plans.

But before I could even ask if she minded, Nipa handed me the bag of cookies and said, "Go. Get an amazing dress for your bat mitzvah. And text me a picture!"

"I will. Especially if it's red."

* * *

Before I knew it, Sara and I were at the boutique, gift certificate in hand. We spent the first fifteen minutes browsing. I held up an outfit now and then for her approval, but she shook her head each time. I was starting to feel discouraged when Sara found a dress buried deep in one of the racks. "What do you think?"

"Is it my size?" I held my breath.

She nodded and smiled.

"And it's not too expensive?"

She looked at the price tag, shook her head, and held the dress out to me. I practically ran to the dressing room.

It was the prettiest dress I'd ever seen: deep purple velvet with a round neck and cap sleeves. I loved everything about it, but the best part was the skirt. It had sequins all over and it shimmered and sparkled whenever I moved. It was perfect for my bat mitzvah, and the party afterward!

I stared at myself in the mirror for a minute or two, then left the dressing room and found Sara. One look at her face told me she loved it as much as I did.

"Oh, Becky. I love it!"

"Me, too."

"Also? I found this to go with it." She handed me a lacy white long-sleeved shrug that also had sequins running through it. "Your bat mitzvah is in January, after all. Those short sleeves are really cute, but they might not keep you warm enough."

I put it on over the dress and it was just right.

"Thank you so much, Sara," I said, hugging her. I carefully

took everything off and she bought the dress and the shrug for me.

"I think I'm starting to look forward to my bat mitzvah," I told her as we headed back to the van.

She laughed. "It's about time. How's that speech coming?" She unlocked the doors and we climbed in.

"Okay, I guess." I shrugged. "Better, anyway. Dad explained how the whole movable sanctuary was about giving God a gift, after all the gifts He gave us. So I'm trying to write about different kinds of gifts I give, and get."

She considered that approach and nodded. "That's good. Everyone can relate to that. You're lucky to have a rabbi in the family."

"And a cool sister." I smiled and waited for Sara to turn on the ignition, but she turned to me instead. She touched the necklace under her sweater, most likely *not* her Star of David. Something told me we were done with bat mitzvah talk and moving onto a different topic.

"Becky . . . Sean and I want to see each other as much as we can over break."

Yep. A *very* different topic. "Umm. Okay?"

"But it's not easy," Sara continued. "Cassidy's going out of town, and Jenna's with her boyfriend, so she can only help once or twice. . . ."

"Help? How?" I suddenly had that roller-coaster sensation. The part where there's a turn so sharp and fast it takes your breath away. Kind of like going from my bat mitzvah dress, and bat mitzvah speech, to dating someone not Jewish. And even though I liked Sam—and loved Sara—I didn't love keeping them a secret.

"The thing is," she was saying, "I hate telling Eema and Abba that I'm going out with Jenna when I'm really seeing Sean." She looked at me, waiting for some kind of response.

"Uh-huh..."

"I was wondering—I mean, you and Sean seem to get along and everything...."

"Uh-huh..." I still had no clue where this was headed, but was pretty sure I wouldn't like it.

"So I was thinking maybe the three of us could hang out."

"What?"

"If you're there, too, I could say, 'Becky and I are going bowling,' only Sean would be there, too. See?"

"I hate bowling."

"That's not the point."

I rubbed my eyes the way Dad did when he was getting a headache. "So we meet up at some bowling alley. Then what? I play video games in the corner? Get something at the snack bar?"

"No! Of course not! You bowl with us. Or, if you don't like bowling, we'll do something else. See a movie, get some pizza, go on a walk in the park..."

I shook my head. "I don't feel good about this. It's been hard enough keeping secrets from Mom and Dad."

"I know. I don't like it, either."

"But this is lying!"

"No! It's not! That's the point. It wouldn't be a lie . . . exactly."

"Not exactly the truth, either."

"Maybe not the *whole* truth."

We sat there for a minute or two, both of us thinking. Neither of us talking. Neither of us even looking at the other.

"Hey." She touched my hand. "I would do it for you. You know I would."

"I know." I pulled my hand away and turned to her. "But that doesn't make it easier. Or right." Unexpected tears appeared out of nowhere—tears I'd been holding inside for a long time. "I mean, doesn't it bother you? Don't you feel kind of bad when Mom and Dad say how proud they are of us, and we're both . . ."

"Becky—"

"They wouldn't be so proud if they knew what we were doing, would they?"

She took a deep breath and let it out. "No. They wouldn't be proud. But maybe, someday, they'll understand."

I wiped my eyes. "Do you really think so?"

"I hope so." She reached into her purse and handed me a tissue. "I'm sorry you're in the middle of all this, but I'm kind of glad, too."

"Why?"

"It's nice, sharing this with someone besides Cassidy and Jenna. Someone at home. You know?"

I did. I understood how hard it was to keep Sam a secret. But it was more than that: it was not being able to share her happiness. Like me not sharing my All-County news. It almost made it less real—and definitely less happy. Keeping secrets wasn't fun; it was hard. Like an itch I couldn't scratch.

She tilted her head. "So . . . ?"

"Okay, okay." I sighed. "We can go bowling, or whatever. So long as no one laughs when I get a gutter ball."

She smiled. "No laughing, I promise. Besides, gutter balls are Sean's specialty." Her phone rang. "Hey, there! We did. . . ." Sara looked at me. "And she looks amazing in it."

I smiled, too, thinking of my new dress.

She nodded. "We talked it over and she's in. Lane seven? Okay . . . See you in fifteen." Her face softened and so did her voice. "Me, too." She ended the call and started the car.

"Wait. We're going bowling *now*?"

"It'll be fun! You'll see."

My mind told me this was why Sara had taken me dress-shopping today.

But my heart refused to listen.

20

TWELVE MINUTES LATER, we were pulling up to Stars and Strikes Bowling Alley. Sara tended to drive a little fast when she was excited.

Or anxious.

Or breathing.

Sam greeted us at the door. He gave my sister a quick kiss, then turned to me and smiled like we were old friends. Like he was glad I came along.

But *I* wasn't. Keeping Sara's secret was one thing; this felt like something else.

"Hey, Trumpet Girl. Nice to see you again."

Sara's eyes narrowed. "Trumpet Girl? Don't you mean flute?"

"It's a long story." He grinned at me.

I didn't grin back.

I followed them inside, feeling like I was betraying my

parents in a whole new way. As I looked through a pile of the ugliest shoes ever made, I wondered how anyone could ever love bowling. By the time I forced my feet into a particularly hideous pair, Sara was already at a lane, setting up the scoreboard, and Sam was at a rack of huge, heavy bowling balls, testing one after another. He waved me over, so I joined him. I wondered if he would thank me for coming, or tell me how he didn't feel right about this, either. . . .

"Here." He handed me a red ball, then an orange one. "See if you like either of these."

Or maybe he just wanted to give me a bowling ball. "Wow. I can actually lift them. They usually weigh a ton."

"I know. I was hoping to find some lighter ones."

"Thanks."

"You're welcome." He smiled at me again, but there was something different about it: it was a sad smile. "I got pretty good at finding the lightest balls for my mom."

I remembered his mom died not that long ago. Did he know that I knew? Should I say something like "I'm sorry for your loss"? People said that at Grandma Rachel's funeral, but it didn't make me feel any better, and it definitely didn't change anything.

Before I figured out if or how I should respond, he said, "Unlike me, she was an excellent bowler. She really loved it. Even when she got sick, we couldn't keep her away." He turned the ball around in his hands. "But the lightweight balls got too heavy for her after a while. . . ." He cleared his throat.

"Anyway, I guess that's why I suggested bowling today. I went all the time after she died. It was almost like she was there with me."

"I think I know what you mean," I told him. "A few weeks after my grandma Rachel died, my family went out for milkshakes, and all six of us ordered peach, even though none of us likes it all that much. But it was her favorite and it reminded us of her." As soon as I said it, I felt embarrassed; it wasn't the same at all. I shouldn't have said—

"Exactly," he said.

We both got quiet for a minute. "Hey," he started, "I hear congratulations are in order, Miss All-County."

"Thanks." I smiled back, but I knew it was a sad smile, like his had been. What was the point of a sad smile, anyway?

I held my breath and waited for him to say how I should tell my parents. How it would only get more complicated with rehearsals and everything. But he just looked at me, and I realized he wasn't thinking all that: *I* was.

"I don't know what to do," I told him.

"You'll figure it out. But if you ever want to talk, I'm around."

"Thanks." Then I realized something. "Uh, Sam? I don't have your number."

He held his hand out and I gave him my phone and he typed it in. "Now you do."

I was pretty sure I'd never need it, but I thanked him anyway. Then we took our balls and headed toward Sara, who was smiling like this would be the most fun ever in the history of bowling.

Turned out she wasn't exaggerating about Sam: he really did specialize in gutter balls. After a while, instead of paying attention to who was winning (Sara, by a landslide), he and I ended up competing to see who got the worst score. It was kind of a fail, but also kind of hilarious.

By the time we finished the game, we were both laughing so hard I didn't even care how bad I was at bowling. Especially since it was time for food, always the best part of any sport, if you ask me. Except for pep band.

"So . . . what do you want to drink?" Sam asked Sara and me as we walked over to the snack bar.

"Lemonade, please," she said.

I was trying to decide between lemonade and orange soda, when Sam smiled at me and said, "Too bad there are no peach milkshakes."

I smiled back. Then, without thinking, asked, "What was your mom's favorite drink?"

"Root beer."

"I'd like a root beer," I said.

"Make it two," Sam told the guy behind the counter. Then he turned to us. "Any food? I know it won't be a cheeseburger."

I looked at Sara, surprised he knew we didn't mix meat and milk.

She smiled at me.

"Curly fries? Pretzels?" Sam waited patiently.

We all settled on the fries, and when the food and drinks came, Sam insisted on treating us. "It's not often I get to hang out with both of you at the same time."

We thanked him, then Sara lifted her cup. "To terrible bowlers, but excellent sports."

Sam took a slurp of his drink, making almost as much noise as Benji, just to make us laugh—which it did.

Fifteen minutes later, Sam crumpled up his napkin and asked, "Okay, who's ready for another battle of the gutter balls?"

I surprised myself by shouting, "I am!"

The second round was almost as funny as the first, and the time went by really fast. Before I knew it, we were returning our shoes and he was kissing Sara goodbye.

He smiled at me. "This was fun."

"Yeah," I told him. "It actually was."

Sam smiled at the two of us. "Have a great time in New York!"

"We will," Sara said.

"I'll try to keep her out of trouble," I told him.

Sara laughed. "You should talk."

We waved at Sam and headed to the car. "We should do this again sometime," Sara suggested.

"Don't push it," I said, but I smiled as I opened the car door and got in.

"So . . . ?" She smiled back. "What do you think of him?"

I sighed. "I already told you. I like him, okay?"

"I know. But . . ." She looked at me.

"But what?"

"I mean . . . You've spent more time with him now, so . . ."

"He's a good guy, all right?" I thought for a few seconds. "If he were Jewish, I might even call him a mensch." Mensch being one of the all-time highest compliments Mom or Dad ever gave.

"Becky! You don't have to be Jewish to be a mensch. It just means you're a good person. That you have integrity. That you're kind."

"In that case, Sam is definitely a mensch."

Sara smiled like she'd just won the lottery or something. "Thank you."

"You're welcome." I paused. "But that doesn't mean I want to go bowling again anytime soon."

NOW

I'M NEVER GOING to love bowling.

The shoes are ugly and the balls are heavy and I hardly ever hit the pins.

Still...

I would give anything to go bowling with them again.

21

THE TRAIN RIDE to New York City was exactly how I'd hoped it would be. Sara and I spent some time doing stuff on our own, like reading and playing games on our phones. But mostly we talked, traded snacks, and took turns playing music for each other in our earbuds. We also tried to guess which Broadway musical Aunt Ruth would take us to this time. That was always Sara's favorite part.

My favorite part was trying a new cupcake place. It seemed like there was always one or two we hadn't visited before, and nobody was better at discovering them than our aunt.

But what Sara and I did most of all on the way up was laugh. She told me some of the crazy stuff that went on backstage at *Les Miz*, and I got her to laugh at a Benji story or two. It not only felt good to laugh so much, it was like we were as close as ever—maybe even closer.

When we arrived at Penn Station a few hours later, we

squeezed past tons of people to finally reach the candy store where our family always met up with Aunt Ruth. Only, for the first time ever, she wasn't waiting there.

"Are we early?" I asked Sara.

"No. Our train actually got here ten minutes late."

"Aunt Ruth is always on time...."

Sara shrugged. "Maybe traffic's worse than usual."

We waited fifteen minutes more, and then I finally saw her coming toward us. At least, I thought it was her. "Is that Aunt Ruth?" I whispered. It had only been a few months since we last saw her, but . . . "Wow. She looks a lot older."

"Shh!" Sara said, even though our aunt was still too far away to hear us. "Just act normal."

A minute later, Aunt Ruth was out of breath and hugging us and apologizing for being late. "I don't know what happened. I must've lost track of the time somehow. Your uncle is away on a business trip...."

"It's fine, Aunt Ruth," Sara said, eyeing me. "Our train was running late, so we basically just got here ourselves."

"Well . . ." Aunt Ruth wiped her damp forehead. "That's a relief."

We stood there, looking at each other and smiling and waiting for the usual routine to start. Aunt Ruth always asked if we wanted some candy since we were at a candy store after all, and we always said no and then she bought some for us anyway. After that, she'd take our whole family to a trendy new café she'd discovered since our last visit.

But this time, it was like we were in a different version of a familiar play, only Sara and I didn't know the new lines.

"Well..." Aunt Ruth said. "Shall we head for home, then?"

"Uh, sure," Sara said. We glanced at each other, confused. "Sounds good."

When we exited Penn Station, everything looked and sounded the same: a million people walking around, sirens blaring and horns honking, skyscrapers and splashy billboards everywhere. But it felt different this time. It felt... quieter.

Aunt Ruth hailed a cab and we piled in. Twenty minutes later, we arrived at her apartment. As soon as she opened the door, I knew things had changed there, too. She usually had lights blazing and fresh flowers all over the place and a crystal-cut bowl filled with butterscotch or cinnamon candies.

But today, all the lights were off, there were no flowers anywhere, and the candy bowl was empty.

"Uncle Jacob is on a business trip," she told us for the second time. "He's so sorry he couldn't be here."

"I know," I said. "You already told—"

"That's a shame." Sara cut me off. "We're sorry, too."

"You can put your suitcases in Miri's room. She's..." Aunt Ruth didn't finish her sentence.

"Thanks." Sara took me by the arm. "C'mon, Becky. Let's unpack."

I followed her down the hall, happy to escape Aunt Ruth

for a little while. We got into Miri's room and Sara shut the door.

"This is bad," I said. "What happened to lunch? There aren't even any candies or flowers around!"

Sara rolled her eyes. "Seriously? *That's* what you're worried about?"

"No. Well, not only that . . ." I sat down on the inflatable mattress that was always set out when we visited. "Aunt Ruth is acting really weird. Mom should've come with us. She'd know what to do. Maybe we should call her."

"No. She'll only get all upset. Just . . . let me think for a minute, okay?"

"Fine." I unzipped my backpack and pulled out the smushed, half-eaten turkey sandwich Mom packed for a snack, and the last few grapes we brought from home.

"Now what are you doing?"

"I'm hungry."

She let out a breath. "Me, too."

I handed her a couple of mushy grapes.

She bit into one and made a face. "They were better on the train."

"Everything was better on the train. Sara, what are we going to do? Should we call Jon?"

She considered. "That's actually not a terrible idea."

Miri's door opened. "Who's hungry?" Aunt Ruth asked.

"Me! Where are we going this time?" I asked, hoping they served pizza. Or chocolate. Or both.

"Not far."

We followed her into the dining room, where soup and sandwiches were already set out on the table.

"I thought instead of going out in the cold to a restaurant, we might eat in for a change," she said.

I shrugged. "It's always cold when we visit. . . ."

Sara pasted on a smile. "Sounds good," she said.

We sat at the table, and I took a bite of turkey sandwich.

"Oh!" Aunt Ruth went to the kitchen and returned with a bowl. "I almost forgot the grapes!"

"Yum," I said.

"Thanks," Sara said.

"So, what are the plans for tonight?" I asked, wondering if Sara or I guessed the right show.

Aunt Ruth stared at her plate. "Actually, I thought it might be nice for Sara to spend some time with her cousin." When she looked at my sister, there was such hope in her eyes, there was no way Sara could say no.

"Can I go, too? I'd love to see Miri," I said.

My aunt frowned. "Maybe next time."

"But—"

Before I could continue, Sara shook her head, so I stopped talking.

"Miri's about half an hour from here," Aunt Ruth continued. "I think her apartment is close to the medical school. . . ."

"You *think*?" I asked. "Haven't you visited?"

My aunt stood. "I'll go get you some money for the cab

rides." She left the room like it was on fire.

My sister glared at me. "What is wrong with you?"

"Whaddaya mean?"

"Of course Aunt Ruth hasn't visited Miri. You know they aren't talking!"

"Because she married someone not Jewish?"

"Yes, Becky. Because she married someone not Jewish." She got up and threw out the rest of her sandwich. "We already talked about this. Remember?"

"I know, but Miri only lives half an hour from here."

"She might as well live on a different planet," Sara said bitterly, dropping her dish into the sink. "I need a shower," she mumbled and walked away.

And just like that, I was all alone.

I quickly finished my sandwich as Aunt Ruth returned with some money.

"Sara is in the shower," I explained.

"Oh, I'll just leave this here," Aunt Ruth said quietly. She put some bills on the table, then walked out, leaving me by myself again. I cleaned up my plate and went back to Miri's room. I called Nipa, but it went straight to voicemail.

It was time to bring in the big guns.

His phone rang once, twice, three times. I was trying to figure out who else to call when he picked up on the fourth ring.

"Hey, Bec. What's up?"

"Jon!" I lowered my voice. "Where are you?"

"I had a hankering for a BLT so I snuck out to get one."

"You're kidding," I said as softly as I could. "Right?"

"Yes, Becky. I'm kidding. Why are you whispering?"

"Because . . ." I shut the door. "Never mind." I sat on the bed.

"Where's Sara?"

"In the shower. Then she's going to see Miri—without me!"

"Okay . . ."

I jumped up. "No! It's not okay! I have to stay here all by myself."

"What happened to Aunt Ruth?"

"I don't know what happened to her! That's why I'm calling!" I started to pace the small bedroom.

"What are you talking about?"

"She came late to pick us up—and she's never late! Then we had turkey sandwiches instead of—"

"You mean, the ones Mom made?"

"No. Well, yes. Those, too. Except they were mushy."

"Becky, you're not making any sense."

"The candy bowl was empty."

"Are you kidding me?" Jon sounded as upset as I was, which made me feel much better. "That does it," he said. "Head back to the train station right now."

"Wait—what?"

"I mean, if there's no candy, what's the point? Why bother visiting at all?"

"This isn't funny, Jon. Really! Aunt Ruth is acting weird.

She won't talk to Miri—she won't even see her, and she only lives half an hour away!"

"Okay, okay. Stop pacing."

"What? How did you know I was—"

"Because I know you. Now sit down and take a breath."

I sat. I breathed.

"Now, start again from when you got off the train."

I explained everything that had happened. When he was finally caught up, I stopped and waited for his reaction.

"Huh."

"That's it? That's all you have to say?"

"I'm not sure what to say," Jon said.

"Great. That really helps." I got up and started pacing again.

"I guess . . . if I were there . . . if Aunt Ruth is that upset about the Miri situation, I would . . ."

"Yeah . . . ?"

"First of all, I would try to be patient with her. Cut her some slack. She's going through a rough time, and obviously isn't herself right now—"

"No kidding."

"And," Jon continued, "if she's too preoccupied to plan outings, maybe I would come up with some."

"Like what?"

"Well, you could always go to the grocery store and stock up on butterscotch candy. . . ."

I tried not to smile.

"Or, I don't know, get her outside. Take a walk around the neighborhood. Maybe go to that park near her apartment."

"I guess we could do that."

"Just . . . be nice."

"I was so excited about this trip, and now it's all messed up."

"Look. I know it's not what you were expecting. And you're kind of in a tough spot. But you can handle this, Bec. It's only a couple of days. . . ."

"I guess."

"Hey—when you get back home, how 'bout I take you out for pizza and you can tell me all about it?"

"Extra cheese and mushrooms?"

"Don't push it."

Just as I was starting to feel better, Sara came in wearing an oversized flannel shirt and a gloomy expression. I'd never seen that shirt before; I wondered if it was Sam's. . . .

"Wanna say hi to Jon?"

"No time. I have to meet Miri."

She left without a smile, or even saying goodbye.

"I've gotta go," Jon said. "I promised Benji we'd hang out. Listen, you'll be back here before you know it. Try to have fun, okay?"

"I'll try."

Dinner was worse than lunch.

I had tried everything Jon suggested, but Aunt Ruth said

she had a headache and didn't want to go to the store or the park or anywhere else but bed.

And Sara was with Miri. So when the two of us finally sat down to eat there was no one for my aunt to talk to except me, and I couldn't talk—at least, not about important stuff.

"So, my dear," she said, leaning in across the table, "tell me everything. What's going on with you?"

"Well . . ." I forged Mom's signature so I could audition for All-County after Dad said I couldn't. And I got in! But I haven't told them. Yeah. I couldn't exactly say that.

"Umm . . ." Sara's dating a really nice guy. But he's not Jewish. Kind of like your son-in-law. Nope. Probably shouldn't say that, either.

"Let's see . . ." I wanted to talk about Ms. T.'s surprise shower, but I was pretty sure my aunt hadn't thrown one for Miri, so that would only make her feel bad.

Of course, there was always my bat mitzvah, but I really didn't want to think—or talk—about that.

By the time I came up with a safe subject, my aunt's eyes glazed over and I felt like a year had passed. "Benji lost a tooth last night," I offered.

She raised her eyebrows. "Oh?"

I smiled. "Mom is the tooth fairy at our house. She likes to leave a pack of sugarless gum." I always thought that was funny, but Aunt Ruth didn't laugh.

"When Miri lost a tooth," she said, "I'd leave her a crisp dollar bill and a mini eraser. Every time I saw a cute one somewhere, I'd buy it and save it for a tooth fairy gift: a flamingo, a basketball, a banana, a rocket ship. . . . She used to love those erasers."

"That's a fun idea," I said. "Maybe we can do it for Benji." But she didn't respond. She just looked like her thoughts were a million miles away.

After dinner we played cards and watched TV, but we were really just waiting for Sara to get back. The longer we waited and the later it got, though, I felt the whole long day catching up with me. After around my twentieth yawn, I excused myself and got ready for bed.

I brushed my teeth, got into my pajamas, and went to put a few things in the top dresser drawer. When I opened it, I found a sandwich bag full of mini erasers.

I took it out and emptied them on my bed; they really were cute. As I looked at each one, I thought about how much fun Aunt Ruth must've had collecting them, and how much Miri must've loved them to keep them all this time.

And I wondered how many erasers it would take to erase all the bad feelings between my aunt and my cousin.

22

I'D TRIED TO stay awake and wait for Sara, but I must've fallen asleep. By the time I woke up the next morning, she and my aunt were already sitting at the kitchen table, so I didn't even have a chance to talk to Sara in private to find out how Miri was doing.

When I joined them, it was obvious they'd already talked about it, because all they discussed over cereal and fruit was today's plans. I could tell something was different, and it wasn't good. Sara barely looked at either of us, and didn't crack a smile even once. But things began to improve the minute we left the building and, before long, it felt like old times again.

First, Aunt Ruth took us to a cool new restaurant called Vic's where the food was great, plus Daniel Radcliffe sat at the booth across from us! At least, I was almost positive it was him; Sara told me to stop staring.

After Vic's we went to a show, only it wasn't a musical. It was *The Play That Goes Wrong*, this goofy murder mystery with a play within a play. The set kept falling apart, the actors forgot their lines and missed their cues.... It was silly and slapstick and I thought it was hilarious.

But my aunt had already seen it, so she only chuckled once or twice, and Sara didn't laugh much, either. Something was definitely on her mind, and I couldn't wait to talk to her about it. Aunt Ruth never left our side for the rest of the day, though, so I didn't have a chance until we arrived back at Penn Station, hugged each other goodbye, and got on the train to return home.

As soon as we got settled in our seats, I asked about Miri, but Sara said she wanted to listen to music for a while. The second time, I barely got a sentence in before she had a text from Sam and forgot all about me.

So I played games on my phone and tried to read some magazines, but I couldn't focus. Then I went to the café car and brought back some junk food to share with Sara, but when I offered, she shook her head and went back to texting Sam.

So I decided I would text Nipa.

Me: Hey.

Nipa: Hey! Where r u?

Me: Train.

Nipa: Uh-oh.

Me: What?

Nipa: 1-word answers = never good. Plus y aren't you talking 2 Sara?

Me: Sam.

Nipa: See? 1-word answer.

Me: Yup.

Nipa: What happened?

It was a good question. I wasn't sure I had a good answer. Suddenly I didn't feel like texting anymore. I had nothing to say . . . but also way too much.

Me: Btr in person.

Nipa: 2morrow?

Me: Yup.

Nipa: TALK 2 HER!!

Me: ok

She signed off with a bunch of heart emojis, and I turned to my sister. "Sara, are you mad at me?"

"What?" She immediately put her phone down and looked at me. "Of course not!"

"Then why won't you talk to me? What happened with Miri? You've been acting weird ever since you saw her."

"Look. I don't mind talking. I just . . . don't want to talk about that."

"Why not?"

"Because . . . it's personal."

"Personal?" I felt my eyes go wide. "We're talking about Miri!"

"No. We're *not* talking about Miri. That's the point."

"I don't understand. You're not the only one who loves her!"

Sara sighed. "I know."

"Then why won't you tell me what happened?"

"Because it's Miri's business and no one else's."

"Then how come she told you?"

"Becky, I'm sorry, but . . ."

"I am so sick of secrets!" I stashed my magazine and phone in the storage compartment in front of my seat and stomped off to the café car again, even though I wasn't hungry. Which was a good thing, because I didn't have any money left anyway.

But it was still better than sitting with Sara.

"Wow," Nipa said. "That doesn't sound good."

I was back in Maryland, spending the night at her house. We were in her kitchen surrounded by two dozen chocolate cupcakes we'd baked to make me "feel better." They normally would, too; but nothing felt normal now.

I stared at the cupcakes. "I thought all the stuff with Sam and All-County would bring us closer. Having each other's backs and everything, you know?"

"Yeah, I know," Nipa said.

"And I was so excited about going to New York! Just Sara and me. I thought we'd stay up late talking and laughing—like we used to. I thought we'd talk about . . . everything."

"Sounds like she talked to Miri instead of you."

"Exactly. And she wouldn't even tell me what they talked about!" I let out a long, sad breath. "There are so many secrets. I can't even keep track anymore."

I watched her divide a big bowl of white icing into four

smaller ones, then we each chose two colors of edible paste her mom had. "What do you think happened at your cousin's?" Nipa asked.

I dipped a toothpick into a tub of royal blue, then swirled it around in the little bowl until all the white disappeared. "I don't know. What do you think?"

Nipa mixed violet into another bowl and frowned. "I have no idea."

I took lemon yellow, hoping a cheerful color would cheer me up . . . but it didn't.

We frosted the cupcakes and decorated them with sprinkles, not talking for a few minutes.

I bit into a pink-iced cupcake but barely tasted it. "I thought Sara and I were done keeping secrets—at least, from each other."

Nipa poured two tall glasses of milk. "Yeah. That's so not fair."

I nodded. "Right? It's messed up! Does she think I won't understand? That I won't take Miri's side?"

"What makes you think there are sides?"

"There are always sides, Nipa. In this case, Aunt Ruth's and Miri's."

She chewed thoughtfully. "And you think Sara's on your cousin's side?"

"That makes the most sense, right? She and Miri are both with someone who isn't Jewish."

She took a long drink of milk, put her glass down, and

looked at me. "I'm not trying to be insensitive or anything—"

"You're never insensitive!"

She bit her lip. "I still don't get what the big deal is. I mean, I get that your dad's a rabbi and Sam's is a reverend—but his dad's okay with it, right?"

"That's what Sam said. And I don't think he'd lie about it."

"Right. So . . . Maybe your parents would be okay with it, too."

"No." I shook my head. "You didn't hear my mom and aunt freaking out about Miri's marriage. And my dad's always telling us not to date non-Jews. It's not that . . . It's hard to explain. It's just . . . it's important to him that we keep our faith. If we all marry someone who isn't Jewish, pretty soon there won't be any Jews left—and there aren't that many of us to begin with. My whole life, I've heard and read about so many Jews who were treated unfairly, who were bullied or even killed just because they were Jewish. Some of my mom's relatives died in the concentration camps, and her grandparents escaped just in time. My dad's grandparents came over from Russia. There were these pogroms there, and his grandfather had to dig his own grave when the soldiers—"

"Okay," Nipa's voice was soft and sad. "I get it. I guess."

"Sometimes I think, if things had been different . . . I wouldn't be here at all."

For a minute or two, neither of us said anything. It was hard, and horrible, to imagine.

"There's so much loss and sadness and sacrifice," I told her.

"Marrying out of our faith feels like a betrayal or something."

"Okay," Nipa said. "Still . . . if Sara's on Miri's side—not to mention her seeing Sam—I understand why your parents would be upset. But why can't she tell *you*?"

We talked in circles awhile longer, then made the paper hearts and flowers for Ms. T's shower that we were going to do before New York. Before Sara took me to get my bat mitzvah dress, and before we went bowling with Sam.

Before we went to New York and everything got messed up again.

We worked for about an hour, then decided we'd do more in the morning and got ready for bed. This was usually my favorite part of our sleepovers. When the lights went out and we gossiped and laughed late into the night.

I knew I could tell Nipa anything, but it was easier in the dark. "I hate that Sara doesn't trust me," I said. "I hate that she's shutting me out—again. I thought we were past that. I mean, she told me all about Sam. . . ."

Nipa was quiet for so long, I wondered if she'd fallen asleep.

"You're right," she finally said softly. "She did tell you about him . . . but you'd already figured it out. In fact, *you* kind of told *her*."

"I guess so," I said quietly. It was true. And suddenly I felt even worse. The only reason Sara had told me her secret was because I'd already guessed it.

23

THE LAST FEW days of winter break came and went; nothing much happened. It was nice being out of school, and fun having Jon around. But I spent most of the time fretting about Sara. She was gone a lot, but even when she was at home, it felt like she was somewhere else.

I missed her. But I was mad at her, too. It was a strange combination; I didn't like it.

And then it was New Year's Eve.

After twelve years of going to bed early on December 31st, the first time I was allowed to stay up until midnight was shaping up to be no fun at all.

Benji had been sick for three days, and now Mom was sick, too.

Dad was out on one of his last-minute emergency visits. Mom always said if he was going to be on call 24/7, maybe he should've been a doctor instead of a rabbi. He'd always just smile and say he was better at spiritual healing than physical.

Since Mom and Dad weren't around, Jon asked Sara and me if we wanted to play Monopoly. I was thinking there had to be something more exciting to do on New Year's Eve; I just didn't know what.

Sara did, though. "No offense, you guys, but this is the worst New Year's Eve ever. I'm going to Cassidy's. A bunch of the pit musicians from the play are hanging out there...."

Of course she had other plans. Maybe she was seeing Cassidy and some of the others from the show, or maybe she was only seeing *one* person from the show. It's not like she told me anything anymore. I was still angry at her for not telling me about Miri last week, so I couldn't help myself from asking, "Just pit? How 'bout stage crew? Or . . . lighting?"

She narrowed her eyes and glared at me.

"Say hi to Cassidy for me," Jon said, ignoring my comment. "And watch out for drunk drivers," he added in a perfect imitation of Mom.

"Hilarious," Sara said, grumpy because of me. She left without a smile or a goodbye.

My brother shrugged and turned to me. "And then there were two."

"Why aren't you with your friends, also?"

"Mom paid me ten bucks to keep you company."

"You should've asked for twenty."

"I did."

I smiled. "Seriously, though? Why spend New Year's Eve here instead of someplace more exciting?"

"There's enough excitement back in L.A. Sometimes it's

nice to be with someone dull and boring." He grinned and raised an eyebrow. "Should we put another log on the fire or call it a night?"

I shrugged. "I guess being with you is better than nothing—even if you *are* dull and boring."

He laughed and threw on another log, and we watched the flames crackle and spark.

It was pretty and soothing and it felt really nice *not* to think about New York and Miri and Aunt Ruth for a change. But I'd gotten an email that morning, with the official rehearsal schedule for All-County, so *that* was on my mind instead. It was the perfect time to tell Jon all about it, especially since it was only the two of us.

I just wasn't sure *how*. . . .

I sat on the floor next to Belle, who rolled over onto her side and purred as I stroked her soft fur. Jon scooped up Beast, who stretched and yawned before settling contentedly in my brother's lap.

Before I figured out what I could and couldn't say, Jon turned to me. "Something on your mind, Bec?"

"Why do you ask?"

"That old poker face of yours," he teased. "Besides, anyone can see you're distracted." He scratched Beast behind the ears. "Even Beast here can sense the tension. He hasn't eaten in five minutes."

I laughed. We all knew Beast's favorite activity was eating.

"Are you gonna tell me"—Jon paused—"or should we play twenty questions?"

I rolled my eyes.

"Okay. Twenty questions it is. Let's see. . . . Are you in some kind of trouble?"

"Seriously? *That's* your first question?"

"Sorry." He held his hands up like he was surrendering. "But are you?"

"No!"

He looked at me a few seconds, then leaned back into the sofa, like he expected this was going to be a long talk. "Is this about your bat mitzvah?"

I shook my head. "I can't give you any details because I made a promise . . . to a friend . . . and I don't want to get them in trouble."

"What did Nipa do?"

"It's not Nipa. Anyway, this friend really wanted to audition for . . . the basketball team."

"You mean, try out?"

"Right. Try out. Only his parents wouldn't let him."

Jon did an exaggerated double take. "Wait, your friend is a boy?"

"Hey! I have plenty of friends who are boys. Anyway, he kind of went behind his parents' backs and tried out. And he got in! I mean, he made the team. Except now it's gonna be hard getting to rehear—to practice. And games. Without them knowing. But if he tells them, they might make him quit."

Jon frowned. "Why didn't they want him to play in the first place?"

"It doesn't matter. The point is—"

"Is it a health issue? Because if that's the case, you should tell your friend to—"

"It's not a health issue, okay? And it's really, really important to my friend because it's, like, the only thing he's good at."

"Wow. That's sad."

"I know, right?" This was going better than I thought. Maybe I could tell him the truth after all!

"The only thing your friend's good at is basketball?"

"What? No! He . . . he *thinks* that's the only thing he's good at. His brother and sister are, like, perfect at everything—kind of like you and Sara."

"What are you talking about?"

I let out a very long breath. "I'm talking about how you always get straight As. And how Sara's been every teacher's pet since, like, kindergarten. I'm talking about your epic bar mitzvah speech and Sara's pitch-perfect chanting. . . ."

"Wow," Jon said. "It's like you're living in an alternate reality." He got up, moved the logs around in the fireplace, and sat back down. "How old were you when I gave my so-called 'epic' speech?"

I shrugged. "I guess around Benji's age."

He laughed. "What you don't remember is that I was so nervous I lost track halfway through, then panicked and broke into a sweat and stood there, paralyzed, in front of the entire congregation."

"What? No, you didn't."

"Yes. I did!" He shook his head. "As for Sara, she practiced her chanting so much she lost her voice. It was hoarse and scratchy and she wanted to cancel the whole thing."

"I remember now! She was drinking tea and lemon juice and honey, but nothing helped. How did I forget that?"

"The point is, both of us were—are—far from perfect. But that's okay." He sat up straight and looked at me. "Bec, listen. Tell your 'friend' that it's not about comparing yourself to other people. All that matters is being the best version of yourself."

The best version of myself.

I could do that. I could be that.

I just had to figure out what it meant. Was the best version of myself playing flute in All-County? Or telling my parents the truth?

For me, New Year's Eve was more than staying up late. More than parties and funny hats, and watching a ball drop at midnight.

It was a chance to start over, do things differently. Do things better.

Sara's secret was exactly that: Sara's. It was mine to keep and hers to tell . . . if she wanted. But All-County was my secret. My choice. My chance to be the best version of myself—whatever that meant, however it turned out.

It was late when Dad got home. I knew he'd be tired, and I knew Mom wasn't feeling great and I could—maybe should—wait until morning. But I also knew if I waited any longer, I might not do it at all.

I hugged Belle, scratched Beast behind his ears, wished Jon a happy New Year, and went upstairs.

Dad saw me in the hall and, even though he looked sleepy, he came over and gave me a hug. "Happy New Year, Rebecca."

"Thanks. You, too."

He let go and turned toward his room: it was now or never. I took a breath. "I know it's late, but can I talk to you and Mom for a minute? It's important."

"Of course."

I followed him into their bedroom, where Mom waved a box of tissues in my general direction and shouted, "Don't come any closer!"

Dad took a chair, and I stayed by the door, desperate to leave but determined to stay.

"Rebecca says she has something important to talk to us about."

They both looked at me and waited.

I cleared my throat and ignored the knots in my stomach and forced myself to look at them. "So . . . remember Rosh Hashanah? When I asked about auditioning for All-County?"

They nodded.

"And Dad said no?"

They nodded again, slower this time.

"I auditioned anyway."

Mom's mouth opened and formed an O while Dad said, "Rebecca, what—?"

I kept going. "I forged Mom's signature. I know it was wrong, but playing the flute is the only thing I'm good at...."

"Becky! Flute is not the only thing you're good at," Mom said. Her words made me feel a little better, but the hurt expression on her face made me feel even worse, so I looked away and focused on Dad.

His face was unreadable.

"I tried to talk to you. I tried to tell you how important music was—is—to me. I thought if I could explain, maybe . . ." I could feel tears start to sting my eyes, but I had to get through this first.

There would be plenty of time for tears later.

"Daddy, I really needed you to understand! But you said no, and I tried to go along with it, but I couldn't." My heart was beating in triple time and I felt cold all over and my hands were sweaty and I wanted to run to my room and pull the blanket over my head . . . except I wasn't done yet.

"I know it was wrong to sign Mom's name. . . ." I looked over at her again, then Dad.

"I'm sorry I forged your signature. And I'm sorry I went behind your back. You don't know how sorry I am! But I had to try. I had to know if I was good enough. And I was. I am."

Somehow, I'd gotten through the whole awful confession without crying . . . but my voice broke with the last three words: "I got in."

I took a breath that was as shaky as the rest of me, then stood there and waited for one—or both—of them to punish me. To yell at me.

At first, neither of them said anything. Then Dad spoke up, but his voice was more sad than angry. "Why are you telling us now, after all this time?"

"I guess 'cause it's New Year's Eve and I'm trying to be the best version of myself? I'm not really sure how to do that, or what it means, exactly. But maybe it means telling the truth, even when it's hard. . . ."

Dad looked at me a few seconds more, then turned to Mom. Mom, who had always encouraged us to follow our dreams. Who had been on my side once but maybe wasn't now and might never be again. Who had trusted me to do the right thing. And suddenly I wondered if having to quit All-County could possibly hurt any more than the disappointment on her face.

"Your mother and I need to discuss this. We'll talk to you tomorrow."

I stood there, wanting to wish Mom a happy New Year, but it felt wrong.

Everything felt wrong.

I turned and closed their door, went to my room, and put my head under the blanket.

NOW

TELLING MY PARENTS the truth had been the hardest thing I'd ever done.

I wish it still was.

24

MY HEAD WAS under the blanket; my thoughts were out of control.

Now that I told Mom and Dad . . . what was going to happen? The first rehearsal for All-County was exactly one week away. That same night would be my thirteenth birthday, too: my teenage years would be off to the worst start in the history of teenagers.

Also, I would be grounded. Forever. Benji would have more of a social life than me.

And how would I explain all this to Ms. T? She'd be so disappointed in me. Maybe angry, too. Whenever she thought of me, she'd only remember the bad thing I did. Plus she'd never trust me again, or give me any solos. On top of all that, her surprise bridal shower was coming up, and we'd worked so hard to make it perfect!

I stuck my head out from under the blanket to look at the

clock. It was after one in the morning, but I was wide awake and feeling extremely sorry for myself when my door burst open. I turned and saw Sara flying into my room.

"Becky! I went in to wish Eema and Abba a happy New Year and I could tell something was wrong, so I asked what happened. . . ." She paced. "I can't believe you told them! Are you okay? What did they say?" She stopped and stared at me.

"They said they'd discuss it and talk to me tomorrow. But it's already tomorrow! Do you think they meant today, or—"

"I can't believe you told them," Sara said again. She sat down next to me.

"Me neither. I can't decide if I was brave or stupid."

She wrapped an arm around me. "Definitely not stupid."

I snuggled closer to her. "They say, 'The truth will set you free.'"

She smiled. "You do realize the rest of that quote is 'but first it will make you miserable.'"

"Actually, I don't even know who said it."

"I think it was originally in the New Testament, but Garfield added that second bit."

I scrunched my nose up. "Garfield the cat?"

Sara laughed. "The president. James A."

"Wait—wasn't he assassinated?"

"Yep."

"A lot of good the truth did him," I commented.

We laughed together and talked awhile longer, then Sara

fell asleep and left me on my own with nothing but worries and what-ifs. I stared up at my plastic stars.

What if Jon's advice was wrong?

What if Mom and Dad wouldn't let me be in All-County? And what if this was my one and only chance?

But most of all, the question I kept coming back to was: What if the best version of myself wasn't good enough?

I must've fallen asleep at some point, because when I woke up, Sara was squished next to me in my twin bed. "Sara!" I tapped her shoulder. "Wake up!" I tapped again. Harder.

"What time is it?" she asked, her eyes still closed.

"It's tomorrow!"

Her eyes snapped open and we looked at each other.

"It's gonna be okay."

I nodded.

"Are you all right?"

I shook my head.

"Can you please say something?"

"What should I do?" I asked her in a panic. "Wait here? Knock on their door and get it over with? Go downstairs and have breakfast and act like everything's fine?"

"Stay put. I'll scope out the situation and come back. I promise I'll put in a good word for you if I can."

She hugged me and left.

Since I was wide awake, I decided to get dressed, but couldn't figure out what to wear. I usually didn't care that much, but maybe it would make a difference somehow . . . like, if I wore a happy, carefree color like pink or yellow, would I be saying I didn't feel bad about what I'd done? That I didn't regret my actions?

If I wore a dark, serious color, would I look sorry? Or guilty? Unable to think clearly, I threw flannel shirts and sweaters and turtlenecks all over my bed and started sorting them by color.

I never realized how much purple I had.

My door burst open again. "Okay, so I heard them talking. . . ."

"Where were they?"

"In their bedroom," Sara informed me.

"So you were eavesdropping," I pointed out.

She put her hands on her hips. "Do you wanna know what they said or not?"

I nodded. I tried to swallow but my mouth was dry.

"The good news is Mom's on your side."

"I knew it!"

"The bad news is Dad isn't."

"I knew that, too. I'm doomed." Since my bed was completely covered, I flopped down on my floor.

"Hey, who's the drama queen around here?"

I couldn't even smile at Sara's favorite joke.

She joined me on the rug. "Listen, we don't know what's going to happen yet."

"Sure we do. Dad always has the last word."

I waited for her to disagree. Instead, all she said was "You sure do like purple."

We stayed there a few minutes, then my stomach growled.

"Breakfast?" she asked.

I shook my head. "I feel safer in here."

"You're being ridiculous."

I shrugged.

"I'll go grab us something and bring it back, okay?" She left before I even answered.

I thought about getting up but didn't have the energy, so I just lay on my back and stared up at my plastic stars. A couple of minutes later, the door opened again. "Did you bring Lucky Charms? Because I could use some luck."

"Becky?" It was Mom. "Where are you?"

I sat up and saw both my parents standing at the door.

"Rebecca, what are you doing on the floor?"

"Oh. Umm . . ." I got up as Dad walked in and stood next to Mom.

Dad took the lead. "Your mother and I talked for a long time. . . ."

"But we didn't quite see eye to eye," Mom said. "We agreed that what you did was wrong. . . ."

"But disagreed as to the consequences," Dad said.

I tried to take a deep breath, but I could barely breathe at all.

"So, we came up with a compromise," Mom said, taking over again. She looked at Dad as if to offer him one last chance to speak up, or maybe disagree. But he only nodded at her. "We looked up the All-County schedule. I believe rehearsals begin on the eighth, yes?"

I nodded. "My birthday," I said softly.

"We're aware," Dad said.

"We've decided to put you on probation," Mom continued. "You have one week to convince us you deserve a second chance."

I let out my breath. "You mean, a chance to be in the band?"

They both nodded.

"What do I have to do to convince you?"

"That," Dad said, "is for you to figure out. We'll let you know our final decision the night before the first rehearsal."

25

IT WAS THE night before my thirteenth birthday. The night before I became a teenager.

I had completed my seven days of probation and had tried to be the absolute best version of myself.

Since I had no idea what it would take to make up for my forgery, I had tried everything I could think of and then some. I had aced two math quizzes, earned a solo in the spring band concert, volunteered at the synagogue to help out with the preschoolers—three times—completed the first draft of my bat mitzvah speech, and had even baked a batch of Dad's favorite oatmeal chocolate chip cookies with Nipa.

The funny and surprising thing was how good I felt about what I'd done. Not the forgery, of course, but all the things afterward. Like finishing my bat mitzvah speech instead of putting it off. Or discovering that helping the little kids on Sunday morning was actually more fun than work. Like, instead of playing a game on my phone, playing a game with Benji.

Speaking of Benji, there was one more thing I had to do to be the best version of myself: help *him* be the best version of himself.

When he broke Mom's vase a few months ago, I'd felt really good about helping him out of a jam. It was the kind of thing Sara would do for me.

But since New Year's Eve, every time I walked by the decorative plate I'd used to replace the vase, all I felt was guilt. I had taught my little brother a bad lesson: when in trouble, find out a way out, keep it a secret, and hope no one discovers the truth.

If I had learned anything in the past couple of weeks, it was that secrets could be exciting and fun, but they could also cause trouble. A lot of trouble. And, sometimes, they ended up hurting the people you loved most.

I knocked on Benji's door (though I was tempted to burst in unannounced).

"Who's there?" he called out.

"Does it matter?" I called back.

"Only if you're a bad guy."

Only sometimes, I thought. The door opened and he grinned at me. "You can come in. You're not a bad guy."

I smiled. "Thanks."

He plopped down on his *Star Wars* bedspread and hugged his Spider-Man doll.

I sat next to him and reached for Spidey. "Y'know, even good guys can do bad things once in a while, especially if it's for a good reason."

"Whaddaya mean?"

"Well, take Spidey here."

"He's a superhero!"

"For sure! But he kept his identity a secret from Aunt May, and from his best friends, too."

"Secrets are cool!"

I sighed, then handed Spidey back and looked around his room, hoping for inspiration, but there was no way around it. When in trouble . . . be honest.

"You're right, Benji. Secrets *are* cool. But it depends on what they are and who you're keeping them from."

He wrinkled his nose, tilted his head, and waited patiently for me to explain.

"Like, if you get Mommy a really fun birthday present and don't tell her what it is? That's a nice kind of secret."

He nodded.

"But . . . when you break her vase, even accidentally, that's not a nice kind."

He smushed Spidey to his chest. "You said it was okay! You said we didn't have to tell her unless she asked."

"You're right. But *I* was wrong. I thought I was helping you, but . . ."

"You were! Mommy never noticed and I never got in trouble."

"I know. But when a superhero makes a mistake, he admits it. Then he says he's sorry and fixes it, or at least tries to."

Benji looked from me to Spidey and back again.

"Now, I'm not a superhero," I told him, "but maybe *you* can be—"

He shook his head. "You gotta be super strong like Spidey or Hulk or Captain America."

"That's what everybody thinks," I said. "Wanna know a secret?"

He nodded.

"It's not about being strong; it's about doing the right thing."

He looked at me and his eyebrows almost touched, which meant he was thinking it over. "Like telling Mommy I broke her vase?"

I nodded.

He looked at me a little longer, then said, "If I tell her, will you come with me?"

"Absolutely."

He stood up and reached for my hand. "Maybe we can both be superheroes."

I definitely was not superhero material, but I had done my best the past week. Now it was out of my hands and up to my parents. I still wanted that All-County seat more than anything but, no matter what happened, I would be okay.

At least, that's what I told myself as I sat in my room and tried *not* to think about the fact it was after nine p.m. and the first All-County rehearsal was less than twenty-four hours away and I still didn't know if I would be there.

I'd played cards with Benji; texted with Jon, who was back in L.A.; and had just gotten off the phone with Nipa when there was a knock at my door.

"Rebecca? May we come in?"

I walked over and opened the door, trying to be calm. Trying to think good thoughts. Trying not to pass out.

"Becky," Mom said, "we wanted to give you your birthday card a few hours early."

"Um . . . thanks?"

She handed me an envelope and I opened it despite sweaty palms and shaky fingers. The card inside was blank, except for one word: YES.

I looked at my parents. "Does this mean . . . ?"

Mom nodded and smiled at me.

I looked over at Dad to be sure he was on board. He smiled, too. "I want you to remember all the good things you can accomplish when you put your mind to it."

"Thanks," I said. "I will."

It was the best birthday card ever, and the best present I could've gotten.

When I woke up the next morning, my first thought was: I am officially a teenager!

My second thought was: tonight is the first All-County rehearsal!

When Mom asked what I wanted for dinner, my answer was: nothing. Like Sara before a performance, I was way too nervous and excited to eat. I just wanted to get to rehearsal already.

When it was finally time, Dad drove me to the same high school where I'd auditioned only a few weeks earlier, while Mom and Sara stayed home to prepare my birthday dinner and cake.

We walked into the building and followed the signs until we reached the band room. We were fifteen minutes early, but I could see a lot of kids already in the room, hanging out in small groups or taking out their instruments and warming up.

"Guess you'd better get in there." Dad settled into one of the chairs in the hall and pulled out a book to read while he waited.

"Guess so." I walked toward the classroom, then stopped and went back to him. "Dad, thanks. For giving me a second chance."

He nodded. "You earned it. Now go in there and show them what you can do."

"I will." I leaned over and hugged him. Then I took a deep breath and opened the door.

There were around thirty of us, including two of my classmates: a cute, shaggy-haired sax player named Cy, and Ethan, Nipa's not-so-secret crush, on trumpet. I was about to go over and say hi when the conductor walked in and everyone went to their sections.

I took a seat in the front with the other four flutists: three girls and one boy.

As I looked around, I thought about how much each one of us wanted to be in that room—how everyone there loved playing music as much as I did. And suddenly I felt a camaraderie I'd never experienced before. An energy that made me feel happy and alive. If this was how Sara felt onstage, I totally got why she wanted to do it forever.

The conductor called the first session to order. He was around Dad's age, with a big red beard, thick glasses, and green eyes that danced when he smiled. And he smiled a lot. He talked a lot, too, and superfast. I had the feeling he was as happy to be there as we were, which made everything even better.

"Welcome, musicians! My name is Mr. Singer, and I will be your conductor for the next six weeks." He looked around the room, taking in each one of us. "Who is excited to be here?"

Everyone raised their hands.

"You call *that* excitement?" He raised his fuzzy eyebrows and waited.

This time, the room erupted in cheers, applause, and whistles.

"That's more like it! I want beautiful, joyful noise here every week."

I did, too. I couldn't wait.

And I couldn't stop smiling.

"Here are the pieces we'll be playing." He passed out

folders with sheet music inside. There were five pieces in all: three classical, one Sousa march, and one Joplin ragtime piece. I was most excited about the Joplin. I'd played some ragtime on my own for fun, but never with a band. I knew it would sound awesome.

We practiced for forty-five minutes, then took a short break and played for another thirty. Mr. Singer told us that after tonight, we'd play close to two hours, but since we hadn't had time to practice the music, we wrapped early. "You are all the best of the best," he said. "So this concert can *be* one of the best. To make that happen, I expect every one of you to take this commitment seriously and to make it a priority."

He didn't have to tell me! Nothing mattered more.

"That means practicing at home on your own and giving it one hundred and ten percent. I assume it's understood that, with only six rehearsals between now and then, you're expected to show up each and every time, unless you have a spectacularly good excuse."

He went over a couple of details and answered a few questions, then told us to practice hard and make him look good—but he said it with a smile.

I chattered at Dad the whole ride back. We stopped at Nipa's on the way home: she was always a guest at my birthday dinners, and I was always a guest at hers. I stopped talking about All-County long enough to go over our plans for Ms. T's upcoming surprise shower next week. And then we were home!

While we all enjoyed a late but delicious dinner of Caesar salad and homemade veggie pizzas, everyone listened as I talked about the rehearsal, the pieces we'd play, Mr. Singer, the other musicians. . . .

"Hey," Sara said as I paused for a drink of water, "is something wrong with your face? You haven't stopped smiling since you got home."

Nipa giggled.

It was totally true.

I smiled some more.

I was thinking the only thing that could've made tonight even more perfect, was if Jon were here to celebrate with us. Just then, my phone chimed from inside my backpack. I looked at Mom.

"Go on—it's probably your big brother."

I ran and grabbed it and, sure enough . . .

"Hey, Bec! Welcome to teenhood."

"Hey, yourself! I was just thinking about you."

"Uh-oh," he joked. "So . . . ? Was All-County everything you'd hoped?"

"More!" And so, for the third time that night, I got to relive the whole thing again. After we hung up, Mom lit thirteen candles and brought my traditional birthday cake—triple chocolate chiffon with marshmallow icing—to the table.

"Close your eyes and make a wish," Sara said with a smile.

"Wish for a puppy from Barks!" Benji suggested, hope in his eyes.

But the truth was I'd already gotten my wish, so I just blew them out.

"Two teenage daughters under one roof!" Dad cried in mock panic. "What have I done to deserve this?"

"Beats me," Sara said, "but it must've been pretty great. Right, Becster?" She pulled me in for a hug. "I can't wait for your concert."

Neither could I.

NOW

MISSED ANOTHER REHEARSAL for All-County.
   I'm not allowed to miss any more.
   After all that's happened,
   I'm wondering if All-County even matters.
   I'm wondering if anything does.

26

IT WAS FINALLY time for Ms. T's surprise shower!

It had taken a lot of planning, work, and—as Sara put it—"pulling more than a few violin strings," but the surprise party had come together beautifully. Since my class was right before lunch, we had decided early on to set up during class and have the party during lunch.

We'd included Ms. T's fiancé, Mr. Davis, from the start because we needed his help. He was thrilled to be a coconspirator, especially since he wasn't invited to the non-surprise shower Ms. T's friends were throwing later on.

The most important thing Mr. Davis did was get the principal on board so we could throw the shower in the first place. He also gave us contact information for people he knew Ms. T would want to come and provided the perfect excuse to keep her away from the classroom so we could get ready: a scheduling meeting "mix-up" with one of the administrators, who was also one of Mr. Davis's best friends. It was conveniently expected to take roughly the same amount of time we needed to get everyone and everything in place.

Turned out, teachers could be very sneaky, too. I wasn't sure if that was good or bad.

Sara got permission to miss a couple of classes and Jenna did, too. Nipa couldn't get out of math class, but sprinted over the second the bell rang. By the time she joined us, our paper hearts and flowers were strung up and food and drinks were set out. Even our special guests—Ms. T's parents, sister, and best friend—were in place.

Now, Nipa and I stood side by side, waiting breathlessly along with close to forty other musicians and a handful of teachers, waiting for me to get a text from Mr. Davis that they were on their way.

After what felt like a year of anticipation, my phone chimed. "Everybody be quiet!" I whisper yelled.

"Try to huddle against the walls or in Ms. T's office," Sara called out.

She turned off the lights and everyone ran to hide as best they could. Nipa and I crouched behind some music stands in the corner and a hush, sprinkled with giggles, fell over the band room.

When I felt like I might pass out from holding my breath, the door finally opened and we heard Mr. Davis ask, "Why are all the lights out?" which was our cue.

Ms. T flicked them on and we all jumped out from our

hiding places and shouted "Surprise!"

"I can't believe it!" she said through happy tears. She looked around the room, taking in the hearts and flowers and familiar faces. When Ms. T saw Sara and Jenna, she hugged them hard. Then she saw her parents and sister and best friend and cried some more.

It was pretty perfect.

"Ms. T," I called out. "Wait 'til you see the cake!" She followed me past the punch bowl and the little sandwiches Sara, Jenna, and I had stayed up half the night putting together. The cake was one of the things I was especially excited about. It had gold and silver musical notes all around the border, and the inscription read, "May you make joyful music together and always be in sync." Nipa and I had come up with the words; I hoped Ms. T would love them as much as we did.

When Ms. T saw the cake, she hugged me, too, then turned to face the crowd. "You guys! This is amazing! As you all know, I am seldom at a loss for words. . . ."

"Boy is that the truth," her sister said.

Then Mr. Davis pulled his bride-to-be in for a hug and a serious kiss, and everyone started applauding.

While everyone filled their plates and cups, Ms. T's mom sliced the cake, even though it was "too beautiful to cut." Then Nipa handed the bride- and groom-to-be an envelope filled with gift cards to their favorite restaurants and stores. Ms. T and Mr. Davis looked at one gift card after another and shook their heads in disbelief. "This is too much," Mr. Davis said, and it looked like he was about to cry, too.

Afterward, Sara, Jenna, Nipa, and I stuck around to clean up, and Ms. T thanked us for at least the thirtieth time. "I will never forget this," she said. "This is the sweetest thing anyone has ever done for me. I have never felt more loved."

She hugged each of us again, and I walked Sara and Jenna to the front entrance before they headed back to their school.

"That could not have gone any better," Jenna said.

"We never could've pulled it off without your help." I turned to Sara, but she didn't look as happy as I felt and I worried something was wrong.

"Is everything okay?" I asked her.

"I guess. I just . . . I wish Miri could've had something like this, too."

I wasn't sure what to say to that. Sure, I felt bad for Miri—but it was her decision to elope and all. Besides, I felt really happy about the shower we just pulled off, and I didn't want to feel sad about Miri—or anything—just then.

"Never mind," Sara said, as much to herself as to me.

She gave me a quick hug and followed Jenna to her car. As we went our separate ways, it started to snow.

It really was a magical day.

27

IT WAS ONE in the morning, and two hours past my bedtime. Past everyone's bedtime. But I couldn't sleep. I was still thinking about how perfect Ms. T's party had been. And how Miri didn't have a party at all. It was strange how differently people could react to the same things. Strange and kind of sad.

I went to my window and looked out at the snow still coming down. Nipa and I were sure tomorrow would be the first snow day of the year. No school buses would be going anywhere in this. We'd already made plans for her to come over and have a baking and movie marathon day.

I watched the snowflakes dance around for a few more minutes, then decided the only thing that would make the snowstorm even better was a steaming mug of hot chocolate. I slipped into my favorite raggedy robe, put on my fuzzy slippers, and headed down to the kitchen.

Sara was already there, her eyes red and her cheeks streaked with tears.

"Sara? What happened? Are you okay?" Why did people always ask that when the person was obviously anything *but* okay?

"Becky." Sara wiped her eyes. "What are you doing up?"

"I couldn't sleep. I was watching the snow and . . . What are *you* doing up?"

She blew her nose. "I couldn't sleep, either."

I forgot all about the hot chocolate and sat down across from her, wanting to say the right thing. Afraid to say the wrong one. Deciding maybe it was best to say nothing at all, just to listen. So I kept my mouth shut and waited.

She looked around to be sure we were alone, which told me that whatever it was had to do with Sam.

"It's okay," I told her. "They're all asleep. Did you and Sam have a fight or something?" But even as I asked, I couldn't imagine it. He really was one of the sweetest guys I knew.

"Of course not." She sort of smiled. "I almost wish we had. It would be easier."

"What would be easier?"

"Everything."

"Sara. What happened?"

"Miri happened."

"What are you talking about?"

She leaned in. "Remember that night I spent with her last month in New York?"

"Yeah." I'd waited so long to hear this, but now I wasn't sure I wanted to after all.

"Everything was fine—better than fine. She and Luke are really, really happy. He cooked a great meal for us, and we talked and laughed. . . . Then Miri said she was desperate for a salted caramel latte at this coffee shop down the block from their apartment. Luke said he had to wake up early—which she must've known—so we went without him." She took a breath. "When we got to the coffee shop, Miri didn't even order the latte. She just wanted to talk in private."

"Why?"

"Because when Miri's around him, she puts on this brave front. This sort of act that everything is wonderful and she couldn't be happier. But the truth is, she's a wreck. Aunt Ruth and Uncle Jacob are making her miserable. Uncle Jacob still refuses to talk to her. And all Aunt Ruth does is beg her to leave Luke."

"What? That's terrible!"

"I know. It's so unfair! Miri really loves him, and they won't even give him a chance! All she wants is for everyone to get along, to be a family. But her parents are forcing her to make a choice: Luke or them."

"It seems like she already chose. I mean, she *married* him."

Sara sighed. "Maybe Miri was hoping Aunt Ruth and Uncle Jacob would change their minds eventually."

"I get why you feel bad for Miri, but I still don't see—"

"Did I tell you that every college Sean applied to is near one that I applied to? And he'll get in, too—every one of them. He's got good grades, ridiculous SAT scores, and an amazing essay all about his mom."

"That's great!"

"It *might* have been, if things were different."

"What 'things'?"

"I don't want him choosing a college because of me!"

"Why not?" I shook my head, not understanding one single part of this weird conversation. "I think it's really nice—"

"Remember how happy Ms. T was today at her shower?" Sara asked, interrupting. "How happy her parents were for her."

"Of course. It couldn't have gone better!"

"I want that, too. When I get married, I want Eema and Abba at my wedding, front and center. I want Abba to walk me down the aisle, or maybe even perform the ceremony! And I want Eema crying happy tears, like Ms. T." Sara wiped the not-happy tears streaming down her face.

"I want one of those corny father and daughter waltzes, and I want to be lifted in a chair while everyone dances the hora all around me. All around *my husband* and me. I want to be surrounded by the people I love most: our parents, Jon, Benji, and you. But that will never happen."

"Sara, you're seventeen! Why are you talking about marriage? You haven't even graduated high school yet! You've got at least four years of college—then Broadway!"

"I may only be seventeen, but I'm old enough to know that I love him—and he loves me. And the longer we're together, the harder it's going to be."

"What is?"

"All of it." Her eyes filled again.

"Maybe you don't have to keep it a secret! Maybe you should just tell Mom and Dad already."

She looked at me. "This isn't All-County Band."

I stared back at her. "What's *that* supposed to mean?"

"It means it's not the same. Mom and Dad will never sign *that* form. And I can't forge their signatures."

"But Sam's dad is okay with it. Maybe—"

"His dad isn't Abba."

"I know, but—"

"Becky. Dad will *never* be okay with this. I can't just do some chores or ace a test or bake him some cookies and change his mind. I can't . . . I can't do this anymore. It's not fair to Sean, or me, or anyone."

"What are you saying?"

She took a shaky breath. "I have to end it."

"What? No . . ."

She gave me a sad smile. "I thought you'd be relieved—no more secrets. No more guilt. No more lies."

"I know, but I think you're making a mistake. If you tell Mom and Dad, the worst that'll happen is you have to break up with him anyway."

She wiped a tear away before it fell. "I'd rather do it on my own terms. Because I *choose* to. Not because I have to."

She turned away and headed for the hall closet. I followed. "What are you doing?"

"I told you, I'm ending it."

"Now? In person?"

"I'm not doing it by text! He deserves better than that." She put on her coat.

"Sara, it's practically one thirty in the morning! Sam is probably sound asleep. His dad, too!"

She let out a breath. "I have to do this before I change my mind." She grabbed Mom's car keys off the hook by the door.

"Wait—please. . . . It's snowing. A ton! At least wait until it stops. It's not safe to drive!"

She put her hands on my shoulders. "I'm sorry I put you in the middle of all this. It wasn't fair, and I never should have done it. Forgive me?"

"There's nothing to forgive."

"Well, thanks for having my back."

"You always have mine," I said softly.

"And I always will." She zipped up her coat. "Hey. No more secrets, okay?"

"No more secrets."

She wrapped her scarf around her shoulders.

"Sara, I really think you should wait."

"I'm sorry. I can't." She put on her gloves and gave me a hug. "I'll be back soon. I promise."

It was the last promise Sara ever made.

And the first one she ever broke.

PART TWO

Now

28

SOMETHING WAKES ME up around three a.m.

It sounds like Mom, only Mom has never, ever sounded like this.

She's screaming and crying and I know I should race downstairs to see what's wrong. But I can't move.

Something unimaginably horrible has happened. Maybe if I stay in bed where it's safe, I'll wake up and everything—everyone—will be fine, and it will all turn out to be a nightmare.

A really terrifying nightmare . . .

I'd meant to stay awake until Sara came back in case she wanted to talk more. In case breaking up with Sam was even harder than she'd expected. In case she needed me to listen to her, the way she always listens to me.

There's a knock on my door and Benji comes in. His hair is sticking up in a million directions and he's wearing his *Star*

Wars pajamas and he looks as scared as I feel.

"Mommy and Daddy are downstairs and there's police and Mommy's crying," he says all in one breath.

I jump out of bed and throw my arms around his skinny little body and hug him hard.

And now it's impossible to pretend everything is fine. Because I know something awful has happened to Sara and nothing will ever be fine again.

I look at my little brother and he looks at me and I would give anything to tell him everything is okay, and don't be scared. But nothing is okay, and *I'm* so scared I can't think.

When I was Benji's age, anytime I got scared, I'd climb into Sara's bed and she'd sing or make me laugh. . . . But I'm not Sara. And she's not here.

"Hey." I do my best to smile at him. "You know what? I think Belle and Beast might be scared. You think maybe you could go to the basement and pet them awhile?"

He nods and looks so serious and so determined to comfort them, it's all I can do not to hug him again. "Thanks, Benji."

I wait until he goes, then force myself to leave my room. As I head downstairs, I hear Dad say, "Thank you for coming," then close the front door.

Maybe it's not as bad as I thought. I mean, "Thank you for coming" is what you say when a neighbor drops by for a visit or a friend comes to your birthday party.

For a minute I almost convince myself that Sara is fine.

Then I hear Mom sobbing again and Dad says, "We should call Jonathan," and I don't even make it down the stairs. I just drop where I am and sit on the step.

"What about Becky and Benji?" Mom asks, her voice already hoarse.

"No," Dad says. "Let them have one more night. . . ."

One more night of what? Peace? Sweet dreams?

One more night of *before* instead of *now*?

"You call Jon," Mom says. "I'll call Ruth."

"Jill . . ." Dad's voice sounds strange. Strangled. "The two of us . . . we need to . . ." His voice cracks and I want to run back to my room and stay there the rest of my life. Because I've *never* heard Dad sound like this.

I've never heard either of my parents sound like they do right now. And that scares me, too.

"What I *need*," Mom says, "is to talk to my sister."

Me, too.

29

I SEE MOM zombie walk into the kitchen holding her phone, fingers clenched and pale, like all the blood has left them.

I see Dad at the foot of the staircase. He looks up at me through red, puffy eyes, obviously surprised to see me there. Then he takes my hand and sits down next to me. "Rebecca... there's been a terrible accident. Sara..." He can't get the words out, just squeezes my hand.

I don't know what to say, so I sit with him, numb all over except for my racing heart that's surely going to explode any second.

I don't mind the silence. I don't mind the waiting.

Waiting is safe. Waiting is better than whatever comes next.

He takes a shaky breath and looks at me. "I am so sorry, but your sister... She was heading home, driving Mom's car. . . . The police said she took a turn too fast and . . . Your mother and I . . ." He wipes his eyes. "We can't understand what she was doing out in the snowstorm in the middle of the night! What could possibly have been so urgent?"

I look away from him but feel him staring at me.

"Rebecca?"

I turn my head and force my eyes to look into his.

He knows I know.

"Come with me." It's not a request. I follow him to his study. He closes the door and turns to me. "Sit."

I lower myself into the chair across from his, but I don't want to be there. I don't want to see the pain he's in. Don't want to answer his questions. And most of all, I don't want to tell Sara's secret.

Maybe now more than ever I owe it to her to keep my promise.

"We are going to sit here," Dad says, "and you are going to tell me every single thing you know."

"But I promised Sara I wouldn't."

"Sara is dead."

I already knew it, in my head. In my heart. In my bones.

But hearing him say it out loud . . .

Before I can tell him even one thing, I start to cry. And I cry so hard and so long it feels like I'll never stop.

He gives me a box of tissues and waits for me to finish crying.

"I'm sorry," I finally say. "I didn't know what to do." I wipe my eyes and nose. "I wanted to tell you, but . . ."

"Tell me now," he says, his voice soft and gentle.

So I do. I tell him everything.

I tell him about Sam rescuing the mouthpiece and me at the football game. And spying on Sara at play practice with Nipa. I tell him about the *Star Wars* necklace and the soup kitchen. About the bowling alley, and Miri and Luke and Aunt Ruth, and Ms. T's surprise shower.

And then I tell him why Sara went out in the snowstorm.

The box of tissues is empty, but my eyes are still full of tears. And all I can think is that I've told Sara's secret and I wonder if she's mad at me.

Does she know I told? Does she care? Does it even matter anymore?

Does anything?

"Thank you for telling me," he says, his voice softer than usual. So soft it's almost a whisper.

"I'm so sorry, Daddy! I'm so . . ." And the tears start to flow again. Tears of sorrow and guilt and pain and regret all rolled into one. Tears for what's happened. Tears for whatever is to come.

Tears for a life now without Sara; a life I can't even begin to imagine.

He comes over and hugs me, and for a minute it feels like it did when I was little and I fell at the playground and he picked me up.

Then the door opens. "Did you get Jon a—" Mom stops

and looks at me. "Becky?"

Dad kisses my forehead. "We'll talk more later."

Mom looks at me, a thousand questions in her eyes—a thousand answers I don't want to give.

"You should try to get some sleep," Dad tells me. "I still need to call your brother and book his flight."

I leave fast, but instead of going to bed I decide to check on Benji. I go to his room, only he's not there, so I head to the basement. Sure enough he's sitting on the floor with Belle and Beast in his lap, all three of them fast asleep. All three of them safe.

I grab the fuzzy green blanket from the back of the couch and cover him with it.

Then I get under it, too, shut my eyes tight, and try to pretend this has all been a horrible dream.

30

I WAKE UP sneezing, covered in a fuzzy green blanket and a fuzzier orange kitten.

Benji opens his eyes, sees Beast practically sitting on my face, and giggles. Belle, not wanting to be left out, leaps onto Benji's chest, which makes me laugh, too.

It feels good to laugh, probably because I spent most of last night crying. I look at my little brother and it's clear he has no idea what happened yet. I wish I could keep it that way.

I wish I could protect him forever.

The best I can do is put it off a little longer. I smile at him. "Hey, wanna have breakfast down here? Wouldn't that be fun? Just the two of us?"

He nods happily; it always takes so little to please him.

"I'll be back in a few minutes, okay? You take care of Belle and Beast while I'm gone."

He nods again and starts petting both cats and telling

them how much he loves them, and his sweetness hurts my heart because I know his carefree childhood is about to end.

I slowly climb the stairs, determined to make the most Benji-friendly breakfast possible—to keep that smile on his face a little longer.

I take one step into the kitchen and stop. My mother is sitting at the table, but it's a version of her I've never seen. Her face is washed out and her hair is a mess and I don't think she's slept since the police came.

"You knew." She stands up and takes a few steps toward me. "You knew about all of it and you didn't say one. Single. Word." She looks so angry that, for the first time in my life, I'm afraid of my own mother.

I take a step back. "Sara made me promise."

"Really? She 'made' you promise?"

She steps closer to me and it's all I can do not to back away. "You let her go." Her voice gets louder every time she speaks, and I worry that Benji will hear her and come running. "You let your sister go out in that dangerous storm!"

"No! I told her not to go! I tried to stop her but—"

"What were you thinking? You . . . let . . . her . . . go." Mom's face is red and her cheeks are streaked with tears.

My own eyes fill with tears, too. "I didn't! I told her—"

"How did you let this happen?" Mom screams at me.

"That's enough!"

I turn to see Dad looking every bit as upset as Mom, only he's upset with *her*, not me. "Sara put her in an impossible situation." He puts his arm around me. "Rebecca was trying to keep a promise."

"A promise?" Mom laughs but it's an ugly sound. "Are you going to stand there and tell me how sacred promises are?"

"Jill. Please. None of us can think clearly right now. You haven't even slept—"

"Don't tell me I'm not thinking clearly. Becky's the one who let Sara drive in a blizzard!"

"It wasn't a blizzard," I say, the words sounding pathetic even as I say them. Is a snowstorm any better? Safer?

"Why is everybody yelling?"

We all turn to see Benji, who looks scared and confused. Dad lets go of me and wraps my little brother in his arms. Mom stares at them, glares at me, and walks away without another word. I hear her bedroom door slam for the first time in my life.

"Rebecca?" Dad looks at me. "Benji and I need to have a little talk. Why don't you go to your room for a few minutes?"

"What about breakfast in the basement?" Benji asks me.

"We'll do it soon, I prom—" No, I am done with promises. "We'll do it soon, okay?"

Benji nods, but without his usual enthusiasm; and all of a sudden, I miss his smile so much.

I wonder if I'll ever see it again after Dad's "little talk."

I give my little brother a quick hug and go to my room. I'm about to call Nipa when I see it's only six a.m. How is that even possible?

I crawl into bed, pull the covers over my head, and pray for sleep.

A knock on my door wakes me up. "Bec?"

"Jon?" I jump up and open the door and he's there. His eyes are bloodshot, and he needs a shave. He looks terrible.

And I have never been happier to see him.

"Hey . . ." He hugs me and we stand there like that for a long time.

"What time is it?" I ask, feeling completely disoriented.

"Around five p.m.," he says.

"I can't believe I fell asleep." I finally let go of him. "I'm really glad you're here. I mean, I wish you didn't need to be, but . . ."

"It's okay. I know what you mean."

I look down the hall and the coast is clear, but I close my door anyway. "Mom is so mad at me. She said I let Sara go out in the storm. . . ."

Jon shakes his head. "Nobody ever 'let' Sara do anything. When she wants to do something, there's no stopping her. I've never known anyone as headstrong as she—"

He stops before he says "is," but can't bring himself to say "was," either. I wonder how long it will be before he can, before any of us can. How long before we get used to "was" instead of "is."

"Listen. Dad's making a million phone calls and I promised I'd help after I take Benji for a walk. Wanna come with?"

"What's Mom doing?"

"She's in her room with Aunt Ruth. Uncle Jacob's with Dad and Benji."

"What? When did they get here?"

He shrugs.

"I should probably call Nipa."

"Okay. We'll talk more later." He squeezes my shoulder and leaves.

I look at my phone and find three texts from Nipa:

Hooray for snow days!

Wanna meet up at the park?

Are you still asleep????

I consider texting her back, but there are some things you just don't do over text. Like tell your best friend your sister is gone . . . or break up with the boy you love.

Nipa answers on the first ring. Fifteen minutes later she's in my room, holding me tight. I can't tell which of us is crying more.

At some point, there's a knock on my door. "Becky, darling?"

"It's my aunt," I tell Nipa. I grab a tissue and hand her the box and go to my door. Aunt Ruth pulls me into a hug so tight I can't breathe. "You poor thing. I am so very sorry!"

Do I thank her? Tell her I'm sorry, too? I don't know what to say. I can barely even think.

I can barely even stand.

As always, Nipa seems to know exactly what I need. She

steps up beside me and puts her arm around me, holding me close. Holding me up.

My aunt smiles at her. "You must be Becky's friend, Nipa! It's so nice to meet you after all these years!" Her smile freezes, then disappears.

There's another awkward silence; the reason they're finally meeting is the worst one imaginable.

"Um . . ." Nipa says. "You, too."

"How is my mom?" I finally blurt out.

Aunt Ruth looks at me. "She's . . . your mother. . . . She needs some . . ."

"Is there anything I can do to help?" my wonderful best friend asks, interrupting the horrible awkwardness.

My aunt turns to Nipa. "Actually, if you could reach out to your classmates and any teachers you think might want to attend the funeral, that would be a tremendous help. I believe Jon contacted Sara's friends, Jenna and Cassidy? They're doing the same for the high school." Aunt Ruth pulls a piece of paper out of her pocket. "I have all the information right here. The funeral is tomorrow morning. . . ."

I feel lightheaded.

Dizzy.

Or maybe I don't feel anything at all because this can't be happening.

My aunt looks at Nipa. "I know it seems hurried. But it's the Jewish way."

"It's the Hindu way, too. People are cremated within

twenty-four hours, then friends and relatives visit family members."

"Sounds a little like sitting shiva...."

I tune them both out. I don't want to hear about sitting shiva, or when and where the funeral is.

Tomorrow morning we're burying my sister.

31

I DON'T HAVE a black dress.

I'm standing in front of my closet, trying to figure out what to wear, when there's a knock on my door.

"Becky?" a voice asks. "Can I come in?"

I open the door and Miri is standing there with her long auburn hair and warm brown eyes.

"Miri?" I whisper.

"I am so sorry—" Her voice breaks. She wraps her arms around me and for a second or two I can almost pretend it's my sister instead of my cousin.

But it isn't.

I want to ask if Luke came with her. And if she and Aunt Ruth are still upset with each other.

I want to tell her life is too short for that.

"Is there anything I can do?" she asks.

I pull out of her embrace. "I don't know what to wear."

I lead her to my closet filled with the bright colors I usually love: cheerful pinks, pretty purples, electric blues, and sunny yellows. She gently sorts through the happy colors that feel so very wrong today.

"How about this?" She pulls out a black-and-white sweater and a black skirt.

I shake my head. "That's my concert outfit." But even as I say it—even as important as music is to me—suddenly it doesn't matter.

Nothing does.

I toss the clothes on my bed.

"Is there anything else I can do?" Miri asks. "Would you like me to bring you some tea or toast?"

"I can't eat."

"Becky . . . I . . ." She takes a shaky breath and blinks away tears. Then she looks at me and there's too much to say, so we just hug again.

"I'd better get dressed." I reach for the skirt that used to make me so happy. I know I'll never wear it again after today.

She touches my shoulder. "I'll see you at synagogue."

The parking lot is packed like it's Yom Kippur, but Dad has his own parking space, so it doesn't matter. The sky is a mixture of white and gray, and the snow is, too. It's cold and windy and I'm glad. The sun doesn't deserve to shine today.

The five of us get out of the minivan: Dad and Jon are in dark suits and black ties, Benji is in his High Holy Day dress clothes, Mom is in a black dress and tears. She's barely looked at me in the past twenty-four hours . . . barely spoken to me, either. Then again, none of us is talking much—even Benji, who looks sad and confused.

We enter the synagogue and immediately head to the small chapel down the hall for privacy. Rabbi Gold is already there, waiting for us. He's one of my father's friends, and he's going to lead the service instead of Dad.

Rabbi Gold gives my father a tight hug and mumbles some words that I can't make out, then shakes hands with the rest of us.

"I am so very sorry," Rabbi Gold says to all of us and no one in particular.

None of us responds.

He clears his throat. "Would any of you like to say a few words at the service?"

None of us responds again—at first.

Then Jon reaches inside his suit jacket and pulls out a folded sheet of paper. "Um . . . I wrote something last night. Could you read it for me?"

I don't know how he managed to do that, but I'm glad he did. Glad someone could.

It takes all my energy and willpower and strength to stand here at all.

Rabbi Gold gently takes the paper from Jon. "I would be honored." There's another silence, then he asks, "Does anyone have any questions?"

I want to ask, "How did God let this happen?" But I don't.

Then he takes five small black ribbons, tears them, and hands one to each of us to pin to our clothes to symbolize our loss. Jon helps Benji with his while the rest of us do our own. It takes me three tries because my fingers are trembling.

"Are you ready?" Rabbi Gold asks in the same gentle voice I've heard Dad use a million times with his own congregants.

Mom stares at him. "How can anyone be ready to bury their child?"

Jon looks at Benji and me. Nods toward the door. We quietly follow him out and down the hall. As horrible as all of this is, I'm grateful Jon's here to take the lead. Grateful that, somehow, he can think clearly. Grateful he can function at all.

The corridor is empty, but I can already hear people speaking softly in the main chapel.

"Jon," I whisper and stop walking. "I can't go in there."

"Me, neither," Benji says.

"I know it's hard, but—"

"No, really." I let go of Jon's hand. "I feel sick. I can't do this."

"Me, too," Benji says.

Jon drops to his knees so he's eye level with our little brother. "We'll get through this together, okay, buddy? You can do this."

Benji nods and Jon hugs him and my heart breaks and I'm so glad Jon is there for Benji.

But I need Sara.

How am I supposed to get through this without her?

Sara always knows what to do, what to say, how to comfort me.

But nothing can comfort me now. Because Sara isn't here.

And I am lost without her.

My body starts to shake and tears start to stream down my face and I can't stop them. I can't stop *any* of this. I need to pause, or rewind.

I need to go back to the last time I was with Sara and do something different. Say something different.

I need to save her.

"Hey," Jon says. "Come here." He puts his arms around me and holds on tight. "I've got you."

"Me, too," Benji says. I feel his skinny arms around me, and I love them both so much, but Sara's arms are the ones I really need.

"Are you ready?" Jon asks in the most tender voice I've ever heard.

"No." I pull away and look up at him. "Are you?"

"No."

He takes my hand and I take Benji's and together the three of us walk into the chapel.

I can't believe what I see: it's literally standing room only. I knew—I know—how beloved Sara was . . . is. But seeing so many people here . . . it takes my breath away.

I see Nipa with her parents. I see Jenna and Cassidy and Marius and Enjolras. I see Ms. T and Mr. Davis and kids from school who I barely even know and it's all overwhelming.

Jon leads Benji and me to the front row, where Aunt Ruth and Uncle Jacob are sitting with Miri. My aunt stands and hugs each of us, and Miri does, too.

As soon as we sit down, our parents come in. Dad has his arm around Mom, who looks like she'll collapse if he lets go. They join us in the front row and my aunt hugs them both. Then Rabbi Gold comes out and takes his place at the podium where Dad has stood so many times over the years.

I try to listen, try to follow along and recite the prayers. But after a while I give up. I just keep staring at the casket in front of us. Keep thinking it's impossible that Sara is in there.

A plain wooden box can't possibly contain someone so full of life.

Suddenly I feel my father's arms around me and I realize I'm crying and shaking and I can't stop. "Shh," he murmurs. He strokes my hair and holds me. Miri hands me a little packet of tissues and I wipe my nose and eyes. When I look over to thank her, I see that she and my aunt are holding hands and I think how happy Sara would be to see that.

I don't remember much of the service, but I do remember Cassidy reading Sara's favorite e. e. cummings poem, "Somewhere I have never travelled." Or trying to. Her voice kept breaking and Rabbi Gold had to read the last few lines because she was crying too hard.

I remember Marius singing the song he and Sara sang

from *Les Miz* when Eponine dies, and I remember hearing people all around me sobbing. And then Ms. T and Mr. Davis sang "For Good," my sister's favorite song from *Wicked*.

But what I remember most is, even though I was surrounded by a roomful of people, I never felt so alone. And I remember feeling—knowing—that the only person who could have made me feel less alone wasn't there.

And never would be again.

32

SIX MEN CARRY the casket out of the chapel.

Dad takes Mom by the hand and I take Benji and Dad gives Jon the car keys and we follow an ugly black hearse to the cemetery, an endless line of cars behind us.

When we get there, we walk to a section that has a dull green canopy and rows of chairs waiting to be filled. It feels like it has dropped ten degrees, but my parents seem unaware of the cold. They huddle with Rabbi Gold, speaking in hushed, solemn voices as the wind picks up.

Jon wraps a scarf around Benji's neck, and I start to shiver, but it's not because of the temperature. It's because of the huge, gaping hole in the ground in front of me.

The hole where the casket will go.

All of a sudden, my chest is tight and I can't breathe.

"You need to sit." There's a gentle hand on my shoulder, and Jon leads me to a seat in the front row. "Breathe with me," he says. "In and out, slowly."

Benji sits next to me, looking worried. Nipa appears seemingly out of nowhere and takes my hand. "Becky. You're gonna be okay," she says.

I turn to face Jon and do my best to match his breathing. I think maybe it's starting to work when Nipa says, "Oh no."

"You!"

I look up and see my mom, who's always cool, calm, and collected in public, approach Reverend McCormick . . . and his son. Sam is pale and looks every bit as awful as my dad, maybe even worse.

"Who's that?" Benji asks.

"I need to go." I jump up and head over to them.

"How dare you show your face here?" Mom stares at Sam, her voice a low growl and her face so furious I barely recognize her.

"I . . ." Sam opens his mouth but nothing else comes out.

"We came to pay our respects," Reverend McCormick says in a soft voice, "not add to your pain."

It's like I'm watching a train wreck about to happen, and there's nothing I can do to stop it.

Mom's fists are clenched and her eyes are harder than I've ever seen them, and I'm afraid she's going to lose it. "You need to leave." She glares at Sam, her voice shaking along with the rest of her.

But *I'm* the one who needs to do something. I need to step between Mom and Sam and speak up. I need to say none of this is his fault. That he and Sara loved each other.

The reverend puts an arm around his son and starts to lead him away, but Sam turns back, his eyes full of tears. "I'm so sorry."

Only he's not looking at Mom. He's looking at me.

"Don't you *ever* speak to her again!" Mom glares at him. "You've caused our family enough suffering."

"Jill." Dad walks up and puts his hand on her arm. "This is not the time or place," he says quietly but firmly.

She rips her arm away and walks over to Aunt Ruth, who pulls her into a hug.

And all I do is watch Sam walk away, even though he has every right to be here.

Even though Sara would *want* him here.

Dad takes my hand and leads me to the front row. Almost all the seats are full now, and I can't help but wonder how many people saw what happened between my mother and Sam.

My father sits on one side of me and Benji's on the other. Mom sits farther down next to Aunt Ruth. I'm glad she's not sitting near me. I'm so angry with her. Jealous, too: she still has her sister. Nipa is right behind me, her hand on my shoulder.

As Rabbi Gold waits for the last few people to take a seat, it starts to snow. It's freezing, but I don't care. All I can think of is how disappointed Sara would be if she'd seen me just now, standing there and doing nothing while our mom attacked the boy she loved.

Rabbi Gold says a few words, then we all rise and he leads us in the kaddish, which I know by heart. *"Yitgadal v'yitkadash sh'mei raba...."*

I said those words at Grandma Rachel's funeral, and at hundreds of Friday night and Saturday morning services for people I didn't even know. But not now.

I can't.

I won't.

If I open my mouth, I will scream.

The snow falls and the wind blows and the casket is lowered into the ground and my father takes a shovel and pours dirt over it.

And I'm never going to see Sara again.

33

ALL I WANT is to go home, go to my room, lock everyone and everything out, and sleep for a thousand years. But I can't because we are holding shiva at our house for the next seven days.

Our house is full of people and a ridiculous amount of food, including countless pound cakes. Pound cake is one of the traditional foods because it's plain, not iced or fancy or especially sweet. Another traditional food is a hard-boiled egg to symbolize the "fullness of life," which makes no sense to me at all.

Sara's life *should* have been full. Full of senior prom and graduation and college and musical theater and . . .

The should-have-beens go on and on in my head. The list, and the loss, is endless.

I close my eyes and try to drown out everyone and everything around me, but it's too crowded and too noisy and I can't.

I open my eyes and see so many familiar faces squeezed into our living room and dining room and hallway. Some of them are smiling—actually smiling!

I see Dad talking with congregants, polite as always, like it's just another day at the synagogue. I see Mom clutching a plate of food someone must've given her, listening to our neighbor talk and talk, but her eyes are empty. I see Jon sitting in a corner speaking softly with Benji. They both look so tired and so sad, I can't stand it.

I can't stand any of it.

I go to the kitchen to escape, but there are people there, too. Luckily it's only my aunt and uncle and cousin.

"What can I get for you, darling?" my aunt asks.

"Can you get rid of all these people?"

"Becky!" Uncle Jacob says. "They're here because they care. They're here to pay their respects."

"Oh yeah? Sam and his dad came to pay their respects and look what happened to them!" My voice is louder than it should be, but I'm way past caring. "Did you see how Mom treated them? Did you hear what she said to them?"

"Who's Sam?" Uncle Jacob asks.

"Becky," Aunt Ruth says, "honey, I know you're upset—"

"Upset? My sister is dead and there are people in the living room smiling like this is a party or something!"

Miri takes my hand. "Hey . . . let's get out of here."

She grabs our coats out of the hall closet and leads me out the side door and down the block, away from everything.

It's the first time all day I feel like I can breathe.

We walk in silence for a while. It's still snowing lightly, and the cold air sends a chill down my body, but I don't mind. The last thing I want is to feel warm and cozy. It would just feel wrong.

"Okay," she says, her hair already covered in snowflakes and her cheeks pink from the cold. "We can stand here or keep walking. Your call."

"Keep walking," I say. "It's only a couple blocks to my school. Okay?"

"Sounds like a plan."

We walk the familiar path that I travel five days a week and end up sitting on a bench outside the school entrance. "We should've brought hot chocolate," Miri says.

"Or a blanket," I suggest.

"Two blankets," she says.

"I'm sorry, Miri."

She puts a gloved hand around me and pulls me in close. "Nothing to be sorry about. In fact, you did me a favor. I didn't want to be there, either."

"Right? Did you see those people smiling? How could they be *smiling*? What is wrong with them?"

"They were telling stories about Sara," she says softly. "Things she said or did. Happy memories."

"Oh." Now I almost wish I'd stayed. I would've liked to hear those stories. "She asked me to keep him a secret," I tell Miri. "Sam."

"And you did. She trusted you, Becky."

It's hard to get the next words out, only I have to. "Maybe if I hadn't kept him a secret, Sara would still be here."

"Oh, Becky . . ." Miri wipes the tears running down my cheeks. "You can't think that."

"Why not? What if it's true? What if this is all my fault?"

Miri puts her hands on my shoulders. "I want you to listen to me, okay? None of this is your fault. Not one bit of it."

"I shouldn't have let her go out in the snowstorm. I should've grabbed the car keys or something."

Miri smiles. "Seriously? When did *anyone* stop Sara from doing *anything*? She always followed her heart."

"Like you?"

Miri stares at me for a second or two, like she's caught off guard. Then she nods. "Like me."

"Miri? Are you glad you married Luke?"

She takes a deep breath and sits back against the cold bench. "I am. But I'm sorry I hurt my parents. And maybe I could've handled things differently. . . ."

"Like how?"

She thinks for a minute or two. Shakes her head. "I don't know. . . . Maybe I could've tried harder to explain that loving Luke doesn't mean I don't love them. And it doesn't mean I won't raise our kids Jewish. He and I have talked about it a lot, and he's fine with that." She gives a sad sort of laugh. "Luke makes a better matzo ball soup than my mom."

"Maybe you *shouldn't* tell her that part." I laugh a little, too. It feels surprising, but good. "Anyway," I tell her, "you still have time. It's not too late."

She hugs me. "I hope you're right."

We sit there, holding hands and shivering in the cold together. After a few minutes, she says, "You know what would be really good right now? A cup of hot tea."

"That actually *does* sound good," I admit. "But I refuse to eat pound cake."

She nods. "Fair enough."

34

WHEN YOU OBSERVE shiva, all the mirrors are covered in the house because we're not supposed to worry about how we look at a terrible time like this. The immediate family sits on low stools, and people visit during the hours my aunt set up.

Some pray with us, others bring meals since no one here has the energy to cook. Our refrigerator and freezer are crammed full of casseroles, and our cabinets are overflowing with bagels and banana bread and pound cake. None of us has much of an appetite, but it doesn't seem to matter. Even the spicy, aromatic veggie dishes from Mrs. Sachdeva, which I usually can't get enough of, don't taste right.

But Nipa still brings them. Every day.

She's been the only bright spot in this impossibly dark week. Still, as glad as I am to see her, as thankful as I am that she's here with me, even our visits are strained and too quiet.

"School was really boring today," she tells me for the fifth time this week.

"Oh yeah?"

She nods. "French is too easy. Math is too hard...."

"Mm."

"Brought your homework." She hands it to me.

Of course she did. She's brought it five days in a row. I take the papers without even glancing at them. "Thanks."

"There's no rush," she assures me. "Everyone is being really nice about it, even Mr. Jenkins," she jokes. My social studies teacher is *not* known for his kindness.

I try to smile, but I doubt it's convincing. We sit in silence for a couple of minutes, trying to figure out what to talk about. We've never had to do that before this past week.

"Miri and her parents left this morning," I blurt out.

"I remember," she says softly. "Is that good or bad?"

I shrug. "Neither. Both? I don't know...."

She waits patiently for me to explain.

"I'm sad they left, but happy Miri and Aunt Ruth are getting along better."

"That makes sense," Nipa says.

And then we're both quiet again.

She stays a little while longer, but I'm not much company. "Well," she says, "guess I'd better go. Homework..."

We both get up. I hug her and thank her for coming.

And then she's gone again.

It's weird; the past five days—except for Nipa—all I've wanted is a break from shiva. A break from visiting hours and platters of food and trying to be polite and grateful when all I really want is for everyone to go away and leave us alone.

But now that it's Friday night, everyone *is* leaving us alone. It's Shabbat, and we won't observe shiva again until tomorrow night. But as bad as it was having company, it's worse without it: too quiet, too empty.

Six minus one equals one chair too many around the dinner table. One voice too few around the house.

It's zero laughter.

Zero singing.

Zero joy.

I've put on my pajamas and brushed my teeth and am heading back to my room when I hear angry voices coming from my parents' room.

Mom and Dad haven't been talking much lately, but now they're arguing, which is way worse.

I should keep walking, but I want to know what they're arguing about. Is it Sam? Is it me?

"Be reasonable," I hear Dad say. "He can still catch up if he leaves on Tuesday."

"No!" Mom shouts. "I am not going to lose another child!"

"Jill, please. He can't stay here forever! You're not being fair to him. Jonathan deserves to—"

"Fair? What does *fair* have to do with any of this?"

"That's not what I—"

"I'll call the college and explain the circumstances," Mom

says. "I'm sure we can get a partial refund...."

"This is not about tuition, and you know it."

"He can go back in the fall," Mom says, not listening to Dad at all.

But I've heard enough. I go to my room and shut the door and think about Jon. Think about how it could be six minus two soon.

I know I don't get a vote, but if I did, I think about how good it's been to have him here the past few days. Then I think about how happy he was when he flew back to school a few weeks ago.

How happy all of us were.

My door opens and Jon is standing at my door. "Hey..."

"Hear anything interesting lately?" he asks, obviously referring to our parents' argument.

"I wouldn't exactly call it interesting."

"Well"—he smiles—"at least they're talking again."

"I wouldn't exactly call it talking," I say. And then I think of something—someone—else. "Do you think Benji heard them 'talking,' too?"

Jon shakes his head. "He's downstairs trying to teach Belle and Beast some tricks."

"Oh yeah? How's that going?"

"About as well as you'd expect. Wanna come see?"

"I do," I say. "We'd better get some extra food to motivate Beast."

"Good idea. Extra food always motivates me, too."

* * *

Shabbat comes and goes and we're back to the last two days of shiva. Back to visitors and plates of food and sitting on stools and quiet conversations and polite behavior. There is one unexpected visitor, though—and it's for me.

Ms. T—or Mrs. Davis now—comes bearing music, not food. After she offers condolences to my parents and a bag full of pencils and lollipops with musical designs to Benji, she wraps me in a huge hug, then Dad suggests we go to the kitchen for some privacy.

After I bring sugar and cream and tea bags to the table, she hands me a folder of new music our class is working on. "In case you need a distraction."

"Thanks." It feels strange seeing her in my house and serving her a cup of mint tea—strange, but nice. We talk about easy things—safe things—like band class, her honeymoon plans for spring break, and of course the wedding she had just a few days ago. I ask if she has any pictures and she pulls out her phone and scrolls through some of her favorites.

"You look so pretty! And so happy."

"Thank you, Becky. Don't think I didn't tell everyone at the wedding about the wonderful surprise shower you threw for me."

"It was Sara's idea," I tell her.

She smiles sadly, and all of a sudden there's this awful, awkward silence . . . one that seems to happen every time Sara's name comes up.

I grip my cup and stare into the liquid inside. "I hate that whenever anyone mentions her, it gets all quiet and sad."

"It's the complete opposite of what Sara was like," Ms. T says.

"Exactly! She would hate this. Everybody sitting around all serious and depressed."

"You're right." She thinks for a minute, then says, "I know it's hard to imagine, but it won't always be this way. The sadness will never go away completely, but it will get easier over time."

"I hope so," I whisper.

She takes a last sip of her tea, then pushes the cup and saucer to the side. "Becky, I called Mr. Singer and explained why you missed last week's rehearsal for All-County."

"I have to miss this week's, too. Shiva isn't over 'til the next morning."

"I know. And so does Mr. Singer." Ms. T lets out a breath. "I don't know if you've been practicing on your own the past few days. . . ."

"Not really." *Not at all.*

"Well, there's still time to catch up, if you want. I can even work with you during lunch or after school. But I'm afraid you can't miss any more rehearsals after this one." She leans closer to me. "I know this is a really difficult time, Becky. So, it's totally your choice. Do you want to continue? If you'd rather sit this one out, you can always try again next year. What do you want to do?"

It's a good question.

And I don't know the answer.

35

SHIVA IS OVER. It's my first day back at school. I was out for seven days, but it feels more like seven years.

Before now, when I wasn't in school because of the flu or something, I would panic about what I'd missed and worry I would never catch up. This time, though, I don't even care, so I guess it's a good thing most of my teachers aren't pressuring me about the missed assignments.

Everything is a little surreal as I walk through the hallways to each of my classes. The first two periods I can't concentrate; it feels like everyone is tiptoeing around me and staring at me. But when I get to band class and take out my flute to warm up with the B-flat scale, I finally start to feel a little more like myself. We're halfway through the first piece when Ms. T—Mrs. Davis—stops to work with the trumpets.

While we wait, I let my eyes wander around the room and that's when I see it, still hanging at the top of the whiteboard:

the banner Sara and Jenna made for the surprise shower.

The shower that was one of the reasons Sara decided to break up with Sam, to drive in a snowstorm. She wanted our family to be at her own shower someday, and her wedding.

But she'll never have a wedding now. Never be a bride. Never walk down the aisle in a lacy white dress or be lifted in a chair during the hora.

And someday, if Jon or Benji or even I get married, she won't be there, either.

Ms. T signals the class to start playing again, but I'm having trouble because the notes are all blurry.

I wipe my eyes and raise my hand and ask if I can go to the restroom. Ms. T nods and I leave as fast as I can. I go to the bathroom and wait for my breathing to slow down, then wipe my face and wash it and wipe it again. I'm throwing the paper towel into the trash when a girl I don't know comes in. She looks at me for a second, like she recognizes me but can't figure out how. Then it hits her.

"You're Sara's sister!"

I hold my breath and wait for her to tell me how sorry she is. Instead she says, "I was at Ms. T's shower. I play oboe in first period band."

"Oh..."

"I saw your sister in *Les Miz*, twice! She made me cry both times!"

"Thanks."

It feels so good *not* to have someone say how sorry she is

for my loss, or how terrible it is that Sara's gone.

To have some random girl be so touched by Sara's performance that she's still remembering it and talking about it months later. There's something so special about that. . . . It makes me really happy—happier than I've been in days.

It makes me feel like Sara is still here.

And that means everything.

Nipa and I have been sitting in the cafeteria for fifteen minutes, and that chance encounter in the restroom is still on my mind. "I mean, it's amazing, right? That she's still thinking about Sara—in a good way. You know?"

"I do." Nipa fishes a mini chocolate chip cookie out of the bag. "That's really something."

"Right?" I lift my sandwich, then put it down again without taking a bite. "I want people to think of Sara, to remember her, months from now. *Years* from now."

"They will," Nipa says with absolute certainty.

"I want to make sure of it."

"How?"

I lift up my sandwich again, and this time I take a big bite out of it. My appetite is back all of a sudden, and I feel energized. I feel like I have a purpose. "I don't know . . . yet," I tell her.

"Well," Nipa says with her usual confidence in me, "you'll figure it out. And when you do? I'm helping."

"You really are the best friend ever," I tell her warmly.

"I know." She smiles at me and I smile back. "So, what happened when you got back to band class?"

"Nothing. I was fine the rest of the time. Except at the end of the period, Ms. T—"

"Mrs. Davis," Nipa corrects with a smile.

"Mrs. Davis asked if I've made a decision about All-County yet."

"Have you?"

I nod. "That girl in the bathroom reminded me that what we do matters. Singing and acting and music, they touch people. Sara loved doing that. And she knew I did, too. She's the one who supported me and tried to convince Mom and Dad to let me audition in the first place. She even drove me there!"

"I remember."

"So, I'm thinking maybe I should see it through, you know?"

"For Sara." Nipa smiles.

I nod again. "For Sara."

I tell Ms. T my decision after school, and she looks as happy about it as I feel. "I'm so glad, Becky. I'll let Mr. Singer know to expect you at next week's rehearsal."

"Thanks."

"And my offer still stands about working with you during lunch or after school, if you like."

"I'll probably take you up on that. I haven't been practicing so much lately." I lift my flute case and turn to leave when she puts a gentle hand on my arm. "How are you?"

People ask all the time, but I know she wants an honest answer. So I think for a minute, and then I tell her the truth. "Not great. But better."

"I'm here if you ever need to talk."

"I know." I smile. "Thanks."

She smiles back and I head out. Now that I've decided to commit to All-County again, I have some serious work to do.

When I get home, the house is quiet.

Dad's back at work. Back to helping other people, despite everything. Maybe *because* of everything. Maybe helping other people helps him, somehow. Or maybe it's a good distraction.

Jon is most likely picking Benji up from school or waiting at the bus stop. There's a part of me that's jealous of their bond; it makes me miss Sara even more. But the better part of me is happy they have each other.

And Mom . . . I don't know what to do about her. She always used to be so busy—at synagogue helping with whatever was needed or visiting a sick congregant or fitting in a few errands when she had time. Now she's almost always in bed. Maybe she's sleeping—she's got to sleep sometime.

I hear her late at night sometimes, walking around, talking on the phone with Aunt Ruth, or having a cup of tea and a quiet conversation with Jon. But never Dad. And never me.

Sure, she'll tell me to feed the cats or take out the recycling or ask me to check Benji's math homework. But nothing more. I think she still blames me for what happened.

Sometimes I still blame myself.

I stop in the living room to pet Belle and scratch Beast on his fuzzy tummy, then head for the kitchen to grab a snack. It feels impossible that just two months ago, Sara and I had so much fun there making Benji's birthday cake and helping Mom with Thanksgiving.

Now the kitchen is quiet and empty, and suddenly I feel such a powerful longing to see Sara sitting at the table, or standing at the counter, that I can't breathe. I drop into the nearest chair, close my eyes, and think of Jon telling me to breathe with him at the cemetery. I inhale and count to three, then exhale and count again, and repeat until my breathing is normal.

The moment finally passes, at least for now. I look around for something to eat, but there isn't much. Most of the shiva food is gone; besides, I couldn't stand one more bite of banana bread or pound cake. Mom hasn't gone to the kosher market since before the funeral, and she hasn't been up to cooking, either. Dad fills in when he can, but half the time he's called away to meetings or congregants, even now.

Jon's been babysitting Benji and doing the laundry, so I've tried to step up and help out, too. I'm not much of a cook, but luckily my brothers aren't fussy, so we get by with pasta or scrambled eggs or sometimes just cereal. One night we ordered pizza, but the delivery girl knew Sara and started crying before we could even tip her.

I grab a half-empty jar of peanut butter but we're out of

jelly, so I take some stale bread and make a PB minus J. The peanut butter sticks to the roof of my mouth, so I pour a glass of milk; one sniff tells me it's gone sour.

I dump it down the drain, grab some water instead, and take that and my sandwich up to my room. I go to my desk and reach for my All-County sheet music folder, but before I even pick it up, my eyes land on my bat mitzvah notebook, which I've neglected along with my music.

To think that was my biggest problem, my biggest worry, at one time. I take a breath, open it, and read my uninspired speech. Read about all the gifts God gave the Jewish people, like freeing us from Egypt when we were slaves, and even—or especially—the gift of life itself.

I stop reading and start thinking about the gift of life being *taken away*, and suddenly I feel the opposite of grateful.

I feel angry.

Cheated.

Betrayed.

I tear out my notes and my speech and rip them into shreds and toss them in my trash can.

"Bec? What're you doing?"

Jon's at my door, looking at me like I've gone insane. And maybe I have.

"Nothing."

"Doesn't look like nothing." He walks over and picks a scrap out of the trash can. "Wait. Is this your bat mitzvah speech?"

"It was. . . ." The piece of paper in my hand can't be more than an inch or two, but I don't care. I tear it into smaller pieces.

"Hey . . ." He takes my hands. "Stop."

I keep tearing. "It's over."

"What do you mean, it's over?" He shakes his head. "It doesn't work like that. You can't just rip up a speech and cancel your bat mitzvah."

I shrug. "That's just it. It's *my* bat mitzvah. And I don't want it anymore."

"You know it's delayed, right? Because of . . . the circumstances."

"The circumstances," I repeat. "It's not delayed, Jon. It's not happening. Ever."

I sit on my bed and he joins me. "Look," he says. "I know you're hurting. We all are. What happened . . . It's still hard to believe. And we'll never be the same—any of us. But that doesn't mean everything stops. It doesn't mean we shut down."

"I'm not shutting down. I'm waking up. Or maybe I'm growing up." I get up. "All I know is I can't stand in front of a bunch of people and give a speech about all the great gifts God has given us when He took away the best gift of all!"

I wait for him to argue with me. To say something smart. To change my mind. But he just sits there looking sad, which is even worse.

"Aren't you gonna say anything?" I ask.

"I'm going back to school." He paused for a second. "Tomorrow."

"Oh." I sit back down and let it sink in. "Good for you," I say, remembering Mom's argument with Dad. Dad was right—Jon should go back to school.

"Bec—"

"No. I mean it. Sara would want you to."

"It's only for a few weeks. . . ."

Then it hits me. As much as I'm going to miss him . . . "It's gonna be hard on Benji."

"He's stronger than you think," Jon says. "Besides, he'll still have you."

I shake my head. "I can barely take care of myself!"

"That's not what Benji thinks. He looks up to you. He told me you're a great big sister."

"Well, if I am, it's because I learned from the best."

I blink away a tear and Jon pulls me in. I rest my head on his shoulder, and we stay like that 'til my phone alarm reminds me it's time for All-County rehearsal.

36

JON PULLS UP in front of the usual place. It's strange to think how excited I was the other times I came here with Dad and Sara. I open my door, but my legs don't move.

"You okay?" Jon asks.

I turn to face him. "It feels different now." I wait for him to ask how, or to give me a pep talk or something.

"I know what you mean," he says. "It's gonna feel different for me, too, back in California. On campus, in classes, at the dorm."

"I thought you wanted to go back to school?"

He smiles. "I thought *you* wanted to go back to All-County?"

"I do. It's just . . ."

"Different."

I nod.

"You know, it's okay to be conflicted. You can be excited about something, but still be, you know . . ."

"Scared? Terrified?"

He laughs. "I was thinking more like slightly anxious. But terrified works, too."

I laugh a little. "Seriously. Will you be okay?"

"We both will. We *all* will, sooner or later. And this"—he nods toward the school—"is proof."

"Proof that we'll be okay?"

"Exactly. Go get 'em."

"Thanks, Jon." I take a deep breath and exit the car.

"Uh, Bec?"

I turn back.

"Forgot something." He holds up my flute.

"Oh!" I reach in and grab it, smiling a little. "Already off to a spectacular start."

"Hey, you've got this."

"That's what Sara said, when she brought me here to audition."

"And she was right."

I smile again. "Yeah. I guess she was."

As I walk down the halls toward band room, I think of that girl who loved Sara's Eponine so much, the one who reminded me how much *I* loved—love—music. I think about how right it felt when I told Nipa and Ms. T that I still want to do All-County.

I stand outside the classroom door and hear the other musicians warming up. Hear Jon say we'll all be okay. Hear Sara say, "You've got this."

And I believe them both.

I open the door and all the flutists stop warming up and look at me. Mr. Singer looks at me, too, then gives a big smile that feels like a warm hug. I smile back and make my way to the flute section.

"Welcome back," one of the other flutists, Katie, says.

"Thanks." I take my seat, open my flute case, and look around the room. Ethan waves from the trumpet section and I wave back.

"I'm glad you're here," the male flutist, Henry, tells me. He leans in and pretends to whisper, "The other girls keep messing up."

"No way!" Katie laughs.

And Henry laughs. And I do, too.

"Miss Myerson?"

I look up at Mr. Singer.

"What should we start with this fine evening?"

He's right. It *is* a fine evening. As I look around the room again, I really am happy to be here. So I choose the one piece guaranteed to help me stay that way. "Joplin."

"Excellent choice."

I put "Maple Leaf Rag" on my music stand and bring my flute to my lips and everything rushes back like it never left: the camaraderie, the excitement. The fun and the joy of being part of something bigger than myself. And the beautiful, beautiful music.

The music most of all.

37

REHEARSAL IS OVER, but I'm just getting started. When we get home, I go straight to my room and practice some more. I'm enjoying it so much, I don't even register the noise downstairs until I pause to grab the next sheet of music.

I run into the kitchen: the smoke detectors are screeching and Mom is screaming and the air is full of smoke as Dad pulls burned brisket out of the oven. Jon grabs a cookie sheet and waves it under the smoke alarm while I open a window and Benji stands in the middle of it all, wide-eyed and scared.

"It's only a piece of meat." Dad reaches for Mom to console her, but she moves away from him, tears streaking her face.

"It's more than that! I wanted to make a nice meal for Jon," she says, sobbing, "before he leaves us."

"Mom." Jon goes over and hugs her. "I'm not *leaving* you. I'm just going *back* to school. I'll be home again before you know it."

The stupid smoke detector goes off again. Benji takes the

cookie sheet Jon was using and waves it around, but he's too short and it doesn't help.

"Good job, buddy." Jon grabs a second cookie sheet. "How 'bout we both do it?"

Benji smiles and they wave their cookie sheets together, almost in sync. It makes me happy and sad at the same time.

"Rebecca?" Dad grabs his cell with one hand and his keys with the other. "Feel like going for a ride?"

Two minutes later we're on the way to our favorite pizza place for an "emergency dinner rescue."

"This is a great idea," I tell him. "You're like an unsung hero."

"We're all doing the best we can."

"Are we?"

He glances my way. I know he would look at me longer if the light wasn't green. "Rebecca . . ."

"Sorry," I say, even though I'm really not. Someone has to say it. "Dad, Mom isn't . . . she's not . . ."

"I know."

Of course he knows. But is he doing anything about it? Is anyone? *Can* anyone?

"I wanted to tell you how pleased I am to hear you playing your flute again," he says, clearly changing the subject. "I heard you practicing in your bedroom. You have a real gift."

His voice is warm and his words are sincere and I know I should feel happy, but instead I feel guilty. When I hear "gift," all I can think of is my speech: the one I'm not giving at the bat mitzvah I'm not having.

I need to tell him. Soon. But Sara's gone and Jon is leaving and Mom is all sad and depressed and it's so peaceful here with him. I hate to ruin it.

"Speaking of gifts," he continues, "how is that speech of yours coming along? Would you like me to take a look?"

I open my mouth, but nothing comes out.

"There's no rush, of course. We're going to reschedule it. With all that's happened, it's permissible. . . . A bat mitzvah is a special thing, Rebecca. It's an important rite of passage, but it's supposed to be a joyful one, too. And it's pretty clear our family needs to heal before we can fully experience joy again and celebrate you the way we should."

I want to ask when we'll "experience joy again," or if we ever will. But as he pulls into the parking lot, what comes out is "I'm not having a bat mitzvah."

He turns the ignition off and looks at me, and I can't believe how bad my timing is. Now it's just the two of us sitting in the parking lot and he can focus completely on me. "What do you mean?"

I take a shaky breath. "I'm sorry, Daddy. But I can't. I *won't*. It just. It doesn't feel *right* anymore. I can't stand up in front of everyone and talk about all the great things God has done and how grateful I am . . . not now."

I close my eyes and wait for him to tell me how disappointed he is, or to insist I have it anyway; I am the rabbi's daughter, after all. How would it look if I canceled my bat mitzvah? If he *allowed* me to cancel it? There's no way he's going to be okay with my decision.

"I understand," he says.

I open my eyes and stare at him, shocked. "You do?"

He takes my gloved hand in his. "Rebecca. We all handle tragedy in different ways. Holocaust survivors, for instance, typically reacted in two very different ways when it came to faith. Some became more religious than ever, grateful to have made it through the concentration camps. Others were so angry at the suffering and loss of life . . . they believed God turned His back on them, so they turned their backs on Him. It's your choice whether you go ahead with your bat mitzvah or not. But I've *tentatively* rescheduled it for May fifteenth. Jon will be home for the summer, and . . ."

"We'll be able to experience joy again?"

He takes a deep breath and lets it out. "I don't know. I hope so, sweetheart. Take your time. Think it over. And we can talk about it some more, too. Anytime. You don't need to make a final decision yet."

I'm pretty sure I have, but he's being so understanding I don't have the heart to say otherwise. So I just nod and mumble, "Okay. I'll think about it."

We leave the car and head over to the pizza place when I see Keisha's Confections next door and get an idea. "Can I run over and get a red velvet cupcake for Mom? Maybe it'll cheer her up."

He smiles. "That's a sweet thought." He hands me some money. "Go ahead and make it half a dozen."

My own smile disappears. We only need five. But before

I can say anything, Dad explains, "Jon can take one for the plane ride."

"Oh, yeah. That's a good idea."

We split up and I walk into the bakery. There's no one behind the counter so I have time to look at all the flavors and decide what to get. Definitely red velvet for Mom, vanilla for Benji . . .

"What can I—"

I look up and see someone walking in from the back room.

I haven't seen him since Sara's funeral. Since my mom yelled at him and his dad. Since . . .

"Hey," Sam says.

I take a breath. "Hey," I whisper.

We stand there and look at each other and neither of us knows what to say.

The door opens and some teenage girls come in, interrupting our awkward silence with their noise and giggling and . . . joy.

"I . . ." I don't know what to say, so I run out of the bakery and wait at the car.

"What happened to the cupcakes?" Dad asks as he hands me the pizza boxes.

My mouth has gone dry. How will he react? Should I make up something? But my mind isn't working, so I just blurt it out before I can think. "Sam works there now." There's no recognition in Dad's eyes. "Sean," I add.

"Oh," Dad says softly. "I didn't know that."

"Me, neither."

He puts his key in the ignition but doesn't start the car.

"Dad, what Mom said to him at the cemetery. It was really awful. *She* was awful. I've never seen her like that! And Sam—he looked so upset! He totally didn't deserve it! I should've spoken up. . . . Sara would have wanted me to. But I didn't and now it's too late and I feel . . ."

"Awful?"

I nod.

He lets out a long breath. "Rebecca. Your mother was not herself that day—none of us were. And, for whatever it's worth, I'm certain both Sean—Sam—and his father understood."

I shrug. "Maybe so. But that doesn't make it right."

"No," Dad says. "It doesn't." He looks at me for a few seconds. "Maybe that part is up to us."

"What do you mean?"

"Well, sometimes when we feel bad about something, it's best to sort it out in person."

"I guess . . . Wait. Do you mean—"

He lifts his eyebrows. "I'm free tomorrow afternoon."

"I've got a practice session with Ms. T after school."

"And after that . . . ?"

I search for an excuse—any excuse—but come up empty.

38

"SO, HOW IS Mrs. Davis?" Dad asks as he picks me up from today's practice session after school. I slide into the front seat with my flute.

"She's great. And she says that I'm pretty much caught up already."

"I'm glad to hear it." He smiles at me. "So, on a scale of one to ten, how excellent is this All-County concert going to be?"

"I'd say somewhere between ten . . . and eleven." I smile back.

"Excellent!"

And then we run out of things to say. Either that, or we're both thinking of what to say when we get to our next stop.

Now that we're on our way, I'm wondering if this is a bad idea. But Dad set it all up because of me, so I'm in no position to bail if I wanted to. Which I don't.

I don't think.

He pulls up in front of a house I've never seen before, and we walk to the door together. He lifts his hand to ring the bell, then pauses and turns to me. "Are you ready, Rebecca?"

"I think so?"

He rings the bell.

The door opens and Reverend McCormick greets us with his usual kind smile and welcomes us into his home.

The home he shares with Sam.

"Thank you again for agreeing to see us, Reverend," Dad says.

"Of course." Reverend McCormick gestures toward a comfy-looking dark green sofa. "Please, make yourselves at home."

Dad nods and we both sit down and it's suddenly really quiet. I thought I knew exactly what I wanted to say, only now it feels all wrong and I'm trying to think of a different way to say it when Sam walks into the room.

"Hey, Becky. Rabbi Myerson."

"Hello, Sean," Dad says.

"Hey, Sam."

The soft, sad look in his eyes catches me off guard and I have this urge to jump up and give him a hug. But I don't.

"Would either of you care for something to drink?" the reverend asks. "Tea? A glass of water?"

I shake my head even though my throat is dry. I'm so scared that, after all this, I'll still say the wrong thing.

"Tea would be perfect," Dad says. "Thank you."

Reverend McCormick smiles and goes to the kitchen.

Suddenly it's very quiet again. And not a good kind of quiet, either. Dad clears his throat and looks at me, like he's waiting for me to start the conversation. Actually, it's not so much a conversation as an apology. For my mom.

But when I look at Sam, I feel like maybe I need to apologize for myself just as much, or maybe even more. For not standing up for him at the cemetery. And for letting Sara drive off in the snowstorm to break up with him.

I never found out what happened when she came here that night. And I suddenly realize that as much as I'm hurting, he is, too.

"I'm so sorry, Sam. . . . I tried to do the right thing but I think I did everything wrong."

"No," he says. "You didn't do anything wrong."

Dad puts his arm around me while I try not to cry. Then Reverend McCormick brings out a pot of tea and Sam gets some cups and the four of us sit together and drink and I start to feel a little better.

Reverend McCormick puts his cup down and looks at Dad and me. "I'm grateful that you came here today. Sara was such a lovely girl. My son, he . . . They—"

"What my dad is trying to say," Sam interrupts, "is that he kept our secret because Sara and I asked him to. He didn't want to—"

"I know all about secrets," I say to no one in particular.

The way Reverend McCormick looks at my dad, it feels

like no one else is even in the room. "I am so profoundly sorry if, in any way, I caused—"

"It wasn't your fault, Dad. I keep telling you that," Sam says gently. "Sara and I . . . we never should have put you in that position." He turns and looks at me. "Or Becky, either."

"Please," my dad says. "Rebecca and I came here to apologize. What happened at the gravesite was inexcusable. My wife—"

Sam's dad waves his hand and cuts Dad off. "No need. Sean and I understand all too well what grief can do."

Sam nods. "When my mother died, I stopped talking."

The reverend nods. "It's true. Not one word for—how long was it?" he asks Sam.

Sam shrugs. "Six, seven weeks?"

"How did you get over it?" I ask him.

He stares at me. "I didn't."

I wonder if that means I'll never get over losing Sara.

"I got *through* it. There's a difference."

"So, how did you get through it?" I ask softly as Dad takes my hand.

"It might not be the same for everyone," Sam says. "But for me, I started volunteering. A lot. Soup kitchens, animal shelters, Special Olympics. I needed to keep busy."

"I think it was more than that," Reverend McCormick says. "I think focusing on others, using your time in ways you found gratifying, gave you a sense of purpose. Of meaning."

Sam considers, then zeroes in on me. "When you lose

someone you love, everything can feel pointless. Things you once thought were important don't seem to matter as much, or at all."

I can't help thinking about my bat mitzvah.

"Another thing that helped me was seeing a grief therapist," Sam says. "She listened when I needed to talk, and talked when I needed to listen."

His dad nods. "She made such an impression on Sean that he's thinking about becoming a therapist himself one day."

I smile for the first time since we walked in the door. "That's awesome."

He smiles back. "Thanks."

We sit for a few more minutes, then my dad and Reverend McCormick take the cups and teapot back to the kitchen, and Sam and I are alone.

It feels strange being with him, and without Sara. All of a sudden, I realize that he was the last person to see her alive.

My stomach hurts and I can barely breathe, but I need to know what she said to him, and what he said to her. "Sam? That night..."

The sudden pain in his eyes tells me he knows exactly what my question will be.

"What happened? What did Sara say?"

He looks at me for a few seconds and I start to wonder if it's too painful or too personal or—

"She said she loved me, but she couldn't see me anymore. That it was too hard."

"And what did you say?"

"I told her I understood. That I wished things were different. I told her I loved her, too. And then she started crying and I tried to hug her but she pulled away and said she had to go."

My face is wet and so is his and I wish I'd never asked and I wish I'd never come and I wish so many things all at once but none of them matter.

"Becky . . . I tried to keep her here. I told her she could sleep on the sofa or wherever she wanted. I told her it was dangerous, that it wasn't safe to drive, but she said she had to get back home. . . ."

"It wasn't your fault, Sam," I whisper.

"It wasn't yours either, Trumpet Girl," he whispers back.

The old nickname feels like a lifetime ago, but it still makes me smile.

He smiles, too.

We wipe our faces and our fathers come back and Dad thanks them again for having us and we say goodbye and walk back to our car.

Before we head home, Dad turns to me and says, "He's a fine young man."

"I know." I hesitate to say anything else, to risk ruining this moment. But I have to. "Dad . . . do you think if I had told you about Sam—or if Sara had—do you think things would have been different?"

"I've been asking myself that same question," he says softly.

Then he's quiet for a minute. "I like to think so. I believe it's always best to 'come clean,' as they say. Keeping secrets may seem noble, but someone almost always gets hurt."

I blink away a tear, surprised I have any left. "I'm so sorry, Daddy."

He covers my hand with his. It feels warm. And strong. "We're all sorry."

"Even Mom?"

"What do you mean?"

"She seems more angry than sorry."

"Well, maybe she's both."

Maybe so, I think to myself: sorry about Sara, and angry with me.

Dad squeezes my hand and turns on the ignition and we head back home.

39

I MUST HAVE gone to all my classes today; I just don't remember what happened in any of them. I was too busy thinking about the visit with Sam last night, and the conversation Dad and I had in the car afterward. Secrets and anger and regrets were all ricocheting around in my brain, making it impossible to concentrate on anything else.

By the time school is over, I'm exhausted. I go straight home, straight to my room, and straight to bed. I'm almost asleep when I hear someone calling my name—a voice I haven't heard in what feels like a really long time. This version, anyway: soft and gentle and *not* angry.

In the old days, I'd stay in bed and shout, "It's open!" But the old days are gone and there's been enough shouting lately. More than enough.

I get out of bed and open the door.

"Your concert is tomorrow night," Mom says.

"I know."

"I wondered if you might like to go shopping for a new outfit, seeing as it's a special occasion."

"Oh . . ." I'm wondering if Dad told her about our conversation. But it doesn't matter. What matters is the warmth in her eyes and how happy I am to see it there again. There's only one possible response. "I'd love to."

Together, we make our way down the stairs and out the front door. "Since Dad's at a meeting and Benji's at Tommy's house," Mom says, "I thought we might treat ourselves to a little snack first, if that sounds good to you."

"I never say no to snacks," I tell her. Which she knows, or at least, she used to.

"How about one of those gooey chocolate cupcakes from Keisha's Confections?"

"Oh. Um . . . Sam works there," I say as we head for the rental car in our driveway. No one's had the energy to find a permanent replacement for the one Sara crashed. The name Sam doesn't register with her. "Sean," I add nervously, afraid of her reaction.

"Oh." Mom pauses at the car door.

We haven't even left our street and I've already managed to ruin our outing.

She taps the button on the car fob and the doors unlock. I slide into the front seat, wondering and worrying about what she'll say next.

Mom looks over at me, her face hard to read. "Why do you call him Sam?"

"It's kind of a long story."

She takes the key out of the ignition and puts it in the cup holder between us. "I have time."

I shrug. "I think it started because he and Sara had the same initials: S-A-M. Nipa noticed it in the program on opening night. And I guess I was used to thinking of him that way and he said it was okay, so it kind of stuck."

"I see." She puts the key back in the ignition but still doesn't turn it. "I understand you and your father paid a visit to the McCormicks," she says, staring out the windshield.

I'm not sure how to respond, so I decide to play it safe and say nothing at all.

"Did it . . . help you?" she asks.

I put on my seatbelt slowly while I think about her question. *Did* it help me? Did it help *anyone*? Or change anything?

"Maybe. I guess. A little? It felt good to clear the air. They were both really nice."

"I'm sure they were." She takes a breath. "You went there to apologize, didn't you?"

That's definitely a question, I just don't know how to answer it. Besides, I'm pretty sure she already knows. I'm trying to figure out what to say without hurting her feelings when she turns and looks at me. "To apologize *for me*. For the way I acted at the cemetery. For the things I said and how I blamed him for . . ." Her eyes fill and suddenly all I want is to comfort her.

"It's okay," I tell her quietly.

"No. It isn't."

"They're not mad at you or anything. Honest."

"*I* am," she says. A tear slides down her cheek. "At least, I *was*. But I didn't know who to be angry *at*. Sara? God?" She shakes her head. "It was so much easier to be angry at Sean. So much easier to blame him..."

"It wasn't his fault," I say softly.

She shakes her head. "No. It wasn't." She wipes her face. "It's taken me some time to realize that. Or maybe I knew it all along. I just didn't... I couldn't..."

"I thought you were mad at me."

"Oh, Becky." She caresses my cheek. "I was mad at everyone. I'm so sorry... sorry I wasn't there when you needed me. Sorry... for all of it."

"I am, too. I'm sorry I forged your signature. And sorry I kept things from you."

"Keeping secrets from the people you love..." Mom shakes her head.

"It's no fun."

"No fun at all," she says. "And the longer you keep them..."

"The worse it feels."

Mom looks at me. "You know, you're hardly the first or even second Myerson woman to keep secrets. I guess it runs in the family."

"What do you mean?"

"Becky... there's something I've never told anyone."

"Even Dad?"

"Even Dad. But I'd like to tell you. If that's okay."

"Okay," I say. "You can tell me."

She takes a breath and lets it out slowly. "When I was younger, my dream was—"

"To become a professional singer. Then you met Dad and your dream changed. That's not a secret."

"The secret is that my dream didn't change. It was . . . *shattered*."

"What happened?"

"I took a bus to New York City—didn't tell a soul. Not my parents, or my best friend . . ."

"Not even Aunt Ruth?"

She shakes her head. "Not even Aunt Ruth. There was this audition for an off-Broadway production of *A Chorus Line*. I waited for hours, along with hundreds of other hopefuls. They finally called my name, and I got up from my seat and walked onto the stage. . . ."

"And then what?"

She shrugs. "I choked. Couldn't do it. Not one single note."

I look at her and want to say something, but my mind is totally blank. My mom just shared a secret with me. A secret she's held onto for a really long time, and I don't know how to react. I don't even understand it.

"What happened? Why did you keep it a secret all this time?"

She pauses for a minute. "I think, back when it happened, I didn't want anyone to know that I had failed. I was so embarrassed. All those hopes . . ."

"But it was one audition," I say. "*One* time. Even if you didn't want to tell anyone about it, you could've have tried again...."

"You're right. I could have. And maybe I should have." Mom gives me a sad smile. "But I wasn't brave. Not like Sara. Sara was fearless." She takes my hand. "And so are you. I could not be any prouder."

And then it's my turn to cry.

She brushes my tears away with her thumb.

"I'm glad you told me your secret."

"So am I."

"And, Mom? I always love listening to you sing."

She kisses my forehead, turns on the ignition.

We haven't even left our driveway yet, but it feels like we've covered a lot of ground.

40

IT'S BEEN ANOTHER day of classes I barely remember; only this time, it's for a good reason: the All-County concert is tonight—finally!

I daydream through school, then go home, wash my hair, and text with Nipa. At dinner, I'm too excited to eat; luckily, Mom understands and says I can make up for it afterward. Then I put on the black skirt and lacy white top we bought yesterday, and the four of us get in the car, stopping to pick up Nipa on the way.

And then we're there. Everyone hugs me and wishes me good luck, then I join my fellow musicians in the band room. The excitement I've been feeling all day is *nothing* compared to this. Everyone is laughing and talking and warming up and it's the best feeling ever.

Or, at least, the best feeling until we walk onstage and there's that magical hush that fills a theater right before a show starts. We take our places—I'm first chair!—and the happiness that comes from doing what I love flows through me.

So much happiness that I start to feel guilty. What right do I have to feel happy when Sara is gone?

But then I look out at the audience and find my parents and my little brother and my best friend. They're all smiling at me and happy for me and I decide if they can be happy, I can, too.

So I raise my flute and let myself get caught up in the music.

The All-County Band is energetic and enthusiastic, and our conductor looks like he's having the time of his life. After the first piece, the audience applauds, then Mr. Singer approaches the microphone and faces the audience.

"Good evening, and welcome to this year's All-County Band!" He waits for the applause to quiet down, then continues. "First, I want to thank this talented group behind me for their tireless efforts and their infectious joy." He turns around and smiles at us, then turns back to the audience. "I thank their music teachers for fostering this love of music in each one of them ... and I thank all the parents out there for supporting these fine musicians, and for schlepping them to rehearsals every week."

The audience applauds again, then we play the three classical pieces in a row. Flawlessly.

And finally, it's time for my favorite number: Scott Joplin's jazzy "Maple Leaf Rag." It always makes me think of those old silent movies with people like Buster Keaton and Charlie Chaplin, and it's impossible not to tap your foot in time to the music and smile.

After the last note, I stand up with the band and take a bow. I see my family stand, too, and smile and cheer and clap with the rest of the audience. And I give myself permission to enjoy the moment.

I also give myself permission to enjoy the turkey tacos Mom makes back at home for the post-concert dinner. Then I make the mistake of remembering my sister and all her post-musical dinners; luckily, just as sadness starts to overtake the happiness, Jon calls for a recap and we FaceTime and I'm okay again.

By the time I get in my pajamas, it's almost midnight. I get into bed, but instead of going to sleep, I start reliving the concert: the preperformance excitement and jitters with my bandmates; walking on the stage and looking out at the audience; Mr. Singer's speech; all the applause. . . .

And then I think about how Sara must have experienced so much of this, too. Every show. Every time. And, as amazing as tonight was, every bit of me wishes she'd been there.

She wanted to be.

She planned to be.

She should have been.

I sit up, more awake than before. I decide maybe a warm cup of milk will help.

As I pad down the hall, it's quiet and dark, except for a light coming from one room: Sara's.

I can't imagine who would be in there, or why. For the first time since the accident, I open her door.

The vanilla-scented perfume she used to wear still lingers in the air. I breathe it in and look around. . . . Then I notice someone is in her bed, squished in between Sara's massive collection of stuffed animals: the ones she'd planned to pack up every summer. But she never did; she never could. Once something found its way to Sara's heart, it stayed there forever.

I tiptoe over to my little brother, wondering if I should let him sleep or get him back to his own bed. I'm pretty sure Mom has no idea he's here; he must've snuck in after she tucked him in.

Before I can decide what to do, Benji opens his eyes. "Sara? Is that you?"

My heart shatters into a million pieces. "No," I whisper. "It's only me."

"Becky? What are you doing here?"

"I could ask you the same question."

He sits up and looks at me as if this is a perfectly ordinary conversation. "I'm keeping Sara's stuffed animals company. They're lonely. They miss her."

I want to ask how long he's been sleeping in here. I want to ask how he goes in and out of Sara's room without anyone noticing.

Instead, I ask, "Can I keep them company, too?"

He nods and moves over, and I squeeze in between him and the ridiculous purple giraffe that's almost as big as he is.

"Hey, Becky?"

"Hmm?"

"Do you think Sara has new stuffed animals where she is?"

I have no clue how to answer. "What do you think?" I ask quietly.

"I hope so," he whispers.

"Me, too, Benji." I put one arm around the giraffe and the other around my brother and before I know it, I fall asleep.

41

WHEN I WAKE up, an oversized purple giraffe is staring at me, and Benji is tugging on my arm and whispering, "Time to get up!"

I roll onto my other side, still a little disoriented and trying to remember why we're in Sara's bed.

"Mommy and Daddy are in the kitchen, so we can go back to our rooms now."

So *that's* how he does it. I tousle his already sleep-tousled hair. "You're pretty smart"—I smile at him—"for a little kid."

He shrugs. "I know."

Something about the confident, self-assured way he says it makes me realize that maybe he's not such a little kid after all. Not anymore. I don't know if that's good or bad.

We leave Sara's room and go our separate, stealthy ways down the hall and back to our own bedrooms. I get dressed and head to the kitchen, where Dad's already taking a last sip of his tea and a last bite of English muffin.

"Hungry?" Mom asks.

I nod.

"Scrambled eggs?"

It's the first time she's offered me anything besides cold cereal or toast since the accident. "Sure. Thanks..."

She pulls the carton of eggs out of the refrigerator as Dad stands and puts a hand on my cheek. "You were really wonderful last night. We're very proud of you, Rebecca."

I hug him. "Thanks, Abba." *Abba.* Sara's name for him—not mine. It just popped out.

I want to take it back because it feels like everyone has stopped breathing and the look on my father's face makes my heart hurt. "I'm sorry! I didn't mean to—"

He pulls me into a hug. "It's nice to have someone call me that again... Becky."

And all of a sudden, we have new names for each other. New names to go with our new lives. And for the first time, I think maybe we'll find our way through this after all.

Find our way to a new normal.

As usual, the highlight of my school day is lunch with Nipa.

"Wow. You ate that in, like, five seconds," she comments as I devour the last crumbs of her samosa and lick my fingers. "Did you skip breakfast again?"

"Not today. Mom made scrambled eggs." I smile, as if it's the best news ever. And maybe it is because Nipa's smile is just as big as mine. For a second or two, I almost tell her about finding Benji in Sara's bed—and joining him. But I decide to keep it to myself.

I'm wondering if I should join him again tonight or if that's a bad idea, when the bell rings. "Hey," I say as we throw our trash out, "wanna hang out after school? Mom's taking Benji to the dentist, so—"

But Nipa shakes her head. "Dad's birthday is tomorrow, so Mom and I are shopping for last-minute gifts. Wanna come with?"

We both know I'll say no. I love her mom, but she's super serious when it comes to shopping, which means Nipa will be gone for hours. "Maybe next time," I tell her.

"Sure." She laughs, knowing exactly what I mean.

A few hours later, though, when the last bell rings and I head to an empty house, I'm kind of wishing I'd gone with Nipa after all. Still, Benji and Mom will be back soon, and I have more than enough homework to keep me busy.

I get the mail on my way to the door, then let myself in. I'm trying to decide if I want popcorn or yogurt for a snack, when something catches my eye in the pile of mail: a big, official-looking envelope from Carnegie Mellon University.

For Sara.

Her number one choice for musical theater.

I feel sick as I stare at the envelope, and I don't know what to do.

Should I open it? Hide it? Throw it away? Leave it for

Mom? What if she can't handle it? Things were finally starting to get a little better. . . . We *all* were starting to get a little better. . . .

I stand there another minute or two, then grab my phone. I try to slow my breathing and listen as it rings once. Twice. Three times . . .

"Bec? I can't really talk—"

"I got the mail and there's an envelope for Sara from Carnegie Mellon and no one's here but me and I don't know what to do. . . ."

The other end is silent for so long I wonder if we've been disconnected. "Jon? Are you there?"

"I'm here." He pauses. "Listen, this envelope, is it thick?"

"Yeah. What does that mean?"

There's silence again. "It means she got in," he says so quietly I can barely hear him.

"Oh." Now I pause, not sure what to say. "So . . . what should I do with it? Mom is finally acting normal again and Dad is happy and—"

"Bec, I'm really sorry," Jon says. "I can't talk right now. I'm on a shoot and everyone's waiting for me."

"But—"

"Put it in your desk and I'll call you as soon as we're done. Okay?"

I nod.

"Bec?"

"Yes. Okay."

He hangs up and I stare at the envelope that's meant for Sara.

I can almost see us gathering around as she opens it, almost hear her shouting, "I got in!" Almost feel her hugging me . . .

I take a shaky breath. I can't do this.

I call Nipa but it goes straight to voicemail. I dial Dad but change my mind and hang up.

I stand there, clenching Sara's big, thick envelope of good news.

Good news she should be celebrating. Good news we all should be celebrating with her. I try to think what she would want me to do.

And then I do it.

"Jon said to put it in my desk, but I couldn't. . . ."

"Did you bring it with you?"

I nod and we sit down on the bench in front of my school. It feels like I left here a week ago, but it's been less than half an hour. I pull the envelope out of my backpack and hand it to Sam.

"It looks like an acceptance letter." He looks at me with the saddest smile I've ever seen. "She did it."

"She'd be so happy," I say quietly.

He nods. "She would."

Neither of us knows what to say after that. All we can do is stare at the big, thick, unopened envelope.

After a while, he looks at me and shakes his head. "I'm sorry, Becky. I can't tell you what to do about this." He hands it back to me. "I think it's better if Jon figures it out with you tonight, like he said."

"Yeah," I whisper, slipping it back into my bag. "Sorry I bothered you. I just . . . I didn't know what else to do."

"Hey. You're never a bother. You know that, right?"

I shrug.

"Besides," he says, "I'm glad you called. I have something for you."

"You do?"

He looks at me with a strange expression. "I was supposed to keep it for your bat mitzvah."

"I'm not having a bat mitzvah."

"I know. Your dad told mine." He pulls a small, gift-wrapped box out of his own backpack with my name on it.

"That's Sara's handwriting."

He nods. "Yeah. We bought it together," he explains. "She wanted me to hold onto it until . . ." He stares at the box for a few seconds, then looks back at me. "Anyway, it's a two-part gift." He pulls his cell phone out. "This is part one. We recorded it at my place." He hands it to me. "Press play whenever you're ready."

Sara's face fills the screen and she's smiling and I'm crying and I can't breathe but somehow I hit play.

"Hey, bat mitzvah girl! If all goes according to plan, tomorrow morning you'll officially become a woman, according to Jewish law, anyway. And I know you'll get all your gifts tomorrow night at the party, but I wanted to give you this tonight."

I pause the video because I don't know if I'm ready for whatever "this" is.

I don't know if I ever will be.

I look up at Sam, who's standing off to the side, watching me.

"It's okay. She'd want you to see it."

I hit play again.

"I know you've heard me sing this five million times and you're probably sick of it. But there's something you need to know. Every time I sang it, I thought of you. So I wanted to sing it one more time, *just* for you. I always tell people that Cassidy and Jenna are my best friends, but the truth is . . . you are. Because of you, Becky, 'I have been changed for good.'"

And I know what she's going to sing before the first note.

And it's beautiful.

I never realized before how perfect the "For Good" lyrics are, especially now. About people coming into our lives for a reason, about rewriting each other's stories and changing each other . . . And maybe never seeing each other again.

And then Sara is talking to me. "If you're lucky, you'll never have to hear me sing this again," she says with a smile. "And in case you think this isn't much of a gift, there's a second one that goes with it.

"Now go and get some sleep. Tomorrow's your big day! I

can't wait to see you up on the bimah. I know you'll be amazing. I love you." And she blows me a kiss and the video ends and she's gone.

I wipe my eyes and look over at Sam.

"You might as well open part two," he says softly, wiping his own eyes.

He holds out a small box, and my fingers tremble as I tear the paper as carefully as I can so I can save it. Because Sara touched it.

I lift the top of the box and see a heart-shaped silver locket on a slender chain.

I look at Sam again.

He nods. "Open it."

Inside is my favorite line from the song Sara just sang: "You'll be with me like a handprint on my heart."

I take a shaky breath and begin to sob. And Sam hugs me and I hug him and we cry together.

42

MY PHONE RINGS.

I let go of Sam, wipe my eyes, and grab my cell in case it's Jon.

But it's not.

"Becky," Mom says, "I decided since Benji and I are already out, we might as well go to the library and the kosher market. Do you need anything?"

What I need is to figure out what to do with Sara's acceptance letter.

What I need is to watch the video again. And again.

What I need is Sara.

I clear my throat. I don't want my mom to know I've been crying. "No, thanks, I'm okay."

We hang up and I turn back to Sam.

"Are you really okay?" he asks.

I shake my head. "Are you?"

He shakes his head, then takes his phone back and asks for my email and sends me the link to Sara's video.

"I think I'm gonna go home now," I tell him. "Thanks for the presents. And thanks for being here."

"Anytime," he says. "I mean it."

I nod. I know he does.

I walk home and go straight up to my room, grateful and relieved to have some time to myself.

I put Sara's envelope in my desk for now, like Jon said. Then I get under my covers and open the link and close my eyes and hold my locket and listen as my sister sings again, just for me.

Then I listen to a different recording from Sara. The same one Mr. Rubenstein made. And I sing along for the first time since she died.

And then, after the music has gone silent, I go to my desk and take out my bat mitzvah notebook.

I finally figured out a way to make sure Sara is remembered.

I don't know how long I spend researching on my computer and taking notes and coming up with ideas. All I know is, by the time Benji walks into my room to say dinner is ready, I'm ready, too.

The food is delicious and the conversation is friendly, but my mind is so full I barely pay attention to either. Full of the hidden envelope in my desk—full of Sam's tears, and Benji with Sara's stuffed animals. Full of the chance meeting with the girl who remembered Sara's performance months later. Full of my new locket and my new idea.

Most of all, full of Sara's face and Sara's voice . . . and Sara's dreams.

After dinner, I clear the table and rinse the dishes. I play cards with Benji and do my homework and wait for Mom to read Benji a bedtime story and tuck him in.

Finally, I hear her close Benji's door, then ask her to join me in Dad's study. She and Dad look at me, and before I can change my mind, I hold up the envelope.

Because I am done with secrets.

"This came in today's mail." I hold my breath and wait for Mom to start crying or run out of the room. But she doesn't do either.

She holds her hand out and takes the envelope and hugs it to her chest. Dad wraps one arm around her and pulls me in with the other.

"Thank you, Becky," he says softly.

We all let go of each other after a few seconds. Mom has tears in her eyes and a sad, sweet smile on her face.

"I'd like to go ahead with my bat mitzvah," I tell them, "if that's okay."

"It is more than okay," Dad says.

"Can we still do it in May? After Jon's back?"

"Absolutely," he says. "I never canceled it."

I take a breath. "There's something else."

"We're listening," Mom says, completely focused on me.

"There's something I want to do—for Sara. And it's really important. I've already figured a lot of it out on my own, but I could use some help with parts of it."

"Whatever you need," Dad says. "We're always here for you."

I take the envelope off his desk and pull out a sheet of paper I'd tucked under the packet and hand it to them.

Their eyes grow wide as Mom reads the heading out loud: "'The Sara A. Myerson Memorial Scholarship for Musical Theater.'"

I watch their faces as they take it all in: the black-and-white photo of Sara as Eponine; a paragraph-long biography all about her gift for, and love of, musical theater. The selection criteria for the award—a video of the candidate singing a Broadway tune and a short essay on what performing means to them.

"I want to give it to a graduating senior who's going to major in musical theater in college." I look at the envelope I'm still holding. "Like Sara would have done."

There are fresh tears in Mom's eyes. "Oh, Becky. This is . . . lovely."

I look at Dad. He takes a minute to speak, and when he does, his voice is soft and it cracks a little. "I think . . . *this* is your mitzvah project."

"But I already have one!"

"Now you have two," he says with a small smile.

I smile back. "I guess you can never have too many."

"You're right about that," he says.

"You're also right about needing a little help setting this up," Mom adds.

Then Dad says, "I happen to know someone who's a bit of an expert in this area. He's already set up several memorial funds for the synagogue."

"Can you introduce us?" I ask.

And then something completely unexpected happens: he laughs.

I stare at him, confused. "What's so funny?"

"You already know him," Dad explains. "He's your bat mitzvah tutor!"

"Mr. Rubenstein?"

He nods.

And then I laugh, too.

43

THE SYNAGOGUE SANCTUARY is crowded and I stand on the bimah in front of the congregation alongside my dad, picking out the faces in the audience who mean the most to me.

My mother and brothers are in the front row, along with Aunt Ruth and Uncle Jacob and Miri. And Luke sitting next to her, holding her hand. Sara would've been so happy to see all of them together.

I see Nipa and her parents sitting with Cassidy and Jenna and so many people from the cast and crew of *Les Miz*. I see Ms. T and Mr. Davis. And then I find Reverend McCormick.

And Sam.

I was allowed to use the same Torah portion, and somehow I chant it, and the prayers that follow, flawlessly. Dad hugs me and Mom joins us and the congregation sings a joyful song and Benji claps and Jon laughs.

And then it's time for my speech. I take a deep breath and look out at all the people who are there. But my mind, and my heart, is with the one who isn't.

"My Torah portion is called *terumah*, which means 'gifts.' It's about God asking for materials, or gifts, to beautify the tabernacle. Materials like colorful yarn, and gold and silver, and precious stones and special oils and spices. God not only lists the kinds of gifts He wants; He even describes how to put the tabernacle together, down to the poles to carry it from place to place.

"The thing is, God didn't command the Jews to give these gifts. He asked only for gifts from every person whose heart so moves him.

"In the end, our gift to Him was really a gift to ourselves: a beautiful, portable gift we could take with us wherever we went, that was there whenever we needed it.

"I've been thinking about gifts a lot lately. Giving them and getting them. People say it's better to give than to receive, but I'm not so sure." Some people in the sanctuary chuckle or smile, and I'm glad because it means they're listening.

"It's not that I don't enjoy giving gifts, especially if they're not too expensive." Some people smile again.

"Every year I volunteer at a local soup kitchen around Thanksgiving, along with the rest of my family. I volunteer here at the synagogue, too, helping the preschoolers on Sunday mornings. And when someone I care about is feeling down, I do my best to cheer them up.

"But the gifts I give don't begin to measure up to the ones I've been given. I recently had the chance to play flute in All-County Band." I look at Ms. T. "Music is definitely one of my favorite gifts." She smiles at me and puts her hand on her heart.

"I've had the same best friend since kindergarten, when we both went for the only available swing at recess. Nipa got to it first, but she let me have it."

I smile at her, and she grins back.

"Then there are the gifts I take for granted, like food and good health and a nice house and a warm bed. But the gift I'm most grateful for is my family. My dad's rabbinic wisdom, my mom's gentle touch—and triple chocolate cake. My big brother Jon's kindness. My little brother Benji's laugh."

I pause for a second or two. I knew this would be the hardest part of the whole service to get through. But it's the most important, too. It's the reason I'm up here in the first place.

I touch my locket and find Sam and we lock eyes.

"The most precious gift of all is my sister, Sara. She should be sitting here in the front row, but she isn't. I'm wearing the dress she chose and the locket she bought. I even chanted the Torah portion she helped me learn.

"My sister believed in me so much that I finally learned to believe in myself. Sara gave me a lifetime's worth of gifts, and the kind of gifts that will last a lifetime. So I want to do the same for her." I take a breath and look at my mom, who nods and smiles at me through her tears. "My mitzvah project is The Sara A. Myerson Memorial Scholarship for Musical Theater.

"Except for the people she loved, Sara loved music more than anything. And I loved her . . ." My voice cracks. I take a few seconds, then keep going—like she would want me to. "I know she is here with me today, and every day from now on, like a handprint on my heart."

44

"YOU DID A good job today."

"Thanks," I say. I'm lying in bed, staring at the stars on my ceiling, and I feel her next to me.

"I liked your speech the most, especially the part about me."

"I figured you would," I say. "I'm glad you did."

I feel her arms around me.

"I miss you," I say.

"I know. But I'll always be here for you, Becky. I promise."

I smile into the darkness. Because when Sara makes a promise, she keeps it.

My bedroom door is open and I wait for Mom to tuck Benji in down the hall. When she goes downstairs, I go to his room.

"Becky? Is that you?"

I smile. "C'mon."

He follows me and stops at Sara's door, but I shake my head. "Just a little further."

He follows me to my room. I close the door and pat my bed. "Hop in."

He climbs up and I turn out the light, then snuggle next to him and we look at the stars on my ceiling.

"Becky? I'm glad you're here."

I put an arm around him. "I'll always be here for you." I squeeze his shoulder. "I promise."

Acknowledgments

It's no *secret* it takes a village to make a book. The *trouble* with acknowledgments is the limited space for unlimited gratitude.

First, thank you to my early readers: Malayna Evans, Penny March, Jesse Milliner, Laura Shovan, and Liz Sues. Your careful reads and thoughtful suggestions are as helpful as they are appreciated! And to Rosa Hsiung (also an early reader), fifty plus years with you as my BFF made writing about Becky and Nipa the easiest part of this story.

Thank you to the following for sharing their time and expertise so generously: musicians and teachers Jeremy Milliner and Joshua Fleming; Aditi Banerjee (baraat!) and Cheryl Jacobson (BARCS!); and Rabbi Doctor Chaim Joseph Wender for explaining that "truth is the center of everything."

Thank you to my dear JPST for navigating, and celebrating, our debut year together, and staying friends ever since: Cory Leonardo, Jessica Kramer, Gillian McDunn, Nicole

Panteleakos, Rajani LaRocca, and, of course, Chris Baron and Josh Levy, my favorite coeditors and collaborators.

Thanks, first and foremost, to my editor, Karen Chaplin, and to the rest of the Quill Tree team: Allison Weintraub, Heather Tamarkin, Joel Tippie, and Andrea Vandergrift. Thanks also to Violet Tobacco, whose beautiful cover hits all the right notes (pun intended).

Thank you as always to agents Liza Fleissig and Ginger Harris-Dontzin for their continuing, unwavering belief in my stories and me.

Finally, thank you to my parents, Freeda and Martin Wender, my husband, Lee Milliner, and our youngest son, Jake. My books would not be here without you.